WHEN KNIGHTHOOD
WAS IN FLOWER

Charles Major

WHEN KNIGHTHOOD WAS IN FLOWER

OR,

The Love Story of Charles Brandon
and Mary Tudor the King's Sister, and
Happening in the Reign of His August
Majesty King Henry the Eighth

JULIA MARLOWE EDITION
WITH SCENES FROM THE PLAY

BIBLIOBAZAAR

WHEN KNIGHTHOOD WAS IN FLOWER

"There lived a Knight, when Knighthood was in flow'r,
Who charmed alike the tilt-yard and the bow'r."

* * * * *

To My Wife

* * * * *

CONTENTS

The Caskodens 17

CHAPTER I 21
The Duel
CHAPTER II 25
How Brandon Came to Court
CHAPTER III 32
The Princess Mary
CHAPTER IV 46
A Lesson in Dancing
CHAPTER V 64
An Honor and an Enemy
CHAPTER VI 74
A Rare Ride to Windsor
CHAPTER VII 82
Love's Fierce Sweetness
CHAPTER VIII 98
The Trouble in Billingsgate Ward
CHAPTER IX 110
Put not your Trust in Princesses
CHAPTER X 125
Justice, O King!
CHAPTER XI 133
Louis XII a Suitor
CHAPTER XII 146
Atonement
CHAPTER XIII 153
A Girl's Consent

CHAPTER XIV 162

In the Siren Country

CHAPTER XV 173

To Make a Man of Her

CHAPTER XVI 181

A Hawking Party

CHAPTER XVII 189

The Elopement

CHAPTER XVIII 203

To the Tower

CHAPTER XIX 212

Proserpina

CHAPTER XX 223

Down into France

CHAPTER XXI 235

Letters from a Queen

*_"Cloth of gold do not despise,_
Though thou be match'd with cloth of frize;
Cloth of frize, be not too bold,
Though thou be match'd with cloth of gold."

* * * * *

---

* Inscription on a label affixed to Brandon's lance under a picture of Mary Tudor
and Charles Brandon, at Strawberry Hill.

THE PLAY

The initial performance of the play was given in St. Louis on the evening of November 26, 1900, and the first New York production was on the fourteenth of the following January.

Its instant and continued success is well known. A prominent dramatic critic of the press has said:

"Julia Marlowe fully realized the popular idea of the Mary described by the novelist. She seemed to revel in the role. With its instantaneous changes from gay daring to anger and fear, from coyness to the dignity that hedges a princess, from resentment to ardent love, the part of Mary Tudor gives Julia Marlowe full scope for the display of her talent. She has never appeared to better or as good advantage as in this play for the reason that it gives opportunity for broader and more effective lights and shades than anything she has hitherto given us."

* * * * *

WHEN KNIGHTHOOD WAS IN FLOWER . . .

The Caskodens

We Caskodens take great pride in our ancestry. Some persons, I know, hold all that to be totally un-Solomonlike and the height of vanity, but they, usually, have no ancestors of whom to be proud. The man who does not know who his great-grandfather was, naturally enough would not care what he was. The Caskodens have pride of ancestry because they know both who and what.

Even admitting that it is vanity at all, it is an impersonal sort of failing, which, like the excessive love of country, leans virtueward; for the man who fears to disgrace his ancestors is certainly less likely to disgrace himself. Of course there are a great many excellent persons who can go no farther back than father and mother, who, doubtless, eat and drink and sleep as well, and love as happily, as if they could trace an unbroken lineage clear back to Adam or Noah, or somebody of that sort. Nevertheless, we Caskodens are proud of our ancestry, and expect to remain so to the end of the chapter, regardless of whom it pleases or displeases.

We have a right to be proud, for there is an unbroken male line from William the Conqueror down to the present time. In this lineal list are fourteen Barons—the title lapsed when Charles I fell—twelve Knights of the Garter and forty-seven Knights of the Bath and other orders. A Caskoden distinguished himself by gallant service under the Great Norman and was given rich English lands and a fair Saxon bride, albeit an unwilling one, as his reward. With this fair, unwilling Saxon bride and her long plait of yellow hair goes a very pretty, pathetic story, which I may tell you at some future time if you take kindly to this. A Caskoden was seneschal to William Rufus, and sat at the rich, half barbaric banquets in the first Great Hall. Still another was one of the doughty barons who wrested from John the Great Charter, England's declaration of independence; another was high in the councils of Henry V. I have omitted one whom I should not fail to mention: Adjodika Caskoden, who was a member of the Dunce Parliament of Henry IV, so called because there were no lawyers in it.

It is true that in the time of Edward IV a Caskoden did stoop to trade, but it was trade of the most dignified, honorable sort; he was a goldsmith, and his guild, as you know, were the bankers and international clearance house for people, king and nobles. Besides, it is stated on good authority that there was a great scandal wherein the goldsmith's wife was mixed up in an intrigue with the noble King Edward; so we learn that even in trade the Caskodens were of honorable position and basked in the smile of their prince. As for myself, I am not one of those who object so much to trade; and I think it contemptible in a man to screw his nose all out of place sneering at it, while enjoying every luxury of life from its profits.

This goldsmith was shrewd enough to turn what some persons might call his ill fortune, in one way, into gain in another. He was one of those happily constituted, thrifty philosophers who hold that even misfortune should not be wasted, and that no evil is so great but the alchemy of common sense can transmute some part of it into good. So he coined the smiles which the king shed upon his wife—he being powerless to prevent, for Edward smiled where he listed, and listed nearly everywhere—into nobles, crowns and pounds sterling, and left a glorious fortune to his son and to his son's son, unto about the fourth generation, which was a ripe old age for a fortune, I think. How few of them live beyond the second, and fewer still beyond the third! It was during the third generation of this fortune that the events of the following history occurred.

Now, it has been the custom of the Caskodens for centuries to keep a record of events, as they have happened, both private and public. Some are in the form of diaries and journals like those of Pepys and Evelyn; others in letters like the Pastons'; others again in verse and song like Chaucer's and the Water Poet's; and still others in the more pretentious form of memoir and chronicle. These records we always have kept jealously within our family, thinking it vulgar, like the Pastons, to submit our private affairs to public gaze.

There can, however, be no reason why those parts treating solely of outside matters should be so carefully guarded, and I have determined to choose for publication such portions as do not divulge family secrets nor skeletons, and which really redound to family honor.

For this occasion I have selected from the memoir of my worthy ancestor and namesake, Sir Edwin Caskoden—grandson of the goldsmith, and Master of the Dance to Henry VIII—the story of Charles Brandon and Mary Tudor, sister to the king.

This story is so well known to the student of English history that I fear its repetition will lack that zest which attends the development of an unforeseen denouement. But it is of so great interest, and is so full, in its sweet, fierce manifestation, of the one thing insoluble by time, Love, that I will nevertheless rewrite it from old Sir Edwin's memoir. Not so much as an historical narrative, although I fear a little history will creep in, despite me, but simply as a picture of that olden long ago, which, try as we will to put aside the hazy, many-folded curtain of time, still retains its shadowy lack of sharp detail, toning down and mellowing the hard aspect of real life—harder and more unromantic even than our own—into the blending softness of an exquisite mirage.

I might give you the exact words in which Sir Edwin wrote, and shall now and then quote from contemporaneous chronicles in the language of his time, but should I so write at all, I fear the pleasure of perusal would but poorly pay for the trouble, as the English of the Bluff King is almost a foreign tongue to us. I shall, therefore, with a few exceptions, give Sir Edwin's memoir in words, spelling and idiom which his rollicking little old shade will probably repudiate as none of his whatsoever. So, if you happen to find sixteenth century thought hob-nobbing in the same sentence with nineteenth century English, be not disturbed; I did it. If the little old fellow grows grandiloquent or garrulous at times—*he* did that. If you find him growing super-sentimental, remember that sentimentalism was the life-breath of chivalry, just then approaching its absurdest climax in the bombastic conscientiousness of Bayard and the whole mental atmosphere laden with its pompous nonsense.

* * * * *

CHAPTER I

The Duel

It sometimes happens, Sir Edwin says, that when a woman will she won't, and when she won't she will; but usually in the end the adage holds good. That sentence may not be luminous with meaning, but I will give you an illustration.

I think it was in the spring of 1509, at any rate soon after the death of the "Modern Solomon," as Queen Catherine called her old father-in-law, the late King Henry VII, that his august majesty Henry VIII, "The Vndubitate Flower and very Heire of both the sayd Linages," came to the throne of England, and tendered me the honorable position of Master of the Dance at his sumptuous court.

As to "worldly goods," as some of the new religionists call wealth, I was very comfortably off; having inherited from my father, one of the counselors of Henry VII, a very competent fortune indeed. How my worthy father contrived to save from the greedy hand of that rich old miser so great a fortune, I am sure I can not tell. He was the only man of my knowledge who did it; for the old king had a reach as long as the kingdom, and, upon one pretext or another, appropriated to himself everything on which he could lay his hands. My father, however, was himself pretty shrewd in money matters, having inherited along with his fortune a rare knack at keeping it. His father was a goldsmith in the time of King Edward, and enjoyed the marked favor of that puissant prince.

Being thus in a position of affluence, I cared nothing for the fact that little or no emolument went with the office; it was the honor which delighted me. Besides, I was thereby an inmate of the king's palace, and brought into intimate relations with the court, and above all, with the finest ladies of the land—the best company a man can keep, since it ennobles his mind with better thoughts, purifies his heart with cleaner motives, and makes him gentle without detracting from his strength. It was an office any lord of the kingdom might have been proud to hold.

Now, some four or five years after my induction into this honorable office, there came to court news of a terrible duel fought down in Suffolk, out of which only one of the four combatants had come alive—two, rather, but one of them in a condition worse than death. The first survivor was a son of Sir William Brandon, and the second was a man called Sir Adam Judson. The story went that young Brandon and his elder brother, both just home from the continental wars, had met Judson at an Ipswich inn, where there had been considerable gambling among them. Judson had won from the brothers a large sum of money which they had brought home; for, notwithstanding their youth, the elder being but twenty-six and the younger about twenty-four years of age, they had gained great honor and considerable profit in wars, especially the younger, whose name was Charles.

It is a little hard to fight for money and then to lose it by a single spot upon the die, but such is the fate of him who plays, and a philosopher will swallow his ill luck and take to fighting for more. The Brandons could have done this easily enough, especially Charles, who was an offhand philosopher, rather fond of a good-humored fight, had it not been that in the course of play one evening the secret of Judson's winning had been disclosed by a discovery that he cheated. The Brandons waited until they were sure, and then trouble began, which resulted in a duel on the second morning following.

This Judson was a Scotch gentleman of whom very little was known, except that he was counted the most deadly and most cruel duelist of the time. He was called the "Walking Death," and it is said took pride in the appellation. He boasted that he had fought eighty-seven duels, in which he had killed seventy-five men, and it was considered certain death to meet him. I got the story of the duel afterwards from Brandon as I give it here.

John was the elder brother, and when the challenge came was entitled to fight first,—a birthright out of which Charles tried in vain to talk him. The brothers told their father, Sir William Brandon, and at the appointed time father and sons repaired to the place of meeting, where they found Judson and his two seconds ready for the fight.

Sir William was still a vigorous man, with few equals in sword play, and the sons, especially the younger, were better men and more skilful than their father had ever been, yet they felt that this duel meant certain death, so great was Judson's fame for skill and cruelty. Notwithstanding they were so handicapped with this feeling of impending evil, they met their duty without a tremor; for the motto of their house was, "*Malo Mori Quam Fedrai.*"

It was a misty morning in March. Brandon has told me since, that when his elder brother took his stand, it was at once manifest that he was Judson's superior, both in strength and skill, but after a few strokes the brother's blade bent double and broke off short at the hilt when it should have gone home. Thereupon, Judson, with a malignant smile of triumph, deliberately selected his opponent's heart and pierced it with his sword, giving the blade a twist as he drew it out in order to cut and mutilate the more.

In an instant Sir William's doublet was off, and he was in his dead son's tracks, ready to avenge him or to die. Again the thrust which should have killed broke the sword, and the father died as the son had died.

After this, came young Charles, expecting, but, so great was his strong heart, not one whit fearing, to lie beside his dead father and brother. He knew he was the superior of both in strength and skill, and his knowledge of men and the noble art told him they had each been the superior of Judson; but the fellow's hand seemed to be the hand of death. An opening came through Judson's unskilful play, which gave young Brandon an opportunity for a thrust to kill, but his blade, like his father's and brother's, bent double without penetrating. Unlike the others, however, it did not break, and the thrust revealed the fact that Judson's skill as a duelist lay in a shirt of mail which it was useless to try to pierce. Aware of this, Brandon knew that victory was his, and that soon he would have avenged the murders that had gone before. He saw that his adversary was strong neither in wind nor arm, and had not the skill to penetrate his guard in a week's trying, so he determined to fight on the defensive until Judson's strength should wane, and then kill him when and how he chose.

After a time Judson began to breathe hard and his thrusts to lack force.

"Boy, I would spare you," he said; "I have killed enough of your tribe; put up your sword and call it quits."

Young Brandon replied: "Stand your ground, you coward; you will be a dead man as soon as you grow a little weaker; if you try to run I will thrust you through the neck as I would a cur. Listen how you snort. I shall soon have you; you are almost gone. You would spare me, would you? I could preach a sermon or dance a hornpipe while I am killing you. I will not break my sword against your coat of mail, but will wait until you fall from weakness and then . . . Fight, you bloodhound!"

Judson was pale from exhaustion, and his breath was coming in gasps as he tried to keep the merciless sword from his throat. At last, by a dexterous twist of his blade, Brandon sent Judson's sword flying thirty feet away. The fellow started to run, but turned and fell upon his knees to beg for life. Brandon's reply was a flashing circle of steel, and his sword point cut lengthwise through Judson's eyes and the bridge of his nose, leaving him sightless and hideous for life. A revenge compared to which death would have been merciful.

The duel created a sensation throughout the kingdom, for although little was known as to who Judson was, his fame as a duelist was as broad as the land. He had been at court upon several occasions, and, at one time, upon the king's birthday, had fought in the royal lists. So the matter came in for its share of consideration by king and courtiers, and young Brandon became a person of interest. He became still more so when some gentlemen who had served with him in the continental wars told the court of his daring and bravery, and related stories of deeds at arms worthy of the best knight in Christendom.

He had an uncle at the court, Sir Thomas Brandon, the king's Master of Horse, who thought it a good opportunity to put his nephew forward and let him take his chance at winning royal favor. The uncle broached the subject to the king, with favorable issue, and Charles Brandon, led by the hand of fate, came to London Court, where that same fate had in keeping for him events such as seldom fall to the lot of man.

* * * * *

CHAPTER II

How Brandon Came to Court

When we learned that Brandon was coming to court, every one believed he would soon gain the king's favor. How much that would amount to none could tell, as the king's favorites were of many sorts and taken from all conditions of men. There was Master Wolsey, a butcher's son, whom he had first made almoner, then chief counselor and Bishop of Lincoln, soon to be Bishop of York, and Cardinal of the Holy Roman Church.

From the other extreme of life came young Thomas, Lord Howard, heir to the Earl of Surrey, and my Lord of Buckingham, premier peer of the realm. Then sometimes would the king take a yeoman of the guard and make him his companion in jousts and tournaments, solely because of his brawn and bone. There were others whom he kept close by him in the palace because of their wit and the entertainment they furnished; of which class was I, and, I flatter myself, no mean member.

To begin with, being in no way dependent on the king for money, I never drew a farthing from the royal treasury. This, you may be sure, did me no harm, for although the king *sometimes* delighted to give, he always hated to pay. There were other good reasons, too, why I should be a favorite with the king. Without meaning to be vain, I think I may presume to say, with perfect truth, that my conversation and manners were far more pleasing and polished than were usual at that day in England, for I made it a point to spend several weeks each year in the noble French capital, the home and center of good-breeding and politeness.

My appointment as Master of the Dance, I am sure, was owing entirely to my manner. My brother, the baron, who stood high with the king, was not friendly toward me because my father had seen fit to bequeath me so good a competency in place of giving it all to the first-born and leaving me dependent upon the tender mercies of an elder brother. So I had no help from him nor from any one else. I was quite small of stature and, therefore, unable to compete, with lance and mace, with bulkier men; but I would bet with any man, of any size, on any game, at any place and time, in any amount; and, if I do say it, who perhaps should not, I basked in the light of many a fair smile which larger men had sighed for in vain.

I did not know when Brandon first came to London. We had all remained at Greenwich while the king went up to Westminster to waste his time with matters of state and quarrel with the Parliament, then sitting, over the amount of certain subsidies.

Mary, the king's sister, then some eighteen or nineteen years of age, a perfect bud, just blossoming into a perfect flower, had gone over to Windsor on a visit to her elder sister, Margaret of Scotland, and the palace was dull enough. Brandon, it seems, had been presented to Henry during this time, at Westminster, and had, to some extent at least, become a favorite before I met him. The first time I saw him was at a joust given by the king at Westminster, in celebration of the fact that he had coaxed a good round subsidy out of Parliament.

The queen and her ladies had been invited over, and it was known that Mary would be down from Windsor and come home with the king and the court to Greenwich when we should return. So we all went over to Westminster the night before the jousts, and were up bright and early next morning to see all that was to be seen.

* * * * *

[Here the editor sees fit to substitute a description of this tournament taken from the quaint old chronicler, Hall.]

The morow beyng after dynner, at tyme conuenenient, the Quene with her Ladyes repaired to see the Iustes, the trompettes blewe vp, and in came many a noble man and Gentleman, rychely appeareiled, takynge vp thir horses, after whome folowed certayne lordes appareiled, they and thir horses, in cloth of Golde and russet and tynsell;

Knyghtes in cloth of Golde, and russet Veluet. And a greate nomber of Gentlemen on fote, in russet satyn and yealow, and yomen in russet Damaske and yealow, all the nether parte of euery mans hosen Skarlet, and yealow cappes.

Then came the kynge vnder a Pauilion of golde, and purpul Veluet embroudered, the compass of the Pauilion about, and valenced with a flat, gold beaten in wyre, with an Imperiall croune in the top, of fyne Golde, his bases and trapper of cloth of Golde, fretted with Damask Golde, the trapper pedant to the tail. A crane and chafron of stele, in the front of the chafro was a goodly plume set full of musers or trimbling spangles of golde. After folowed his three aydes, euery of them vnder a Pauilion of Crymosyn Damaske & purple. The nomber of Gentlemen and yomen a fote, appareiled in russet and yealow was clxviii. Then next these Pauilions came xii chyldren of honor, sitting euery one of them on a greate courser, rychely trapped, and embroudered in seuerall deuises and facions, where lacked neither brouderie nor goldsmythes work, so that euery chyld and horse in deuice and fascion was contrary to the other, which was goodly to beholde.

Then on the counter parte, entered a Straunger, fyrst on horsebacke in a long robe of Russet satyne, like a recluse or a religious, and his horse trapped in the same sewte, without dromme or noyse of mynstrelsye, puttinge a byll of peticion to the Quene, the effect whereof was, that if it would please her to license hym to runne in her presence, he would do it gladly, and if not, then he would departe as he came. After his request was graunted, then he put off hys sayd habyte and was armed at all peces with ryche bases & horse, also rychely trapped, and so did runne his horse to the tylte end, where dieurs men on fote appareiled in Russet satyn awaited on him. Thereupon the Heraulds cryed an Oyez! and the grownd shoke with the trompe of rushynge stedes. Wonder it were to write of the dedes of Armes which that day toke place, where a man might haue seen many a horse raysed on highe with galop, turne and stoppe, maruaylous to behold. C.xiv staves were broke and the kynge being lusty, he and the straunger toke the prices.

* * * * *

When the queen had given the stranger permission to run, and as he moved away, there was a great clapping of hands and waving of trophies among the ladies, for he was of such noble mien and comely face as to attract the gaze of every one away from even the glittering person of his majesty the king.

His hair, worn in its natural length, fell in brown curls back from his forehead almost to the shoulder, a style just then new, even in France. His eyes were a deep blue, and his complexion, though browned by exposure, held a tinge of beauty which the sun could not mar and a girl might envy. He wore neither mustachio nor beard, as men now disfigure their faces—since Francis I took a scar on his chin—and his clear cut profile, dilating nostrils and mobile, though firm-set mouth, gave pleasing assurance of tenderness, gentleness, daring and strength.

I was standing near the queen, who called to me: "Who is the handsome stranger that so gracefully asked our license to run?"

"I can not inform your majesty. I never saw him until now. He is the goodliest knight I have ever beheld."

"That he is," replied the queen; "and we should like very much to know him. Should we not, ladies?" There was a chorus of assent from a dozen voices, and I promised, after the running, to learn all about him and report.

It was at this point the heralds cried their "Oyes," and our conversation was at an end for the time.

As to height, the stranger was full six feet, with ample evidence of muscle, though no great bulk. He was grace itself, and the king afterwards said he had never seen such strength of arm and skill in the use of the lance—a sure harbinger of favor, if not of fortune, for the possessor.

After the jousting the Princess Mary asked me if I could yet give her an account of the stranger; and as I could not, she went to the king.

I heard her inquire:

"Who was your companion, brother?"

"That is a secret, sister. You will find out soon enough, and will be falling in love with him, no doubt. I have always looked upon you as full of trouble for me in that respect; you will not so much as glance at anyone I choose for you, but I suppose would be ready enough with your smiles for some one I should not want."

"Is the stranger one whom you would not want?" asked Mary, with a dimpling smile and a flash of her brown eyes.

"He most certainly is," returned the king.

"Then I will fall in love with him at once. In fact, I don't know but I have already."

"Oh, I have no doubt of that; if I wanted him, he might be Apollo himself and you would have none of him." King Henry had been compelled to refuse several very advantageous alliances because this fair, coaxing, self-willed sister would not consent to be a part of the moving consideration.

"But can you not tell me who he is, and what his degree?" went on Mary in a bantering tone.

"He has no degree; he is a plain, untitled soldier, not even a knight; that is, not an English knight. I think he has a German or Spanish order of some sort."

"Not a duke; not an earl; not even a baron or knight? Now he has become interesting."

"Yes, I suppose so; but don't bother me."

"Will he be at the dance and banquet to-night?"

"No! No! Now I must go; don't bother me, I say." And the king moved away.

That night we had a grand banquet and dance at Westminster, and the next day we all, excepting Lady Mary, went back to Greenwich by boat, paying a farthing a head for our fare. This was just after the law fixing the boat fare, and the watermen were a quarreling lot, you may be sure. One farthing from Westminster to Greenwich! Eight miles. No wonder they were angry.

The next day I went back to London on an errand, and over to Wolsey's house to borrow a book. While there Master Cavendish, Wolsey's secretary, presented me to the handsome stranger, and he proved to be no other than Charles Brandon, who had fought the terrible duel down in Suffolk. I could hardly believe that so mild-mannered and boyish a person could have taken the leading part in such a tragedy. But with all his gentleness there was an underlying dash of cool daring which intimated plainly enough that he was not all mildness.

We became friends at once, drawn together by that subtle human quality which makes one nature fit into another, resulting in friendship between men, and love between men and women.

We soon found that we had many tastes in common, chief among which was the strongest of all congenial bonds, the love of books. In fact we had come to know each other through our common love of reading, for he also had gone to Master Cavendish, who had a fine library, to borrow some volumes to take with him down to Greenwich.

Brandon informed me he was to go to Greenwich that day, so we determined to see a little of London, which was new to him, and then take boat in time to be at the palace before dark.

That evening, upon arriving at Greenwich, we hunted up Brandon's uncle, the Master of Horse, who invited his nephew to stay with him for the night. He refused, however, and accepted an invitation to take a bed in my room.

The next day Brandon was installed as one of the captains of the king's guard, under his uncle, but with no particular duties, except such as should be assigned him from time to time. He was offered a good room on one of the lower floors, but asked, instead, to be lodged in the attic next to me. So we arranged that each had a room opening into a third that served us alike for drawing-room and armory.

Here we sat and talked, and now and then one would read aloud some favorite passage, while the other kept his own place with finger between the leaves. Here we discussed everything from court scandal to religion, and settled to our own satisfaction, at least, many a great problem with which the foolish world is still wrestling.

We told each other all our secrets, too, for all the world like a pair of girls. Although Brandon had seen so much of life, having fought on the continent ever since he was a boy, and for all he was so much a man of the world, yet had he as fresh and boyish a heart as if he had just come from the clover fields and daisies. He seemed almost diffident, but I soon learned that his manner was but the cool gentleness of strength.

Of what use, let me ask, is a friend unless you can unload your heart upon him? It matters not whether the load be joy or sorrow; if the former, the need is all the greater, for joy has an expansive power, as some persons say steam has, and must escape from the heart upon some one else.

So Brandon told me of his hopes and aspirations, chief among which was his desire to earn, and save, enough money to pay the debt against his father's estate, which he had turned over to his younger brother and sisters. He, as the eldest, could have taken it all, for his father had died without a will, but he said there was not enough to divide, so he had given it to them and hoped to leave it clear of debt; then for New Spain, glory and fortune, conquest and yellow gold. He had read of the voyages of the great Columbus, the Cabots, and a host of others, and the future was as rosy as a Cornish girl's cheek. Fortune held up her lips to him, but—there's often a sting in a kiss.

* * * * *

CHAPTER III

The Princess Mary

Now, at that time, Mary, the king's sister, was just ripening into her greatest womanly perfection. Her skin was like velvet; a rich, clear, rosy snow, with the hot young blood glowing through it like the faint red tinge we sometimes see on the inner side of a white rose leaf. Her hair was a very light brown, almost golden, and fluffy, soft, and fine as a skein of Arras silk. She was of medium height, with a figure that Venus might have envied. Her feet and hands were small, and apparently made for the sole purpose of driving mankind distracted. In fact, that seemed to be the paramount object in her creation, for she had the world of men at her feet. Her greatest beauty was her glowing dark brown eyes, which shone with an ever-changing luster from beneath the shade of the longest, blackest upcurving lashes ever seen.

Her voice was soft and full, and, except when angry, which, alas, was not infrequent, had a low and coaxing little note that made it irresistible; she was a most adroit coaxer, and knew her power full well, although she did not always plead, having the Tudor temper and preferring to command—when she could. As before hinted, she had coaxed her royal brother out of several proposed marriages for her, which would have been greatly to his advantage; and if you had only known Henry Tudor, with his vain, boisterous, stubborn violence, you could form some idea of Mary's powers by that achievement alone.

Will Sommers, the fool, one day spread through court an announcement that there would be a public exhibition in the main hall of the palace that evening, when the Princess Mary would perform the somewhat alarming, but, in fact, harmless, operation of wheedling the king out of his ears. This was just after she had coaxed him to annul a marriage contract which her father had made for her with Charles of Germany, then heir to the greatest inheritance that ever fell to the lot of one man—Spain, the Netherlands, Austria, and heaven only knows what else.

She had been made love to by so many men, who had lost their senses in the dazzling rays of her thousand perfections—of whom, I am ashamed to say, that I, for a time, had been insane enough to be one—that love had grown to be a sort of joke with her, and man, a poor, contemptible creature, made to grovel at her feet. Not that she liked or encouraged it; for, never having been moved herself, she held love and its sufferings in utter scorn. Man's love was so cheap and plentiful that it had no value in her eyes, and it looked as if she would lose the best thing in life by having too much of it.

Such was the royal maid to whose tender mercies, I now tell you frankly, my friend Brandon was soon to be turned over. He, however, was a blade of very different temper from any she had known; and when I first saw signs of a growing intimacy between them I felt, from what little I had seen of Brandon, that the tables were very likely to be turned upon her ladyship. Then thought I, "God help her," for in a nature like hers, charged with latent force, strong and hot and fiery as the sun's stored rays, it needed but a flash to make it patent, when damage was sure to follow for somebody—probably Brandon.

Mary did not come home with us from Westminster the morning after the joustings, as we had expected, but followed some four or five days later, and Brandon had fairly settled himself at court before her arrival. As neither his duties nor mine were onerous, we had a great deal of time on our hands, which we employed walking and riding, or sitting in our common room reading and talking. Of course, as with most young men, that very attractive branch of natural history, woman, was a favorite topic, and we accordingly discussed it a great deal; that is, to tell the exact truth, *I* did. Although Brandon had seen many an adventure during his life on the continent, which would not do to write down here, he was as little of a boaster as any man I ever met, and, while I am in the truth-telling business, I was as great a braggart of my inches as ever drew the long-bow—in that line, I mean. Gods! I flush up hot, even now, when I think of it. So I talked a great deal and found myself infinitely pleased with Brandon's conversational powers, which were rare; being no less than the capacity for saying nothing, and listening politely to an infinite deal of the same thing, in another form, from me.

I remember that I told him I had known the Princess Mary from a time when she was twelve years old, and how I had made a fool of myself about her. I fear I tried to convey the impression that it was her exalted rank only which made her look unfavorably upon my passion, and suppressed the fact that she had laughed at me good humoredly, and put me off as she would have thrust a poodle from her lap. The truth is, she had always been kind and courteous to me, and had admitted me to a degree of intimacy much greater than I deserved. This, partly at least, grew out of the fact that I helped her along the thorny path to knowledge; a road she traveled at an eager gallop, for she dearly loved to learn—from curiosity perhaps.

I am sure she held me in her light, gentle heart as a dear friend, but while her heart was filled with this mild warmth for me, mine began to burn with the flame that discolors everything, and I saw her friendliness in a very distorting light. She was much kinder to me than to most men, but I did not see that it was by reason of my absolute harmlessness; and, I suppose, because I was a vain fool, I gradually began to gather hope—which goes with every vain man's love—and what is more, actually climbed to the very apex of idiocy and declared myself. I well knew the infinite distance between us; but like every other man who came within the circle of this charming lodestone I lost my head, and, in short, made a greater fool of myself than I naturally was—which is saying a good deal for that time in my life, God knows!

I knew vaguely but did not fairly realize how utterly beyond my reach in every way she was until I opened the flood-gates of my passion—as I thought it—and saw her smile, and try to check the coming laugh. Then came a look of offended dignity, followed by a quick softening glance.

"Leave me one friend, I pray you, Edwin. I value you too highly to lose, and esteem you too much to torment. Do not make of yourself one of those fools who feel, or pretend to feel, I care not which, such preference for me. You cannot know in what contempt a woman holds a man who follows her though she despises him. No man can beg a woman's love; he must command it; do not join their ranks, but let us be good friends. I will tell you the plain truth; it would be no different were we both of the same degree; even then I could not feel toward you as you think you wish, but I can be your friend, and will promise to be that always, if you will promise never again to speak of this to me."

I promised solemnly and have always kept my word, as this true, gracious woman, so full of faults and beauties, virtues and failings, has, ever since that day and moment, kept hers. It seemed that my love, or what I supposed was love, left my heart at once, frozen in the cold glint of her eyes as she smiled upon my first avowal; somewhat as disease may leave the sickened body upon a great shock. And in its place came the restful flame of a friend's love, which so softly warms without burning. But the burning! There is nothing in life worth having compared with it for all its pains and agonies. Is there?

"Now if you must love somebody," continued the princess, "there is Lady Jane Bolingbroke, who is beautiful and good, and admires you, and, I think, could learn to—" but here the lady in question ran out from behind the draperies, where, I believe, she had been listening to it all, and put her hand over her mistress' mouth to silence her.

"Don't believe one word she says, Sir Edwin," cried Lady Jane; "if you do I never *will* like you." The emphasis on the "will" held out such involuntary promise in case I did not believe the princess, that I at once protested total want of faith in a single syllable she had said about her, and vowed that I knew it could not be true; that I dared not hope for such happiness.

You see, I had begun to make love to Jane almost before I was off my knees to Mary, and, therefore, I had not been much hurt in Mary's case. I had suffered merely a touch of the general epidemic, not the lingering, chronic disease that kills.

Then I knew that the best cure for the sting which lies in a luckless love is to love elsewhere, and Jane, as she stood there, so *petite*, so blushing and so fair, struck me as quite the most pleasing antidote I could possibly find, so I began at once to administer to myself the delightful counter-irritant. It was a happy thought for me; one of those which come to a man now and then, and for which he thanks his wits in every hour of his after life.

But the winning of Jane was not so easy a matter as my vanity had prompted me to think. I started with a handicap, since Jane had heard my declaration to Mary, and I had to undo all that before I could do anything else. Try the same thing yourself with a spirited girl, naturally laughter-loving and coy, if you think it a simple, easy undertaking. I began to fear I should need another antidote long before I heard her sweet soul-satisfying "yes." I do not believe, however, I could have found in the whole world an antidote to my love for Jane. You see I tell you frankly that I won her, and conceal nothing, so far as Jane and I are concerned, for the purpose of holding you in suspense. I have started out to tell you the history of two other persons—if I can ever come to it—but find a continual tendency on the part of my own story to intrude, for every man is a very important personage to himself. I shall, however, try to keep it out.

In the course of my talk with Brandon I had, as I have said, told him the story of Mary, with some slight variations and coloring, or rather discoloring, to make it appear a little less to my discredit than the barefaced truth would have been. I told him also about Jane; and, I grieve and blush to say, expressed a confidence in that direction I little felt.

It had been perhaps a year since my adventure with Mary, and I had taken all that time trying to convince Jane that I did not mean a word I had said to her mistress, and that I was very earnest in everything I said to her. But Jane's ears would have heard just as much had they been the pair of beautiful little shells they so much resembled. This troubled me a great deal, and the best I could hope was that she held me on probation.

On the evening of the day Mary came home to Greenwich, Brandon asked: "Who and what on earth is this wonderful Mary I hear so much about? They say she is coming home to-day, and the court seems to have gone mad about it; I hear nothing but 'Mary is coming! Mary is coming! Mary! Mary!' from morning until night. They say Buckingham is beside himself for love of her. He has a wife at home, if I am right, and is old enough to be her father. Is he not?" I assented; and Brandon continued: "A man who will make such a fool of himself about a woman is woefully weak. The men of the court must be poor creatures."

He had much to learn about the power of womanhood. There is nothing on earth—but you know as much about it as I do.

"Wait until you see her," I answered, "and you will be one of them, also. I flatter you by giving you one hour with her to be heels over head in love. With an ordinary man it takes one-sixtieth of that time; so you see I pay a compliment to your strength of mind."

"Nonsense!" broke in Brandon. "Do you think I left all my wits down in Suffolk? Why, man, she is the sister of the king, and is sought by kings and emperors. I might as well fall in love with a twinkling star. Then, besides, my heart is not on my sleeve. You must think me a fool; a poor, enervated, simpering fool like—like—well, like one of those nobles of England. Don't put me down with them, Caskoden, if you would remain my friend."

We both laughed at this sort of talk, which was a little in advance of the time, for a noble, though an idiot, to the most of England was a noble still, God-created and to be adored.

Another great bond of sympathy between Brandon and myself was a community of opinion concerning certain theories as to the equality of men and tolerance of religious thought. We believed that these things would yet come, in spite of kingcraft and priestcraft, but wisely kept our pet theories to ourselves: that is, between ourselves.

Of what use is it to argue the equality of human kind to a man who honestly thinks he is better than any one else, or to one who really believes that some one else is better than he; and why dispute about the various ways of saving one's soul, when you are not even sure you have a soul to save? When I open my mouth for public utterance, the king is the best man in Christendom, and his premier peer of the realm the next best. When the king is a Catholic I go to Mass; since, praised be the Lord, I have brains enough not to let my head interfere with the set ways of a stone wall.

Now, when Mary returned the whole court rejoiced, and I was anxious for Brandon to meet her and that they should become friends. There would be no trouble in bringing this meeting about, since, as you know, I was upon terms of intimate friendship with Mary, and was the avowed, and, as I thought, at least hoped, all but accepted lover of her first lady in waiting and dearest friend, Lady

Jane Bolingbroke. Brandon, it is true, was not noble; not even an English knight, while I was both knighted and noble; but he was of as old a family as England boasted, and near of kin to some of the best blood of the land. The meeting came about sooner than I expected, and was very near a failure. It was on the second morning after Mary's arrival at Greenwich. Brandon and I were walking in the palace park when we met Jane, and I took the opportunity to make these, my two best-loved friends, acquainted.

"How do you do, Master Brandon?" said Lady Jane, holding out her plump little hand, so white and soft, and dear to me. "I have heard something of you the last day or so from Sir Edwin, but had begun to fear he was not going to give me the pleasure of knowing you. I hope I may see you often now, and that I may present you to my mistress."

With this, her eyes, bright as overgrown dew-drops, twinkled with a mischievous little smile, as if to say: "Ah, another large handsome fellow to make a fool of himself."

Brandon acquiesced in the wish she had made, and, after the interchange of a few words, Jane said her mistress was waiting at the other side of the grounds, and that she must go. She then ran off with a laugh and a courtesy, and was soon lost to sight behind the shrubbery at the turning of the walk.

In a short time we came to a summer house near the marble boat-landing, where we found the queen and some of her ladies awaiting the rest of their party for a trip down the river, which had been planned the day before. Brandon was known to the queen and several of the ladies, although he had not been formally presented at an audience. Many of the king's friends enjoyed a considerable intimacy with the whole court without ever receiving the public stamp of recognition, socially, which goes with a formal presentation.

The queen, seeing us, sent me off to bring the king. After I had gone, she asked if any one had seen the Princess Mary, and Brandon told her Lady Jane had said she was at the other side of the grounds. Thereupon her majesty asked Brandon to find the princess and to say that she was wanted.

Brandon started off and soon found a bevy of girls sitting on some benches under a spreading oak, weaving spring flowers. He had never seen the princess, so could not positively know her.

As a matter of fact, he did know her, as soon as his eyes rested on her, for she could not be mistaken among a thousand—there was no one like her or anything near it. Some stubborn spirit of opposition, however, prompted him to pretend ignorance. All that he had heard of her wonderful power over men, and the servile manner in which they fell before her, had aroused in him a spirit of antagonism, and had begotten a kind of distaste beforehand. He was wrong in this, because Mary was not a coquette in any sense of the word, and did absolutely nothing to attract men, except to be so beautiful, sweet and winning that they could not let her alone; for all of which surely the prince of fault-finders himself could in no way blame her.

She could not help that God had seen fit to make her the fairest being on earth, and the responsibility would have to lie where it belonged—with God; Mary would have none of it. Her attractiveness was not a matter of volition or intention on her part. She was too young for deliberate snare-setting—though it often begins very early in life—and made no effort to attract men. Man's love was too cheap a thing for her to strive for, and I am sure, in her heart, she would infinitely have preferred to live without it—that is, until the right one should come. The right one is always on his way, and, first or last, is sure to come to every woman—sometimes, alas! too late—and when he comes, be it late or early, she crowns him, even though he be a long-eared ass. Blessed crown! and thrice-blessed blindness—else there were fewer coronations.

So Brandon stirred this antagonism and determined not to see her manifold perfections, which he felt sure were exaggerated; but to treat her as he would the queen—who was black and leathery enough to frighten a satyr—with all respect due to her rank, but with his own opinion of her nevertheless, safely stored away in the back of his head.

Coming up to the group, Brandon took off his hat, and, with a graceful little bow that let the curls fall around his face, asked: "Have I the honor to find the Princess Mary among these ladies?"

Mary, who I know you will at once say was thoroughly spoiled, without turning her face toward him, replied:

"Is the Princess Mary a person of so little consequence about the court that she is not known to a mighty captain of the guard?"

He wore his guardsman's doublet, and she knew his rank by his uniform. She had not noticed his face.

Quick as a flash came the answer: "I can not say of what consequence the Princess Mary is about the court; it is not my place to determine such matters. I am sure, however, she is not here, for I doubt not she would have given a gentle answer to a message from the queen. I shall continue my search." With this, he turned to leave, and the ladies, including Jane, who was there and saw it all and told me of it, awaited the bolt they knew would come, for they saw the lightning gathering in Mary's eyes.

Mary sprang to her feet with an angry flush in her face, exclaiming: "Insolent fellow, I am the Princess Mary; if you have a message, deliver it and be gone." You may be sure this sort of treatment was such as the cool-headed, daring Brandon would repay with usury; so, turning upon his heel and almost presenting his back to Mary, he spoke to Lady Jane:

"Will your ladyship say to her highness that her majesty, the queen, awaits her coming at the marble landing?"

"No need to repeat the message, Jane," cried Mary. "I have ears and can hear for myself." Then turning to Brandon: "If your insolence will permit you to receive a message from so insignificant a person as the king's sister, I beg you to say to the queen that I shall be with her presently."

He did not turn his face toward Mary, but bowed again to Jane.

"May I ask your ladyship further to say for me that if I have been guilty of any discourtesy I greatly regret it. My failure to recognize the Princess Mary grew out of my misfortune in never having been allowed to bask in the light of her countenance. I cannot believe the fault lies at my door, and I hope for her own sake that her highness, on second thought, will realize how ungentle and unkind some one else has been." And with a sweeping courtesy he walked quickly down the path.

"The insolent wretch!" cried one.

"He ought to hold papers on the pillory," said another.

"Nothing of the sort," broke in sensible, fearless little Jane; "I think the Lady Mary was wrong. He could not have known her by inspiration."

"Jane is right," exclaimed Mary, whose temper, if short, was also short-lived, and whose kindly heart always set her right if she but gave it a little time. Her faults were rather those of education than of nature. "Jane is right; it was what I deserved. I did not think when I spoke, and did not really mean it as it sounded. He acted like a man, and looked like one, too, when he defended himself. I warrant the pope at Rome could not run over him with impunity. For once I have found a real live man, full of manliness. I saw him in the lists at Windsor a week ago, but the king said his name was a secret, and I could not learn it. He seemed to know you, Jane. Who is he? Now tell us all you know. The queen can wait."

And her majesty waited on a girl's curiosity.

I had told Jane all I knew about Brandon, so she was prepared with full information, and gave it. She told the princess who he was; of his terrible duel with Judson; his bravery and adventures in the wars; his generous gift to his brother and sisters, and lastly, "Sir Edwin says he is the best-read man in the court, and the bravest, truest heart in Christendom."

After Jane's account of Brandon, they all started by a roundabout way for the marble landing. In a few moments whom did they see, coming toward them down the path, but Brandon, who had delivered his message and continued his walk. When he saw whom he was about to meet, he quickly turned in another direction. The Lady Mary had seen him, however, and told Jane to run forward and bring him to her. She soon overtook him and said:

"Master Brandon, the princess wishes to see you." Then, maliciously: "You will suffer this time. I assure you she is not used to such treatment. It was glorious, though, to see you resent such an affront. Men usually smirk and smile foolishly and thank her when she smites them."

Brandon was disinclined to return.

"I am not in her highness's command," he answered, "and do not care to go back for a reprimand when I am in no way to blame."

"Oh, but you must come; perhaps she will not scold this time," and she put her hand upon his arm, and laughingly drew him along. Brandon, of course, had to submit when led by so sweet a captor—anybody would. So fresh, and fair, and lovable was Jane, that I am sure anything masculine *must* have given way.

Coming up to the princess and her ladies, who were waiting, Jane said: "Lady Mary, let me present Master Brandon, who, if he has offended in any way, humbly sues for pardon." That was the one thing Brandon had no notion on earth of doing, but he let it go as Jane had put it, and this was his reward:

"It is not Master Brandon who should sue for pardon," responded the princess, "it is I who was wrong. I blush for what I did and said. Forgive me, sir, and let us start anew." At this she stepped up to Brandon and offered him her hand, which he, dropping to his knee, kissed most gallantly.

"Your highness, you can well afford to offend when you have so sweet and gracious a talent for making amends. 'A wrong acknowledged,' as some one has said, 'becomes an obligation.'" He looked straight into the girl's eyes as he said this, and his gaze was altogether too strong for her, so the lashes fell. She flushed and said with a smile that brought the dimples:

"I thank you; that is a real compliment." Then laughingly: "Much better than extravagant comments on one's skin, and eyes, and hair. We are going to the queen at the marble landing. Will you walk with us, sir?" And they strolled away together, while the other girls followed in a whispering, laughing group.

Was there ever so glorious a calm after such a storm?

"Then those mythological compliments," continued Mary, "don't you dislike them?"

"I can't say that I have ever received many—none that I recall," replied Brandon, with a perfectly straight face, but with a smile trying its best to break out.

"Oh! you have not? Well! how would you like to have somebody always telling you that Apollo was humpbacked and misshapen compared with you; that Endymion would have covered his face had he but seen yours, and so on?"

"I don't know, but I think I should like it—from some persons," he replied, looking ever so innocent.

This savored of familiarity after so brief an acquaintance, and caused the princess to glance up in slight surprise; but only for the instant, for his innocent look disarmed her.

"I have a mind to see," she returned, laughing and throwing her head back, as she looked up at him out of the corner of her lustrous eyes. "But I will pay you a better compliment. I positively thank you for the rebuke. I do many things like that, for which I am always sorry. Oh! you don't know how difficult it is to be a good princess." And she shook her head, with a gathering of little trouble-wrinkles in her forehead, as much as to say, "There is no getting away from it, though." Then she breathed a soft little sigh of tribulation as they walked on.

"I know it must be a task to be good when everybody flatters even one's shortcomings," said Brandon, and then continued in a way that, I am free to confess, was something priggish: "It is almost impossible for us to see our own faults, even when others are kind enough to point them out, for they are right ugly things and unpleasant to look upon. But lacking those outside monitors, one must all the more cultivate the habit of constant inlooking and self-examination. If we are only brave enough to confront our faults and look them in the face, ugly as they are, we shall be sure to overcome the worst of them. A striving toward good will achieve at least a part of it."

"Oh!" returned the princess, "but what *is* good and what *is* wrong? So often we can not tell them apart until we look back at what we have done, and then it is all too late. I truly wish to be good more than I desire anything else in the world. I am so ignorant and helpless, and have such strong inclinations to do wrong that sometimes I seem to be almost all wrong. The priests say so much, but tell us so little. They talk about St. Peter and St. Paul, and a host of other saints and holy fathers and what-nots, but fail to tell us what we need every moment of our lives; that is, how to know the right when we see it, and how to do it; and how to know the wrong and how to avoid it. They ask us to believe so much, and insist that faith is the sum of virtue, and the lack of it the sum of sin; that to faith all things are added; but we might believe every syllable of their whole disturbing creed, and then spoil it all through blind ignorance of what is right and what is wrong."

"As to knowing right and wrong," replied Brandon, "I think I can give you a rule which, although it may not cover the whole ground, is excellent for every-day use. It is this: Whatever makes others unhappy is wrong; whatever makes the world happier is good. As to how we are always to do this, I can not tell you. One has to learn that by trying. We can but try, and if we fail altogether, there is still virtue in every futile effort toward the right."

Mary bent her head as she walked along in thought.

"What you have said is the only approach to a rule for knowing and doing the right I have ever heard. Now what do you think of me as a flatterer? But it will do no good; the bad is in me too strong; it always does itself before I can apply any rule, or even realize what is coming." And again she shook her head with a bewitching little look of trouble.

"Pardon me, your highness; but there is no bad *in* you. It has been put *on* you by others, and is all on the outside; there is none of it in your heart at all. That evil which you think comes out of you, simply falls from you; your heart is all right, or I have greatly misjudged you." He was treating her almost as if she were a child.

"I fear, Master Brandon, you are the most adroit flatterer of all," said Mary, shaking her head and looking up at him with a side glance, "people have deluged me with all kinds of flattery—I have the different sorts listed and labeled—but no one has ever gone to the extravagant length of calling me good. Perhaps they think I do not care for that; but I like it best. I don't like the others at all. If I am beautiful or not, it is as God made me, and I have nothing to do with it, and desire no credit, but if I could only be good it might be my own doing, perhaps, and I ought to have praise. I wonder if there is really and truly any good in me, and if you have read me aright." Then looking up at him with a touch of consternation: "Or are you laughing at me?"

Brandon wisely let the last suggestion pass unnoticed.

"I am sure that I am right; you have glorious capacities for good, but alas! corresponding possibilities for evil. It will eventually all depend upon the man you marry. He can make out of you a perfect woman, or the reverse." Again there was the surprised expression in Mary's face, but Brandon's serious look disarmed her.

"I fear you are right, as to the reverse, at any rate; and the worst of it is, I shall never be able to choose a man to help me, but shall sooner or later be compelled to marry the creature who will pay the greatest price."

"God forbid!" said Brandon reverently.

They were growing rather serious, so Mary turned the conversation again into the laughing mood, and said, with a half sigh: "Oh! I hope you are right about the possibilities for good, but you do not know. Wait until you have seen more of me."

"I certainly hope I shall not have long to wait."

The surprised eyes again glanced quickly up to the serious face, but the answer came: "That you shall not:—but here is the queen, and I suppose we must have the benediction." Brandon understood her hint—that the preaching was over,—and taking it for his dismissal, playfully lifted his hands in imitation of the old Bishop of Canterbury, and murmured the first line of the Latin benediction. Then they both laughed and courtesied, and Brandon walked away.

* * * * *

CHAPTER IV

A Lesson in Dancing

I laughed heartily when Jane told me of the tilt between Brandon and Princess Mary, the latter of whom was in the habit of saying unkind things and being thanked for them.

Brandon was the wrong man to say them to, as Mary learned. He was not hot-tempered; in fact, just the reverse, but he was the last man to brook an affront, and the quickest to resent, in a cool-headed, dangerous way, an intentional offense.

He respected himself and made others do the same, or seem to do so, at least. He had no vanity—which is but an inordinate desire for those qualities that bring self-respect, and often the result of conscious demerit—but he knew himself, and knew that he was entitled to his own good opinion. He was every inch a man, strong, intelligent and brave to temerity, with a reckless disregard of consequences, which might have been dangerous had it not been tempered by a dash of prudence and caution that gave him ballast.

I was not surprised when I heard of the encounter; for I knew enough of him to be sure that Mary's high-handedness would meet its counterpart in my cool friend Brandon. It was, however, an unfortunate victory, and what all Mary's beauty and brightness would have failed to do, her honest, open acknowledgment of wrong, following so quickly upon the heels of her fault, accomplished easily. It drew him within the circle of her fatal attractions, and when Jane told me of it, I knew his fate was sealed, and that, sooner or later, his untouched heart and cool head would fall victim to the shafts that so surely winged all others.

It might, and probably would, be "later," since, as Brandon had said, he was not one of those who wear the heart upon the sleeve. Then he had that strong vein of prudence and caution, which, in view of Mary's unattainableness, would probably come to his help. But never was man's heart strong enough to resist Mary Tudor's smile for long.

There was this difference between Brandon and most others—he would be slow to love, but when love should once fairly take root in his intense nature, he would not do to trifle with.

The night after the meeting, Mary cuddled up to Jane, who slept with her, and whispered, half bashfully:

"Tell me all about Brandon; I am interested in him. I believe if I knew more persons like him I should be a better girl, notwithstanding he is one of the boldest men I ever knew. He says anything he wishes, and, with all his modest manner, is as cool with me as if I were a burgher's daughter. His modesty is all on the outside, but it is pretty, and pretty things must be on the outside to be useful. I wonder if Judson thought him modest?"

Jane talked of Brandon to Mary, who was in an excellent humor, until the girls fell asleep.

When Jane told me of this I became frightened; for the surest way to any woman's heart is to convince her that you make her better, and arouse in her breast purer impulses and higher aspirations. It would be bad enough should Brandon fall in love with the princess, which was almost sure to happen, but for them to fall in love with each other meant Brandon's head upon the block, and Mary's heart bruised, broken and empty for life. Her strong nature, filled to the brim with latent passion, was the stuff of which love makes a conflagration that burns to destruction; and should she learn to love Brandon, she would move heaven and earth to possess him.

She whose every desire from childhood up had been gratified, whose every whim seemed to her a paramount necessity, would stop at nothing when the dearest wish a woman's heart can coin was to be gained or lost. Brandon's element of prudence might help him, and might forestall any effort on his part to win her, but Mary had never heard of prudence, and man's caution avails but little when set against woman's daring. In case they both should love, they were sure to try for each other, and in trying were equally sure to find ruin and desolation.

A few evenings after this I met the princess in the queen's drawing-room. She beckoned me to her, and, resting her elbows on the top of a cabinet, her chin in her hands, said: "I met your friend, Captain Brandon, a day or two ago. Did he tell you?"

"No," I answered; "Jane told me, but he has not mentioned it."

It was true Brandon had not said a word of the matter, and I had not spoken of it, either. I wanted to see how long he would remain silent concerning an adventure that would have set most men of the court boasting at a great rate. To have a tilt with the ever-victorious Mary, and to come off victor, was enough, I think, to loosen any tongue less given to bragging than Brandon's.

"So," continued Mary, evidently somewhat piqued, "he did not think his presentation to me a thing worth mentioning? We had a little passage-at-arms, and, to tell you the truth, I came off second best, and had to acknowledge it, too. Now, what do you think of this new friend of yours? And he did not boast about having the better of me? After all, there is more virtue in his silence than I at first thought." And she threw back her head, and clapped her hands and laughed with the most contagious little ripple you ever heard. She seemed not to grieve over her defeat, but dimpled as though it were a huge joke, the thought of which rather pleased her than otherwise. Victory had grown stale for her, although so young.

"What do I think of my new friend?" I repeated after her; and that gave me a theme upon which I could enlarge eloquently. I told her of his learning, notwithstanding the fact that he had been in the continental wars ever since he was a boy. I repeated to her stories of his daring and bravery, that had been told to me by his uncle, the Master of the Horse, and others, and then I added what I knew Lady Jane had already said. I had expected to be brief, but to my surprise found a close and interested listener, even to the twice-told parts, and drew my story out a little, to the liking of us both.

"Your friend has an earnest advocate in you, Sir Edwin," said the princess.

"That he has," I replied. "There is nothing too good to say of him."

I knew that Mary, with her better, clearer brain, held the king almost in the palm of her hand, so I thought to advance Brandon's fortune by a timely word.

"I trust the king will see fit to favor him, and I hope that you will speak a word in his behalf, should the opportunity occur."

"What in the name of heaven have we to give him?" cried Mary impatiently, for she kept an eye on things political, even if she were only a girl—"the king has given away everything that can be given, already, and now that the war is over, and men are coming home, there are hundreds waiting for more. My father's great treasure is squandered, to say nothing of the money collected from Empson, Dudley, and the other commissioners. There is nothing to give unless it be the titles and estate of the late Duke of Suffolk. Perhaps the king will give these to your paragon, if you will paint him in as fair a light as you have drawn him for me." Then throwing back her head with a laugh, "Ask him."

"It would be none too much for his deserts," I replied, falling in with her humor.

"We will so arrange it then," went on Mary, banteringly; "Captain Brandon no longer, but Charles Brandon, Duke of Suffolk. How sounds it, Master Caskoden?"

"Sweet in my ears," I replied.

"I really believe you would have the king's crown for him, you absurd man, if you could get it. We must have so interesting a person at court; I shall at least see that he is presented to the queen at once. I wonder if he dances; I suppose not. He has probably been too busy cutting and thrusting." And she laughed again at her own pleasantry.

When the mirth began to gather in her face and the dimples came responsive to her smiles; when she threw back her perfectly poised head, stretching her soft, white throat, so full and round and beautiful, half closing her big brown eyes till they shone again from beneath the shade of those long, black sweeping lashes; when her red lips parted, showing her teeth of pearl, and she gave the little clap of her hands—a sort of climax to the soft, low, rippling laugh—she made a picture of such exquisite loveliness that it is no wonder men were fools about her, and caught love as one catches a contagion. I had it once, as you already know, and had recovered.

All that prevented a daily relapse was my fair, sweet antidote, Jane, whose image rested in my heart, a lasting safeguard.

"I wonder if your prodigy plays cards; that is, such as we ladies play?" asked Mary. "You say he has lived much in France, where the game was invented, but I have no doubt he would scorn to waste his time at so frivolous a pursuit, when he might be slaughtering armies single-handed and alone."

"I do not know as to his dancing and card-playing, but I dare venture a wager he does both," I replied, not liking her tone of sarcasm. She had yet to learn who Brandon was.

"I will hazard ten crowns," said Mary quickly, for she loved a wager and was a born gambler.

"Taken," said I.

"We will try him on both to-morrow night in my drawing-room," she continued. "You bring him up, but tell no one. I will have Jane there with her lute, which will not frighten you away, I know, and we will try his step. I will have cards, too, and we shall see what he can do at triumph. Just we four—no one else at all. You and Jane, the new Duke of Suffolk and I. Oh! I can hardly wait," and she fairly danced with joyous anticipation.

The thing had enough irregularity to give it zest, for while Mary often had a few young people in her drawing-room, the companies were never so small as two couples only, and the king and queen, to make up for greater faults, were wonderful sticklers in the matter of little proprieties.

The ten-crown wager, too, gave spice to it, but to do her justice she cared very little for that. The princess loved gambling purely for gambling's sake, and with her, the next best thing to winning was losing.

When I went to my room that night, I awakened Brandon and told him of the distinguished honor that awaited him.

"Well! I'll be"—but he did not say what he would "be." He always halted before an oath, unless angry, which was seldom, but then beware!—he had learned to swear in Flanders. "How she did fly at me the other morning. I never was more surprised in all my life. For once I was almost caught with my guard down, and did not know how to parry the thrust. I mumbled over some sort of a lame retaliation and beat a retreat. It was so unjust and uncalled-for that it made me angry; but she was so gracious in her amends that

I was almost glad it happened. I like a woman who can be as savage as the very devil when it pleases her; she usually has in store an assortment of possibilities for the other extreme."

"She told me of your encounter," I returned, "but said she had come off second best, and seemed to think her overthrow a huge joke."

"The man who learns to know what a woman thinks and feels will have a great deal of valuable information," he replied; and then turned over for sleep, greatly pleased that one woman thought as she did.

I was not sure he would be so highly flattered if he knew that he had been invited to settle a wager, and to help Mary to a little sport.

As to the former, I had an interest there myself, although I dared not settle the question by asking Brandon if he played cards and danced; and, as to the matter of Mary's sport, I felt there was but little, if any, danger of her having too much of it at his expense, Brandon being well able to care for himself in that respect.

The next evening, at the appointed time, we wended our way, by an unfrequented route, and presented ourselves, as secretly as possible, at the drawing-room of the princess.

The door was opened by Lady Jane, and we met the two girls almost at the threshold. I had told Brandon of the bantering conversation about the title and estates of the late Duke of Suffolk, and he had laughed over it in the best of humor. If quick to retaliate for an intentional offense, he was not thin-skinned at a piece of pleasantry, and had none of that stiff, sensitive dignity, so troublesome to one's self and friends.

Now, Jane and Mary were always bantering me because I was short, and inclined to be—in fact—round, but I did not care. It made them laugh, and their laughing was so contagious it made me laugh, too, and we all enjoyed it. I would give a pound sterling any time for a good laugh; and that, I think, is why I have always been—round.

So, upon entering, I said:

"His grace, the Duke of Suffolk, ladies."

They each made a sweeping courtesy, with hand on breast, and gravely saluted him:

"Your grace! good even'."

Brandon's bow was as deep and graceful, if that were possible, as theirs, and when he moved on into the room it was with a little halt in his step, and a big blowing out of the cheeks, in ludicrous imitation of his late lamented predecessor, that sent the girls into peals of soft laughter and put us all at our ease immediately.

Ah! what a thing it is to look back upon; that time of life when one finds his heaven in a ready laugh!

"Be seated all," said the princess. "This is to be without ceremony, and only we four. No one knows a word of it. Did you tell any one, Sir Edwin?"

"Perish the thought," I exclaimed.

She turned her face toward Brandon, "—but I know you did not. I've heard how discreet you were about another matter. Well, no one knows it then, and we can have a famous evening. You did not expect this, Master Brandon, after my reception of you the other morning? Were you not surprised when Sir Edwin told you?"

"I think I can safely say that I was prepared not to be surprised at anything your highness might graciously conclude to do—after my first experience," he answered, smiling.

"Indeed?" returned Mary with elevated eyebrows, and a rising inflection on the last syllable of the word. It was now her turn for a little surprise. "Well, we'll try to find some way to surprise you one of these days;" and the time came when she was full of surprises for him. Mary continued: "But let us not talk about the other day. Of what use are 'other days,' anyway? Before the evening is over, Master Brandon, we want you to give us another sermon," and she laughed, setting off three other laughs as hearty and sincere as if she had uttered the rarest witticism on earth.

The princess had told Jane and Jane had told me of the "Sermon in the Park," as Mary called it.

"Jane needs it as much as I," said the princess.

"I can't believe that," responded Brandon, looking at Jane with a softening glance quite too admiring and commendatory to suit me; for I was a jealous little devil.

The eyebrows went up again.

"Oh! you think she doesn't? Well, in truth, Master Brandon, there is one failing that can not be laid at your door; you are no flatterer." For answer Brandon laughed, and that gave us the cue, and away we went in a rippling chorus, all about nothing. Some persons may call our laughter foolish, but there are others who consider it the height of all wisdom. St. George! I'd give my Garter for just one other laugh like that; for just one other hour of youth's dancing blood and glowing soul-warmth; of sweet, unconscious, happy heart-beat and paradise-creating joy in everything.

After a few minutes of gay conversation, in which we all joined, Mary asked: "What shall we do? Will one of you suggest something?"

Jane sat there looking so demure you would have thought mischief could not live within a league of her, but those very demure girls are nearly always dangerous. She said, oh! so innocently:

"Would you like to dance? If so, I will play." And she reached for her lute, which was by her side.

"Yes, that will be delightful. Master Brandon, will you dance with me?" asked the princess, with a saucy little laugh, her invitation meaning so much more to three of us than to Brandon. Jane and I joined in the laugh, and when Mary clapped her hands that set Brandon off, too, for he thought it the quaintest, prettiest little gesture in the world, and was all unconscious that our laugh was at his expense.

Brandon did not answer Mary's invitation—the fit of laughter had probably put it out of his mind—so she, evidently anxious to win or lose her wager at once, again asked him if he danced.

"Oh, pardon me. Of course. Thank you." And he was on his feet beside her chair in an instant ready for the dance. This time the girl's laugh, though equally merry, had another tone, for she knew she had lost.

Out they stepped upon the polished floor, he holding her hand in his, awaiting the pause in the music to take the step. I shall never forget the sight of those two standing there together—Mary, dark-eyed and glowing; Brandon, almost rosy, with eyes that held the color of a deep spring sky, and a wealth of flowing curls crowning his six feet of perfect manhood, strong and vigorous as a young lion. Mary, full of beauty-curves and graces, a veritable Venus in her teens, and Brandon, an Apollo, with a touch of Hercules, were a complement each to the other that would surely make a perfect one.

When the music started, off they went, heel and toe, bow and courtesy, a step forward and a step back, in perfect time and rhythm—a poem of human motion. Could Brandon dance? The princess had her answer in the first ten steps. Nothing could be more graceful than Brandon's dancing, unless it were Mary's. Her slightest movement was grace itself. When she would throw herself backward in thrusting out her toe, and then swing forward with her head a little to one side, her uplifted arm undulating like the white neck of a swan,—for her sleeve, which was slit to the shoulder, fell back and left it bare,—she was a sight worth a long journey to see. And when she looked up to Brandon with a laugh in her brown eyes, and a curving smile just parting her full, red lips, that a man would give his very luck to—but I had better stop.

"Was there ever a goodlier couple?" I asked Jane, by whose side I sat.

"Never," she responded as she played, and, strange to say, I was jealous because she agreed with me. I was jealous because I feared it was Brandon's beauty to which she referred. That I thought would naturally appeal to her. Had he been less handsome, I should perhaps have thought nothing of it, but I knew what my feelings were toward Mary, and I judged, or rather misjudged, Jane by myself. I supposed she would think of Brandon as I could not help thinking of Mary. Was anything in heaven or earth ever so beautiful as that royal creature, dancing there, daintily holding up her skirts with thumb and first finger, just far enough to show a distracting little foot and ankle, and make one wish he had been born a sheep rather than a sentient man who had to live without Mary Tudor? Yet, strange as it may seem, I was really and wholly in love with Jane; in fact, I loved no one but Jane, and my feeling of intense admiration for Mary was but a part of man's composite inconstancy.

A woman—God bless her—if she really loves a man, has no thought of any other; one at a time is all-sufficient; but a man may love one woman with the warmth of a simoon, and at the same time feel like a good healthy south wind toward a dozen others. That is the difference between a man and a woman—the difference between the good and the bad. One average woman has enough goodness in her to supply an army of men.

Mary and Brandon went on dancing long after Jane was tired of playing. It was plain to see that the girl was thoroughly enjoying it. They kept up a running fire of small talk, and laughed, and smiled, and bowed, and courtesied, all in perfect time and grace.

It is more difficult than you may think, if you have never tried, to keep up a conversation and dance La Galliard, at the same time—one is apt to balk the other—but Brandon's dancing was as easy to him as walking, and, although so small a matter, I could see it raised him vastly in the estimation of both girls.

"Do you play triumph?" I heard Mary ask in the midst of the dancing.

"Oh! yes," replied Brandon, much to my delight, as the princess threw a mischievous, knowing glance over her shoulder to see if I had heard. She at once saw I had, and this, of course, settled the wager.

"And," continued Brandon, "I also play the new game, 'honor and ruff,' which is more interesting than triumph."

"Oh! do you?" cried Mary. "That will more than compensate for the loss of my ten crowns. Let us sit down at once; I have been wishing to learn, but no one here seems to know it. In France, they say, it is the only game. I suppose there is where you learned it? Perhaps you know their new dances too! I have heard they are delightful!"

"Yes, I know them," replied Brandon.

"Why, you are a perfect treasure; teach me at once. How now, Master of the Dance? Here is your friend outdoing you in your own line."

"I am glad to hear it," I returned.

"If Lady Jane will kindly play some lively air, written in the time of 'The Sailor Lass,' I will teach the Lady Mary the new dance," said Brandon.

Jane threw one plump little knee over the other and struck up "The Sailor Lass." After she had adjusted the playing to Brandon's suggestion, he stepped deliberately in front of Mary, and, taking her right hand in his left, encircled her waist with his right arm. The girl was startled at first and drew away. This nettled Brandon a little, and he showed it plainly.

"I thought you wished me to teach you the new dance?" he said.

"I do, but—but I did not know it was danced that way," she replied with a fluttering little laugh, looking up into his face with a half shy, half apologetic manner, and then dropping her lashes before his gaze.

"Oh, well!" said Brandon, with a Frenchman's shrug of the shoulders, and then moved off as if about to leave the floor.

"But is that really the way you—they dance it? With your—their arm around my—a lady's waist?"

"I should not have dared venture upon such a familiarity otherwise," answered Brandon, with a glimmer of a smile playing around his lips and hiding in his eyes.

Mary saw this shadowy smile, and said: "Oh! I fear your modesty will cause you hurt; I am beginning to believe you would dare do anything you wish. I more than half suspect you are a very bold man, notwithstanding your smooth, modest manner."

"You do me foul wrong, I assure you. I am the soul of modesty, and grieve that you should think me bold," said Brandon, with a broadening smile.

Mary interrupted him. "Now, I do believe you are laughing at me—at my prudery, I suppose you think it."

Mary would rather have been called a fool than a prude, and I think she was right. Prudery is no more a sign of virtue than a wig is of hair. It is usually put on to hide a bald place.

The princess stood irresolute for a moment, in evident hesitation and annoyance.

"You are grieving because I think you bold! And yet you stand there laughing at me to my face. I think so more than ever now. I know it. Oh, you make me angry! Don't! I do not like persons who anger me and then laugh at me." This turned Brandon's smile into a laugh which he could not hold back.

Mary's eyes shot fire, and she stamped her foot, exclaiming: "Sir, this goes beyond all bounds; I will not tolerate your boldness another moment." I thought she was going to dismiss him, but she did not. The time had come when he or she must be the master.

It was a battle royal between the forces on the floor, and I enjoyed it and felt that Brandon would come out all right.

He said good-humoredly: "What, shall you have all the laugh in your sleeve at my expense? Do you expect to bring me here to win a wager for you, made on the assumption of my stupidity and lack of social accomplishments, and then complain when it comes my turn to laugh? I think I am the one who should be offended, but you see I am not."

"Caskoden, did you tell him?" demanded Mary, evidently referring to the wager.

"He said not a word of it," broke in Brandon, answering for me; "I should have been a dullard, indeed, not to have seen it myself after what you said about the loss of your ten crowns; so let us cry quits and begin again."

Mary reluctantly struck her flag.

"Very well, I am willing," she said laughingly; "but as to your boldness, I still insist upon that; I forgive you, however, this time." Then, half apologetically, "After all, it is not such a grievous charge to make. I believe it never yet injured any man with women; they rather like it, I am afraid, however angry it makes them. Don't they, Jane?"

Jane, of course, "did not know," so we all laughed, as usual, upon the slightest pretext, and Mary, that fair bundle of contradictions and quick transitions, stepped boldly up to Brandon, with her colors flying in her cheeks, ready for the first lesson in the new dance.

She was a little frightened at his arm around her waist, for the embrace was new to her—the first touch of man—and was shy and coy, though willing, being determined to learn the dance. She was an apt pupil and soon glided softly and gracefully around the room with unfeigned delight; yielding to the new situation more easily as she became accustomed to it.

This dance was livelier exercise than La Galliard, and Mary could not talk much for lack of breath. Brandon kept the conversation going, though, and she answered with glances, smiles, nods and monosyllables—a very good vocabulary in its way, and a very good way, too, for that matter.

Once he said something to her, in a low voice, which brought a flush to her cheeks, and caused her to glance quickly up into his face. By the time her answer came they were nearer us, and I heard her say: "I am afraid I shall have to forgive you again if you are not careful. Let me see an exhibition of that modesty you so much boast," But a smile and a flash of the eyes went with the words, and took all the sting out of them.

After a time the dancers stopped, and Mary, with flushed face and sparkling eyes, sank into a chair, exclaiming: "The new dance is delightful, Jane. It is like flying; your partner helps you so. But what would the king say? And the queen? She would simply swoon with horror. It is delightful, though." Then, with more confusion in her manner than I had ever before seen: "That is, it is delightful if one chooses her partner."

This only made matters worse, and gave Brandon an opportunity.

"Dare I hope?" he asked, with a deferential bow.

"Oh, yes; you may hope. I tell you frankly it was delightful with you. Now, are you satisfied, my modest one? Jane, I see we have a forward body here; no telling what he will be at next," said Mary, with evident impatience, rapidly swaying her fan. She spoke almost sharply, for Brandon's attitude was more that of an equal than she was accustomed to, and her royal dignity, which was the artificial part of her, rebelled against it now and then in spite of her real inclinations. The habit of receiving only adulation, and living on a pinnacle above everybody else, was so strong from continued practice, that it appealed to her as a duty to maintain that elevation. She had never before been called upon to exert herself in that direction, and the situation was new. The servile ones with whom she usually associated maintained it for her; so she now felt, whenever she thought of it, that she was in duty bound to clamber back, at least part of the way, to her dignity, however pleasant it was, personally, down below in the denser atmosphere of informality.

In her heart the princess preferred, upon proper occasions, such as this, to abate her dignity, and often requested others to dispense with ceremony, as, in fact, she had done with us earlier in the evening. But Brandon's easy manner, although perfectly respectful and elegantly polite, was very different from anything she had ever known. She enjoyed it, but every now and then the sense of her importance and dignity—for you must remember she was the first princess of the blood royal—would supersede even her love of enjoyment, and the girl went down and the princess came up. Besides, she half feared that Brandon was amusing himself at her expense, and that, in fact, this was a new sort of masculine worm. Really, she sometimes doubted if it were a worm at all, and did not know what to expect, nor what she ought to do.

She was far more girl than princess, and would have preferred to remain merely girl and let events take the course they were going, for she liked it. But there was the other part of her which was princess, and which kept saying: "Remember who you are," so she was plainly at a loss between natural and artificial inclinations contending unconsciously within her.

Replying to Mary's remark over Jane's shoulder, Brandon said:

"Your highness asked us to lay aside ceremony for the evening, and if I have offended I can but make for my excuse my desire to please you. Be sure I shall offend no more." This was said so seriously that his meaning could not be misunderstood. He did not care whether he pleased so capricious a person or not.

Mary made no reply, and it looked as if Brandon had the worst of it.

We sat a few minutes talking, Mary wearing an air of dignity. Cards were proposed, and as the game progressed she gradually unbent again and became as affable and familiar as earlier in the evening. Brandon, however, was frozen. He was polite, dignified and deferential to the ladies, but the spirit of the evening was gone, since he had furnished it all with his free, off-hand manner, full of life and brightness.

After a short time, Mary's warming mood failing to thaw our frozen fun-maker, and in her heart infinitely preferring pleasure to dignity, she said: "Oh, this is wearisome. Your game is far less entertaining than your new dance. Do something to make me laugh, Master Brandon."

"I fear you must call in Will Sommers," he replied, "if you wish to laugh. I can not please you in both ways, so will hold to the one which seems to suit the princess."

Mary's eyes flashed and she said ironically:

"That sounds very much as though you cared to please me in any way." Her lips parted and she evidently had something unkind ready to say; but she held the breath she had taken to speak it with, and, after one or two false starts in as many different lines, continued: "But perhaps I deserve it, I ask you to forgive me, and hereafter desire you three, upon all proper occasions, when we are by ourselves, to treat me as one of you—as a woman—a girl, I mean. Where is the virtue of royalty if it only means being put upon a pinnacle above all the real pleasures of life, like foolish old Stylites on his column? The queen is always preaching to me about the strict maintenance of my 'dignity royal,' as she calls it, and perhaps she is right; but out upon 'dignity royal' say I; it is a terrible nuisance. Oh, you don't know how difficult it is to be a princess and not a fool. There!" And she sighed in apparent relief.

Then turning to Brandon: "You have taught me another good lesson, sir, and from this hour you are my friend, if you will be, so long as you are worthy—no, I do not mean that; I know you will always be worthy—but forever. Now we are at rights again. Let us try to remain so—that is, I will," and she laughingly gave him her hand, which he, rising to his feet, bowed low over and kissed, rather fervently and lingeringly, I thought.

Hand-kissing was new to us in England, excepting in case of the king and queen at public homage. It was a little startling to Mary, though she permitted him to hold her hand much longer than there was any sort of need—a fact she recognized, as I could easily see from her tell-tale cheeks, which were rosy with the thought of it.

So it is when a woman goes on the defensive prematurely and without cause; it makes it harder to apply the check when the real need comes.

After a little card-playing, I expressed regret to Jane that I could not have a dance with her for lack of music.

"I will play, if the ladies permit," said Brandon; and he took Lady Jane's lute and played and sang some very pretty little love songs and some comic ones, too, in a style not often heard in England, so far away from the home of the troubadour and lute. He was full of surprises, this splendid fellow, with his accomplishments and graces.

When we had danced as long as we wished—that is, as Jane wished—as for myself, I would have been dancing yet—Mary again asked us to be seated. Jane having rested, Brandon offered to teach her the new dance, saying he could whistle an air well enough to give her the step. I at once grew uneasy with jealous suspense, for I did *not* wish Brandon to dance in that fashion with Jane, but to my great relief she replied:

"No; thank you; not to-night." Then shyly glancing toward me: "Perhaps Sir Edwin will teach me when he learns. It is his business, you know."

Would I? If a month, night and day, would conquer it, the new dance was as good as done for already. That was the first real mark of favor I ever had from Jane.

We now had some songs from Mary and Jane; then I gave one, and Brandon sang again at Mary's request. We had duets and quartets and solos, and the songs were all sweet, for they came from the heart of youth, and went to the soul of youth, rich in its God-given fresh delight in everything. Then we talked, and Mary, and Jane, too, with a sly, shy, soft little word now and then, drew Brandon out to tell of his travels and adventures. He was a pleasing talker, and had a smooth, easy flow of words, speaking always in a low, clear voice, and with perfect composure. He had a way of looking first one auditor and then another straight in the eyes with a magnetic effect that gave to everything he said an added interest. Although at that time less than twenty-five years old, he was really a learned man, having studied at Barcelona, Salamanca and Paris. While there had been no system in his education, his mind was a sort of knowledge junk-shop, wherein he could find almost anything he wanted. He spoke German, French and Spanish, and seemed to know the literature of all these languages.

He told us he had left home at the early age of sixteen as his uncle's esquire, and had fought in France, then down in Holland with the Dutch; had been captured by the Spanish and had joined the Spanish army, as it mattered not where he fought, so that there was a chance for honorable achievement and a fair ransom now and then. He told us how he had gone to Barcelona and Salamanca, where he had studied, and thence to Granada, among the Moors; of his fighting against the pirates of Barbary, his capture by them, his slavery and adventurous escape; and his regret that now drowsy peace kept him mewed up in a palace.

"It is true," he said, "there is a prospect of trouble with Scotland, but I would rather fight a pack of howling, starving wolves than the Scotch; they fight like very devils, which, of course, is well; but you have nothing after you have beaten them, not even a good whole wolf skin."

In an unfortunate moment Mary said: "Oh, Master Brandon, tell us of your duel with Judson."

Thoughtful, considerate Jane frowned at the princess in surprise, and put her finger on her lips.

"Your ladyship, I fear I can not," he answered, and left his seat, going over to the window, where he stood, with his back toward us, looking out into the darkness. Mary saw what she had done, and her eyes grew moist, for, with all her faults, she had a warm, tender heart and a quick, responsive sympathy. After a few seconds of painful silence, she went softly over to the window where Brandon stood.

"Sir, forgive me," she said, putting her hand prettily upon his arm. "I should have known. Believe me, I would not have hurt you intentionally."

"Ah! my lady, the word was thoughtlessly spoken, and needs no forgiveness; but your heart shows itself in the asking, and I thank you: I wanted but a moment to throw off the thought of that terrible day." Then they came back together, and the princess, who had tact enough when she cared to use it, soon put matters right again.

I started to tell one of my best stories in order to cheer Brandon, but in the midst of it, Mary, who, I had noticed, was restless and uneasy, full of blushes and hesitancy, and with a manner as new to her as the dawn of the first day was to the awakening world, abruptly asked Brandon to dance with her again. She had risen and was standing by her chair, ready to be led out.

"Gladly," answered Brandon, as he sprang to her side and took her hand. "Which shall it be, La Galliard or the new dance?" And Mary standing there, the picture of waiting, willing modesty, lifted her free hand to his shoulder, tried to raise her eyes to his, but failed, and softly said: "The new dance."

This time the dancing was more soberly done, and when Mary stopped it was with serious, thoughtful eyes, for she had felt the tingling of a new strange force in Brandon's touch. A man, not a worm, but a real man, with all the irresistible infinite attractions that a man may have for a woman—the subtle drawing of the lodestone for the passive iron—had come into her life. Doubly sweet it was to her intense, young virgin soul, in that it first revealed the dawning of that two-edged bliss which makes a heaven or a hell of earth— of earth, which owes its very existence to love.

I do not mean that Mary was in love, but that she had met, and for the first time felt the touch, yes even the subtle, unconscious, dominating force so sweet to woman, of the man she could love, and had known the rarest throb that pulses in that choicest of all God's perfect handiwork—a woman's heart—the throb that goes before—the John, the Baptist, as it were, of coming love.

It being after midnight, Mary filled two cups of wine, from each of which she took a sip, and handed them to Brandon and me. She then paid me the ten crowns, very soberly thanked us and said we were at liberty to go.

The only words Brandon ever spoke concerning that evening were just as we retired:

"Jesu! she is perfect. But you were wrong, Caskoden. I can still thank God I am not in love with her. I would fall upon my sword if I were."

I was upon the point of telling him she had never treated any other man as she had treated him, but I thought best to leave it unsaid. Trouble was apt to come of its own accord soon enough.

In truth, I may as well tell you, that when the princess asked me to bring Brandon to her that she might have a little sport at his expense, she looked for a laugh, but found a sigh.

* * * * *

CHAPTER V

An Honor and an Enemy

A day or two after this, Brandon was commanded to an audience, and presented to the king and queen. He was now eligible to all palace entertainments, and would probably have many invitations, being a favorite with both their majesties. As to his standing with Mary, who was really the most important figure, socially, about the court, I could not exactly say. She was such a mixture of contradictory impulses and rapid transitions, and was so full of whims and caprice, the inevitable outgrowth of her blood, her rank and the adulation amid which she had always lived, that I could not predict for a day ahead her attitude toward any one. She had never shown so great favor to any man as to Brandon, but just how much of her condescension was a mere whim, growing out of the impulse of the moment, and subject to reaction, I could not tell. I believed, however, that Brandon stood upon a firmer foundation with this changing, shifting, quicksand of a girl than with either of their majesties.

In fact, I thought he rested upon her heart itself. But to guess correctly what a girl of that sort will do, or think, or feel would require inspiration.

Of course most of the entertainments given by the king and queen included as guests nearly all the court, but Mary often had little fêtes and dancing parties which were smaller, more select and informal. These parties were really with the consent and encouragement of the king, to avoid the responsibility of not inviting everybody. The larger affairs were very dull and smaller ones might give offense to those who were left out. The latter, therefore, were turned over to Mary, who cared very little who was offended or who was not, and invitations to them were highly valued.

One afternoon, a day or two after Brandon's presentation, a message arrived from Mary, notifying me that she would have a little fête that evening in one of the smaller halls and directing me to be there as Master of the Dance. Accompanying the message was a note from no less a person than the princess herself, inviting Brandon.

This was an honor indeed—an autograph invitation from the hand of Mary! But the masterful rascal did not seem to consider it anything unusual, and when I handed him the note upon his return from the hunt, he simply read it carelessly over once, tore it in pieces and tossed it away. I believe the Duke of Buckingham would have given ten thousand crowns to receive such a note, and would doubtless have shown it to half the court in triumphant confidence before the middle of the night. To this great Captain of the guard it was but a scrap of paper. He was glad to have it nevertheless, and, with all his self-restraint and stoicism, could not conceal his pleasure.

Brandon at once accepted the invitation in a personal note to the princess. The boldness of this actually took my breath, and it seems at first to have startled Mary a little, also. As you must know by this time, her "dignity royal" was subject to alarms, and quite her most troublesome attribute—very apt to receive damage in her relations with Brandon.

Mary did not destroy Brandon's note, despite the fact that her sense of dignity had been disturbed by it, but after she had read it slipped off into her private room, read it again and put it on her escritoire. Soon she picked it up, reread it, and, after a little hesitation, put it in her pocket. It remained in the pocket for a moment or two, when out it came for another perusal, and then she unfastened her bodice and put it in her bosom. Mary had been so intent upon what she was doing that she had not seen Jane, who was sitting quietly in the window, and, when she turned and saw her, she was so angry she snatched the note from her bosom and threw it upon the floor, stamping her foot in embarrassment and rage.

"How dare you watch me, hussy?" she cried. "You lurk around as still as the grave, and I have to look into every nook and corner, wherever I go, or have you spying on me."

"I did not spy upon you, Lady Mary," said Jane quietly.

"Don't answer me; I know you did. I want you to be less silent after this. Do you hear? Cough, or sing, or stumble; do something, anything, that I may hear you."

Jane rose, picked up the note and offered it to her mistress, who snatched it with one hand, while she gave her a sharp slap with the other. Jane ran out, and Mary, full of anger and shame, slammed the door and locked it. The note, being the cause of all the trouble, she impatiently threw to the floor again, and went over to the window bench, where she threw herself down to pout. In the course of five minutes she turned her head for one fleeting instant and looked at the note, and then, after a little hesitation, stole over to where she had thrown it and picked it up. Going back to the light at the window, she held it in her hand a moment and then read it once, twice, thrice. The third time brought the smile, and the note nestled in the bosom again.

Jane did not come off so well, for her mistress did not speak to her until she called her in that evening to make her toilet. By that time Mary had forgotten about the note in her bosom; so when Jane began to array her for the dance, it fell to the floor, whereupon both girls broke into a laugh, and Jane kissed Mary's bare shoulder, and Mary kissed the top of Jane's head, and they were friends again.

So Brandon accepted Mary's invitation and went to Mary's dance, but his going made for him an enemy of the most powerful nobleman in the realm, and this was the way of it.

These parties of Mary's had been going on once or twice a week during the entire winter and spring, and usually included the same persons. It was a sort of coterie, whose members were more or less congenial, and most of them very jealous of interlopers. Strange as it may seem, uninvited persons often attempted to force themselves in, and all sorts of schemes and maneuvers were adopted to gain admission. To prevent this, two guardsmen with halberds were stationed at the door. Modesty, I might say, neither thrives nor is useful at court.

When Brandon presented himself at the door his entrance was barred, but he quickly pushed aside the halberds and entered. The Duke of Buckingham, a proud, self-important individual, was standing near the door and saw it all. Now Buckingham was one of those unfortunate persons who never lose an opportunity to make a mistake, and being anxious to display his zeal on behalf of the princess stepped up to prevent Brandon's entrance.

"Sir, you will have to move out of this," he said pompously. "You are not at a jousting bout. You have made a mistake and have come to the wrong place."

"My Lord of Buckingham is pleased to make rather more of an ass of himself than usual this evening," replied Brandon with a smile, as he started across the room to Mary, whose eye he had caught. She had seen and heard it all, but instead of coming to his relief stood there laughing to herself. At this Buckingham grew furious and ran around ahead of Brandon, valiantly drawing his sword.

"Now, by heaven! fellow, make but another step and I will run you through," he said.

I saw it all, but could hardly realize what was going on, it came so quickly and was over so soon. Like a flash Brandon's sword was out of its sheath, and Buckingham's blade was flying toward the ceiling. Brandon's sword was sheathed again so quickly that one could hardly believe it had been out at all, and, picking up Buckingham's, he said with a half-smothered laugh:

"My lord has dropped his sword." He then broke its point with his heel against the hard floor, saying: "I will dull the point, lest my lord, being unaccustomed to its use, wound himself." This brought peals of laughter from everybody, including the king. Mary laughed also, but, as Brandon was handing Buckingham his blade, came up and demanded:

"My lord, is this the way you take it upon yourself to receive my guests? Who appointed you, let me ask, to guard my door? We shall have to omit your name from our next list, unless you take a few lessons in good manners." This was striking him hard, and the quality of the man will at once appear plain to you when I say that he had often received worse treatment, but clung to the girl's skirts all the more tenaciously. Turning to Brandon the princess said:

"Master Brandon, I am glad to see you, and regret exceedingly that our friend of Buckingham should so thirst for your blood." She then led him to the king and queen, to whom he made his bow, and the pair continued their walk about the room. Mary again alluded to the skirmish at the door, and said laughingly:

"I would have come to your help, but I knew you were amply able to take care of yourself. I was sure you would worst the duke in some way. It was better than a mummery, and I was glad to see it. I do not like him."

The king did not open these private balls, as he was supposed, at least, not to be their patron, and the queen, who was considerably older than Henry, was averse to such things. So the princess opened her own balls, dancing for a few minutes with the floor entirely to herself and partner. It was the honor of the evening to open the ball with her, and quite curious to see how men put themselves in her way and stood so as to be easily observed and perchance chosen. Brandon, after leaving Mary, had drifted into a corner of the room back of a group of people, and was talking to Wolsey—

who was always very friendly to him—and to Master Cavendish, a quaint, quiet, easy little man, full of learning and kindness, and a warm friend to the Princess Mary.

It was time to open the ball, and, from my place in the musicians' gallery, I could see Mary moving about among the guests, evidently looking for a partner, while the men resorted to some very transparent and amusing expedients to attract her attention. The princess, however, took none of the bidders, and soon, I noticed, she espied Brandon standing in the corner with his back toward her.

Something told me she was going to ask him to open the dance, and I regretted it, because I knew it would set every nobleman in the house against him, they being very jealous of the "low-born favorites," as they called the untitled friends of royalty. Sure enough, I was right. Mary at once began to make her way over to the corner, and I heard her say: "Master Brandon, will you dance with me?"

It was done prettily. The whole girl changed as soon as she found herself in front of him. In place of the old-time confidence, strongly tinged with arrogance, she was almost shy, and blushed and stammered with quick coming breath, like a burgher maid before her new-found gallant. At once the courtiers made way for her, and out she walked, leading Brandon by the hand. Upon her lips and in her eyes was a rare triumphant smile, as if to say:

"Look at this handsome new trophy of my bow and spear."

I was surprised and alarmed when Mary chose Brandon, but when I turned to the musicians to direct their play, imagine, if you can, my surprise when the leader said:

"Master, we have our orders for the first dance from the princess."

Imagine, also, if you can, my double surprise and alarm, nay, almost my terror, when the band struck up Jane's "Sailor Lass." I saw the look of surprise and inquiry which Brandon gave Mary, standing there demurely by his side, when he first heard the music, and I heard her nervous little laugh as, she nodded her head, "Yes," and stepped closer to him to take position for the dance. The next moment she was in Brandon's arms, flying like a sylph about the room. A buzz of astonishment and delight greeted them before they were half way around, and then a great clapping of hands, in which the king himself joined. It was a lovely sight, although, I think, a graceful woman is more beautiful in La Galliard than any other dance, or, in fact, any other situation in which she can place herself.

After a little time the Dowager Duchess of Kent, first lady in waiting to the queen, presented herself at the musicians' gallery and said that her majesty had ordered the music stopped, and the musicians, of course, ceased playing at once. Mary thereupon turned quickly to me:

"Master, are our musicians weary that they stop before we are through?"

The queen answered for me in a high-voiced Spanish accent: "I ordered the music stopped; I will not permit such an indecent exhibition to go on longer."

Fire sprang to Mary's eyes and she exclaimed: "If your majesty does not like the way we do and dance at my balls you can retire as soon as you see fit. Your face is a kill-mirth anyway." It never took long to rouse her ladyship.

The queen turned to Henry, who was laughing, and angrily demanded:

"Will your majesty permit me to be thus insulted in your very presence?"

"You got yourself into it; get out of it as best you can. I have often told you to let her alone; she has sharp claws." The king was really tired of Catherine's sour frown before he married her. It was her dower of Spanish gold that brought her a second Tudor husband.

"Shall I not have what music and dances I want at my own balls?" asked the princess.

"That you shall, sister mine; that you shall," answered the king. "Go on master, and if the girl likes to dance that way, in God's name let her have her wish. It will never hurt her; we will learn it ourself, and will wear the ladies out a-dancing."

After Mary had finished the opening dance there was a great demand for instruction. The king asked Brandon to teach him the steps, which he soon learned to perform with a grace perhaps equaled by no living creature other than a fat brown bear. The ladies were at first a little shy and inclined to stand at arm's length, but Mary had set the fashion and the others soon followed. I had taken a fiddler to my room and had learned the dance from Brandon; and was able to teach it also, though I lacked practice to make my step perfect. The princess had needed no practice, but had danced beautifully from the first, her strong young limbs and supple body taking as naturally to anything requiring grace of movement as a cygnet to water.

This, thought I, is my opportunity to teach Jane the new dance. I wanted to go to her first, but was afraid, or for some reason did not, and took several other ladies as they came. After I had shown the step to them I sought out my sweetheart. Jane was not a prude, but I honestly believe she was the most provoking girl that ever lived. I never had succeeded in holding her hand even the smallest part of an instant, and yet I was sure she liked me very much; almost sure she loved me. She feared I might unhinge it and carry it away, or something of that sort, I suppose. When I went up and asked her to let me teach her the new dance, she said:

"I thank you, Edwin; but there are others who are more anxious to learn than I, and you had better teach them first."

"But I want to teach you. When I wish to teach them I will go to them."

"You did go to several others before you thought of coming to me," answered Jane, pretending to be piqued. Now that was the unkindest thing I ever knew a girl to do—refuse me what she knew I so wanted, and then put the refusal on the pretended ground that I did not care much about it. I so told her, and she saw she had carried things too far, and that I was growing angry in earnest. She then made another false, though somewhat flattering, excuse:

"I could not bear to go through that dance before so large a company. I should not object so much if no one else could see—that is, with you—Edwin." "Edwin!" Oh! so soft and sweet! The little jade! to think that she could hoodwink me so easily, and talk me into a good humor with her soft, purring "Edwin." I saw through it all quickly enough, and left her without another word. In a few minutes she went into an adjoining room where I knew she was alone. The door was open and the music could be heard there, so I followed.

"My lady, there is no one to see us here; I can teach you now, if you wish," said I.

She saw she was cornered, and replied, with a toss of her saucy little head: "But what if I do not wish?"

Now this was more than I could endure with patience, so I answered: "My young lady, you shall ask me before I teach you."

"There are others who can dance it much better than you," she returned, without looking at me.

"If you allow another to teach you that dance," I responded, "you will have seen the last of me." She had made me angry, and I did not speak to her for more than a week. When I did—but I will tell you of that later on. There was one thing about Jane and the new step: so long as she did not know it, she would not dance it with any other man, and foolish as my feeling may have been, I could not bear the thought of her doing it. I resolved that if she permitted another man to teach her that dance it should be all over between us. It was a terrible thought to me, that of losing Jane, and it came like a very stroke upon my heart. I would think of her sweet little form, so compact and graceful; of her gray, calm eyes, so full of purity and mischief; of her fair oval face, almost pale, and wonder if I could live without the hope of her. I determined, however, that if she learned the new dance with any other man I would throw that hope to the winds, whether I lived or died. St. George! I believe I should have died.

The evening was devoted to learning the new dance, and I saw Mary busily engaged imparting information among the ladies. As we were about to disperse I heard her say to Brandon:

"You have greatly pleased the king by bringing him a new amusement. He asked me where I learned it, and I told him you had taught it to Caskoden, and that I had it from him. I told Caskoden so that he can tell the same story."

"Oh! but that is not true. Don't you think you should have told him the truth, or have evaded it in some way?" asked Brandon, who was really a great lover of the truth, "when possible," but who, I fear on this occasion, wished to appear more truthful than he really was. If a man is to a woman's taste, and she is inclined to him, he lays up great stores in her heart by making her think him good; and shameful impositions are often practiced to this end.

Mary flushed a little and answered, "I can't help it. You do not know. Had I told Henry that we four had enjoyed such a famous time in my rooms he would have been very angry, and——and——you might have been the sufferer."

"But might you not have compromised matters by going around the truth some way, and leaving the impression that others were of the party that evening?"

That was a mistake, for it gave Mary an opportunity to retaliate: "The best way to go around the truth, as you call it, is by a direct lie. My lie was no worse than yours. But I did not stop to argue about such matters. There is something else I wished to say. I want to tell you that you have greatly pleased the king with the new dance. Now teach him 'honor and ruff' and your fortune is made. He has had some Jews and Lombards in of late to teach him new games at cards, but yours is worth all of them." Then, somewhat hastily and irrelevantly, "I did not dance the new dance with any other gentleman——but I suppose you did not notice it," and she was gone before he could thank her.

* * * * *

CHAPTER VI

A Rare Ride to Windsor

The princess knew her royal brother. A man would receive quicker reward for inventing an amusement or a gaudy costume for the king than by winning him a battle. Later in life the high road to his favor was in ridding him of his wife and helping him to a new one—a dangerous way though, as Wolsey found to his sorrow when he sank his glory in poor Anne Boleyn.

Brandon took the hint and managed to let it be known to his play-loving king that he knew the latest French games. The French Duc de Longueville had for some time been an honored prisoner at the English court, held as a hostage from Louis XII, but de Longueville was a blockhead, who could not keep his little black eyes off our fair ladies, who hated him, long enough to tell the deuce of spades from the ace of hearts. So Brandon was taken from his duties, such as they were, and placed at the card table. This was fortunate at first; for being the best player the king always chose him as his partner, and, as in every other game, the king always won. If he lost there would soon be no game, and the man who won from him too frequently was in danger at any moment of being rated guilty of the very highest sort of treason. I think many a man's fall, under Henry VIII, was owing to the fact that he did not always allow the king to win in some trivial matter of game or joust. Under these conditions everybody was anxious to be the king's partner. It is true he frequently forgot to divide his winnings, but his partner had this advantage, at least: there was no danger of losing. That being the case, Brandon's seat opposite the king was very likely to excite envy, and the time soon came, Henry having learned the play, when Brandon had to face someone else, and the seat was too costly for a man without a treasury. It took but a few days to put Brandon *hors de combat*, financially, and he would have been in a bad plight had not Wolsey come to his relief. After that, he played and paid the king in his own coin.

This great game of "honor and ruff" occupied Henry's mind day and night during a fortnight. He feasted upon it to satiety as he did with everything else; never having learned not to cloy his appetite by over-feeding. So we saw little of Brandon while the king's fever lasted, and Mary said she wished she had remained silent about the cards. You see, she could enjoy this new plaything as well as her brother; but the king, of course, must be satisfied first. They both had enough eventually; Henry in one way, Mary in another.

One day the fancy struck the king that he would rebuild a certain chapel at Windsor; so he took a number of the court, including Mary, Jane, Brandon and myself, and went with us up to London, where we lodged over night at Bridewell House. The next morning—as bright and beautiful a June day as ever gladdened the heart of a rose—we took horse for Windsor; a delightful seven-league ride over a fair road.

Mary and Jane traveled side by side, with an occasional companion or two, as the road permitted. I was angry with Jane, as you know, so did not go near the girls; and Brandon, without any apparent intention one way or the other, allowed events to adjust themselves, and rode with Cavendish and me.

We were perhaps forty yards behind the girls, and I noticed after a time that the Lady Mary kept looking backward in our direction, as if fearing rain from the east. I was in hopes that Jane, too, would fear the rain, but you would have sworn her neck was stiff, so straight ahead did she keep her face. We had ridden perhaps three leagues, when the princess stopped her horse and turned in her saddle. I heard her voice, but did not understand what she said.

In a moment some one called out: "Master Brandon is wanted." So that gentleman rode forward, and I followed him. When we came up with the girls, Mary said: "I fear my girth is loose."

Brandon at once dismounted to tighten it, and the others of our immediate party began to cluster around.

Brandon tried the girth.

"My lady, it is as tight as the horse can well bear," he said.

"It is loose, I say," insisted the princess, with a little irritation; "the saddle feels like it. Try the other." Then turning impatiently to the persons gathered around: "Does it require all of you, standing there like gaping bumpkins, to tighten my girth? Ride on; we can manage this without so much help." Upon this broad hint everybody rode ahead while I held the horse for Brandon, who went on with his search for the loose girth. While he was looking for it Mary leaned over her horse's neck and asked: "Were you and Cavendish settling all the philosophical points now in dispute, that you found him so interesting?"

"Not all," answered Brandon, smiling.

"You were so absorbed, I supposed it could be nothing short of that."

"No," replied Brandon again. "But the girth is not loose."

"Perhaps I only imagined it," returned Mary carelessly, having lost interest in the girth.

I looked toward Jane, whose eyes were bright with a smile, and turned Brandon's horse over to him. Jane's smile gradually broadened into a laugh, and she said: "Edwin, I fear my girth is loose also."

"As the Lady Mary's was?" asked I, unable to keep a straight face any longer.

"Yes," answered Jane, with a vigorous little nod of her head, and a peal of laughter.

"Then drop back with me," I responded.

The princess looked at us with a half smile, half frown, and remarked: "Now you doubtless consider yourselves very brilliant and witty."

"Yes," returned Jane maliciously, nodding her head in emphatic assent, as the princess and Brandon rode on before us.

"I hope she is satisfied now," said Jane *sotto voce* to me.

"So you want me to ride with you?" I replied.

"Yes," nodded Jane.

"Why?" I asked.

"Because I want you to," was the enlightening response.

"Then why did you not dance with me the other evening?"

"Because I did *not* want to."

"Short but comprehensive," thought I, "but a sufficient reason for a maiden."

I said nothing, however, and after a time Jane spoke: "The dance was one thing and riding with you is another. I did not wish to dance with you, but I do wish to ride with you. You are the only gentleman to whom I would have said what I did about my girth being loose. As to the new dance, I do not care to learn it because I would not dance it with any man but you, and not even with you—yet." This made me glad, and coming from coy, modest Jane meant a great deal. It meant that she cared for me, and would, some day, be mine; but it also meant that she would take her own time and her own sweet way in being won. This was comforting, if not satisfying, and loosened my tongue: "Jane, you know my heart is full of love for you—"

"Will the universe crumble?" she cried with the most provoking little laugh. Now that sentence was my rock ahead, whenever I tried to give Jane some idea of the state of my affections. It was a part of the speech which I had prepared and delivered to Mary in Jane's hearing, as you already know. I had said to the princess: "The universe will crumble and the heavens roll up as a scroll ere my love shall alter or pale." It was a high-sounding sentence, but it was not true, as I was forced to admit, almost with the same breath that spoke it. Jane had heard it, and had stored it away in that memory of hers, so tenacious in holding to everything it should forget. It is wonderful what a fund of useless information some persons accumulate and cling to with a persistent determination worthy of a better cause. I thought Jane never would forget that unfortunate, abominable sentence spoken so grandiloquently to Mary. I wonder what she would have thought had she known that I had said substantially the same thing to a dozen others. I never should have won her in that case. She does not know it yet, and never shall if I can prevent. Although dear Jane is old now, and the roses on her cheeks have long since paled, her gray eyes are still there, with their mischievous little twinkle upon occasion, and—in fact, Jane can be as provoking as ever when she takes the fancy, for she is as sure of my affection now as upon the morning of that rare ride to Windsor. Aye, surer, since she knows that in all these years it has changed only to grow greater and stronger and truer in the fructifying light of her sweet face, and the nurturing warmth of her pure soul. What a blessed thing it is for a man to love his wife and be satisfied with her, and to think her the fairest being in all the world; and how thrice happy is he who can stretch out the sweetest season of his existence, the days of triumphant courtship, through the flying years of all his life, and then lie down to die in the quieted ecstasy of a first love.

So Jane halted my effort to pour out my heart, as she always did.

"There is something that greatly troubles me," she said.

"What is it?" I asked in some concern.

"My mistress," she answered, nodding in the direction of the two riding ahead of us. "I never saw her so much interested in any one as she is in your friend, Master Brandon. Not that she is really in love with him as yet perhaps, but I fear it is coming and I dread to see it. She has never been compelled to forego anything she wanted, and her desires are absolutely imperative. They drive her, and she is helpless against them. She would not and could not make the smallest effort to overcome them. I think it never occurred to her that such a thing could be necessary; everything she wants she naturally thinks is hers by divine right. There has been no great need of such an effort until now, but your friend Brandon presents it. I wish he were at the other side of the world. I think she feels that she ought to keep away from him before it is too late, both for his sake and her own, but she is powerless to deny herself the pleasure of being with him, and I do not know what is to come of it all. That incident of the loose girth is an illustration. Did you ever know anything so bold and transparent? Any one could see through it, and the worst of all is she seems not to care if every one does see. Now look at them ahead of us! No girl is so happy riding beside a man unless she is interested in him. She was dull enough until he joined her. He seemed in no hurry to come, so she resorted to the flimsy excuse of the loose girth to bring him. I am surprised that she even sought the shadow of an excuse, but did not order him forward without any pretense of one. Oh! I don't know what to do. It troubles me greatly. Do you know the state of his feelings?"

"No," I answered, "but I think he is heart-whole, or nearly so. He told me he was not fool enough to fall in love with the king's sister, and I really believe he will keep his heart and head, even at that dizzy height. He is a cool fellow, if there ever was one."

"He certainly is different from other men," returned Jane. "I think he has never spoken a word of love to her. He has said some pretty things, which she has repeated to me; has moralized to some extent, and has actually told her of some of her faults. I should like to see anyone else take that liberty. She seems to like it from him, and says he inspires her with higher, better motives and a yearning to be good; but I am sure he has made no love to her."

"Perhaps it would be better if he did. It might cure her," I replied.

"Oh! no! no! not now; at first, perhaps, but not now. What I fear is that if he remains silent much longer she will take matters in hand and speak herself. I don't like to say that—it doesn't sound well—but she is a princess, and it would be different with her from what it would be with an ordinary girl; she might have to speak first, or there might be no speaking from one who thought his position too far beneath hers. She whose smallest desires drive her so, will never forego so great a thing as the man she loves only for the want of a word or two."

Then it was that Jane told me of the scene with the note, of the little whispered confidence upon their pillows, and a hundred other straws that showed only too plainly which way this worst of ill winds was blowing—with no good in it for any one. Now who could have foretold this? It was easy enough to prophesy that Brandon would learn to love Mary, excite a passing interest, and come off crestfallen, as all other men had done. But that Mary should love Brandon, and he remain heart-whole, was an unlooked-for event—one that would hardly have been predicted by the shrewdest prophet.

What Lady Jane said troubled me greatly, as it was but the confirmation of my own fears. Her opportunity to know was far better than mine, but I had seen enough to set me thinking.

Brandon, I believe, saw nothing of Mary's growing partiality at all. He could not help but find her wonderfully attractive and interesting, and perhaps it needed only the thought that she might love him, to kindle a flame in his own breast. But at the time of our ride to Windsor, Charles Brandon was not in love with Mary Tudor, however near it he may unconsciously have been. He would whistle and sing, and was as light-hearted as a lark—I mean when away from the princess as well as with her—a mood that does not go with a heart full of heavy love, of impossible, fatal love, such as his would have been for the first princess of the first blood royal of the world.

But another's trouble could not dim the sunlight in my own heart, and that ride to Windsor was the happiest day of my life up to that time. Even Jane threw off the little cloud our forebodings had gathered, and chatted and laughed like the creature of joy and gladness she was. Now and then her heart would well up so full of the sunlight and the flowers, and the birds in the hedge, aye, and of the contagious love in my heart, too, that it poured itself forth in a spontaneous little song which thrills me even now.

Ahead of us were the princess and Brandon. Every now and then her voice came back to us in a stave of a song, and her laughter, rich and low, wafted on the wings of the soft south wind, made the glad birds hush to catch its silvery note. It seemed that the wild flowers had taken on their brightest hue, the trees their richest Sabbath-day green, and the sun his softest radiance, only to gladden the heart of Mary that they might hear her laugh. The laugh would have come quite as joyously had the flowers been dead and the sun black, for flowers and sunlight, south wind, green pastures and verdant hills, all were riding by her side. Poor Mary! Her days of laughter were numbered.

We all rode merrily on to Windsor, and when we arrived it was curious to see the great nobles, Buckingham, both the Howards, Seymour and a dozen others stand back for plain Charles Brandon to dismount the fairest maiden and the most renowned princess in Christendom. It was done most gracefully. She was but a trifle to his strong arms, and he lifted her to the sod as gently as if she were a child. The nobles envied Brandon his evident favor with this unattainable Mary and hated him accordingly, but they kept their thoughts to themselves for two reasons: First, they knew not to what degree the king's favor, already marked, with the help of the princess might carry him; and second, they did not care to have a misunderstanding with the man who had cut out Adam Judson's eyes.

We remained at Windsor four or five days, during which time the king made several knights. Brandon would probably have been one of them, as everybody expected, had not Buckingham related to Henry the episode of the loose girth, and adroitly poisoned his mind as to Mary's partiality. At this the king began to cast a jealous eye on Brandon. His sister was his chief diplomatic resource, and when she loved or married, it should be for Henry's benefit, regardless of all else.

Brandon and the Lady Mary saw a great deal of each other during this little stay at Windsor, as she always had some plan to bring about a meeting, and although very delightful to him, it cost him much in royal favor. He could not trace this effect to its proper cause and it troubled him. I could have told him the reason in two words, but I feared to put into his mind the thought that the princess might learn to love him. As to the king, he would not have cared if Brandon or every other man, for that matter, should go stark mad for love of his sister, but when she began to show a preference he grew interested, and it was apt sooner or later to go hard with the fortunate one. When we went back to Greenwich Brandon was sent on a day ahead.

* * * * *

CHAPTER VII

Love's Fierce Sweetness

After we had all returned to Greenwich the princess and Brandon were together frequently. Upon several occasions he was invited, with others, to her parlor for card playing. But we spent two evenings, with only four of us present, prior to the disastrous events which changed everything, and of which I am soon to tell you. During these two evenings the "Sailor Lass" was in constant demand.

This pair, who should have remained apart, met constantly in and about the palace, and every glance added fuel to the flame. Part of the time it was the princess with her troublesome dignity, and part of the time it was Mary—simply girl. Notwithstanding these haughty moods, anyone with half an eye could see that the princess was gradually succumbing to the budding woman; that Brandon's stronger nature had dominated her with that half fear which every woman feels who loves a strong man—stronger than herself.

One day the rumor spread through the court that the old French king, Louis XII, whose wife, Anne of Brittany, had just died, had asked Mary's hand in marriage. It was this, probably, which opened Brandon's eyes to the fact that he had been playing with the very worst sort of fire; and first made him see that in spite of himself, and almost without his knowledge, the girl had grown wonderfully sweet and dear to him. He now saw his danger, and struggled to keep himself beyond the spell of her perilous glances and siren song. This modern Ulysses made a masterful effort, but alas! had no ships to carry him away, and no wax with which to fill his ears. Wax is a good thing, and no one should enter the Siren country without it. Ships, too, are good, with masts to tie one's self to, and sails and rudder, and a gust of wind to waft one quickly past the island. In fact, one cannot take too many precautions when in those enchanted waters.

Matters began to look dark to me. Love had dawned in Mary's breast, that was sure, and for the first time, with all its fierce sweetness. Not that it had reached its noon, or anything like it. In truth, it might, I hoped, die in the dawning, for my lady was as capricious as a May day; but it was love—love as plain as the sun at rising. She sought Brandon upon all occasions, and made opportunities to meet him; not openly—at any rate, not with Brandon's knowledge, nor with any connivance on his part, but apparently caring little what he or any one else might see. Love lying in her heart had made her a little more shy than formerly in seeking him, but her straightforward way of taking whatever she wanted made her transparent little attempts at concealment very pathetic.

As for Brandon, the shaft had entered his heart, too, poor fellow, as surely as love had dawned in Mary's, but there was this difference: With our princess—at least I so thought at the time— the sun of love might dawn and lift itself to mid-heaven and glow with the fervent ardor of high noon—for her blood was warm with the spark of her grandfather's fire—and then sink into the west and make room for another sun to-morrow. But with Brandon's stronger nature the sun would go till noon and there would burn for life. The sun, however, had not reached its noon with Brandon, either; since he had set his brain against his heart, and had done what he could to stay the all-consuming orb at its dawning. He knew the hopeless misery such a passion would bring him, and helped the good Lord, in so far as he could, to answer his prayer, and lead him not into temptation. As soon as he saw the truth, he avoided Mary as much as possible.

As I said, we had spent several evenings with Mary after we came home from Windsor, at all of which her preference was shown in every movement. Some women are so expressive under strong emotion that every gesture, a turn of the head, a glance of the eyes, the lifting of a hand or the poise of the body, speaks with a tongue of eloquence, and such was Mary. Her eyes would glow with a soft fire when they rested upon him, and her whole person told all too plainly what, in truth, it seemed she did not care to hide. When others were present she would restrain herself somewhat, but with only Jane and myself, she could hardly maintain a seemly reserve. During all this time Brandon remained cool and really seemed unconscious of his wonderful attraction for her. It is hard to understand why he did not see it, but I really believe he did not. Although he was quite at ease in her presence, too much so, Mary sometimes thought, and strangely enough sometimes told him in a fit of short-lived, quickly repented anger that always set him laughing, yet there was never a word or gesture that could hint of undue familiarity. It would probably have met a rebuff from the princess part of her; for what a perversity, both royal and feminine, she wanted all the freedom for herself. In short, like any other woman, she would rather love than be loved, that is, until surrender day should come; then of course . . .

After these last two meetings, although the invitations came frequently, none was accepted. Brandon had contrived to have his duties, ostensibly at least, occupy his evenings, and did honestly what his judgment told him was the one thing to do; that is, remain away from a fire that could give no genial warmth, but was sure to burn him to the quick. I saw this only too plainly, but never a word of it was spoken between us.

The more I saw of this man, the more I respected him, and this curbing of his affections added to my already high esteem. The effort was doubly wise in Brandon's case. Should love with his intense nature reach its height, his recklessness would in turn assert itself, and these two would inevitably try to span the impassable gulf between them, when Brandon, at least, would go down in the attempt. His trouble, however, did not make a mope of him, and he retained a great deal of his brightness and sparkle undimmed by what must have been an ache in his heart. Though he tried, without making it too marked, to see as little of Mary as possible, their meeting once in a while could not be avoided, especially when one of them was always seeking to bring it about. After a time, Mary began to suspect his attempts to avoid her, and she grew cold and distant through pique. Her manner, however, had no effect upon Brandon, who did not, or at least appeared not to notice it. This the girl could not endure, and lacking strength to resist her heart, soon returned to the attack.

Mary had not seen Brandon for nearly two weeks, and was growing anxious, when one day she and Jane met him in a forest walk near the river. Brandon was sauntering along reading when they overtook him. Jane told me afterwards that Mary's conduct upon coming up to him was pretty and curious beyond the naming. At first she was inclined to be distant, and say cutting things, but when Brandon began to grow restive under them and showed signs of turning back, she changed front in the twinkling of an eye and was all sweetness. She laughed and smiled and dimpled, as only she could, and was full of bright glances and gracious words.

She tried a hundred little schemes to get him to herself for a moment—the hunting of a wild flower or a four-leaved clover, or the exploration of some little nook in the forest toward which she would lead him—but Jane did not at first take the hint and kept close at her heels. Mary's impulsive nature was not much given to hinting—she usually nodded and most emphatically at that—so after a few failures to rid herself of her waiting lady she said impatiently: "Jane, in the name of heaven don't keep so close to us. You won't move out of reach of my hand, and you know how often it inclines to box your ears."

Jane did know, I am sorry for Mary's sake to say, how often the fair hand was given to such spasms; so with this emphasized hint she walked on ahead, half sulky at the indignity put upon her, and half amused at her whimsical mistress.

Mary lost no time, but began the attack at once.

"Now, sir, I want you to tell me the truth; why do you refuse my invitations and so persistently keep away from me? I thought at first I would simply let you go your way, and then I thought I—would not. Don't deny it. I know you won't. With all your faults, you don't tell even little lies; not even to a woman—I believe. Now there is a fine compliment—is it not?—when I intended to scold you!" She gave a fluttering little laugh, and, with hanging head, continued: "Tell me, is not the king's sister of quality sufficient to suit you? Perhaps you must have the queen or the Blessed Virgin? Tell me now?" And she looked up at him, half in banter, half in doubt.

"My duties——," began Brandon.

"Oh! bother your duties. Tell me the truth."

"I will, if you let me," returned Brandon, who had no intention whatever of doing anything of the sort. "My duties now occupy my time in the evening—"

"That will not do," interrupted Mary, who knew enough of a guardsman's duty to be sure it was not onerous. "You might as well come to it and tell the truth; that you do not like our society." And she gave him a vicious little glance without a shadow of a smile.

"In God's name, Lady Mary, that is not it," answered Brandon, who was on the rack. "Please do not think it. I cannot bear to have you say such a thing when it is so far from the real truth."

"Then tell me the real truth."

"I cannot; I cannot. I beg of you not to ask. Leave me! or let me leave you. I refuse to answer further." The latter half of this sentence was uttered doggedly and sounded sullen and ill-humored, although, of course, it was not so intended. He had been so perilously near speaking words which would probably have lighted, to their destruction—to his, certainly—the smoldering flames within their breast that it frightened him, and the manner in which he spoke was but a tone giving utterance to the pain in his heart.

Mary took it as it sounded, and, in unfeigned surprise, exclaimed angrily: "Leave you? Do I hear aright? I never thought that I, the daughter and sister of a king, would live to be dismissed by a—by a—any one."

"Your highness—" began Brandon; but she was gone before he could speak.

He did not follow her to explain, knowing how dangerous such an explanation would be, but felt that it was best for them both that she should remain offended, painful as the thought was to him.

Of course, Mary's womanly self-esteem, to say nothing of her royal pride, was wounded to the quick, and no wonder.

Poor Brandon sat down upon a stone, and, as he longingly watched her retiring form, wished in his heart he were dead. This was the first time he really knew how much he loved the girl, and he saw that, with him at least, it was a matter of bad to worse; and at that rate would soon be—worst.

Now that he had unintentionally offended her, and had permitted her to go without an explanation, she was dearer to him than ever, and, as he sat there with his face in his hands, he knew that if matters went on as they were going, the time would soon come when he would throw caution to the dogs and would try the impossible—to win her for his own. Caution and judgment still sat enthroned, and they told him now what he knew full well they would not tell him after a short time—that failure was certain to follow the attempt, and disaster sure to follow failure. First, the king would, in all probability, cut off his head upon an intimation of Mary's possible fondness for him; and, second, if he should be so fortunate as to keep his head, Mary could not, and certainly would not, marry him, even if she loved him with all her heart. The distance between them was too great, and she knew too well what she owed to her position. There was but one thing left—New Spain; and he determined while sitting there to sail with the next ship.

The real cause of Brandon's manner had never occurred to Mary. Although she knew her beauty and power, as she could not help but know it—not as a matter of vanity, but as a matter of fact—yet love had blinded her where Brandon was concerned, and that knowledge failed to give her light as to his motives, however brightly it might illumine the conduct of other men toward whom she was indifferent.

So Mary was angry this time; angry in earnest, and Jane felt the irritable palm more than once. I, too, came in for my share of her ill temper, as most certainly would Brandon, had he allowed himself to come within reach of her tongue, which he was careful not to do. An angry porcupine would have been pleasant company compared with Mary during this time. There was no living with her in peace. Even the king fought shy of her, and the queen was almost afraid to speak. Probably so much general disturbance was never before or since collected within one small body as in that young Tartar-Venus, Mary. She did not tell Jane the cause of her vexation, but only said she "verily hated Brandon," and that, of course, was the key to the whole situation.

After a fortnight, this ill-humor began to soften in the glowing warmth of her heart, which was striving to reassert itself, and the desire to see Brandon began to get the better of her sense of injury.

Brandon, tired of this everlasting watchfulness to keep himself out of temptation, and, dreading at any moment that lapse from strength which is apt to come to the strongest of us, had resolved to quit his place at court and go to New Spain at once. He had learned, upon inquiry, that a ship would sail from Bristol in about twenty days, and another six weeks later. So he chose the former and was making his arrangements to leave as soon as possible.

He told me of his plans and spoke of his situation: "You know the reason for my going," he said, "even if I have never spoken of it. I am not much of a Joseph, and am very little given to running away from a beautiful woman, but in this case I am fleeing from death itself. And to think what a heaven it would be. You are right, Caskoden; no man can withstand the light of that girl's smile. I am unable to tell how I feel toward her. It sometimes seems that I can not live another hour without seeing her; yet, thank God, I have reason enough left to know that every sight of her only adds to an already incurable malady. What will it be when she is the wife of the king of France? Does it not look as if wild life in New Spain is my only chance?"

I assented as we joined hands, and our eyes were moist as I told him how I should miss him more than anyone else in all the earth—excepting Jane, in mental reservation.

I told Jane what Brandon was about to do, knowing full well she would tell Mary; which she did at once.

Poor Mary! The sighs began to come now, and such small vestiges of her ill-humor toward Brandon as still remained were frightened off in a hurry by the fear that she had seen the last of him.

She had not before fully known that she loved him. She knew he was the most delightful companion she had ever met, and that there was an exhilaration about his presence which almost intoxicated her and made life an ecstasy, yet she did not know it was love. It needed but the thought that she was about to lose him to make her know her malady, and meet it face to face.

Upon the evening when Mary learned all this, she went into her chamber very early and closed the door. No one interrupted her until Jane went in to robe her for the night, and to retire. She then found that Mary had robed herself and was lying in bed with her head covered, apparently asleep. Jane quietly prepared to retire, and lay down in her own bed. The girls usually shared one couch, but during Mary's ill-temper she had forced Jane to sleep alone.

After a short silence Jane heard a sob from the other bed, then another, and another.

"Mary, are you weeping?" she asked.

"Yes."

"What is the matter, dear?"

"Nothing," with a sigh.

"Do you wish me to come to your bed?"

"Yes, I do." So Jane went over and lay beside Mary, who gently put her arms about her neck.

"When will he leave?" whispered Mary, shyly confessing all by her question.

"I do not know," responded Jane, "but he will see you before he goes."

"Do you believe he will?"

"I know it;" and with this consolation Mary softly wept herself to sleep.

After this, for a few days, Mary was quiet enough. Her irritable mood had vanished, but Jane could see that she was on the lookout for some one all the time, although she made the most pathetic little efforts to conceal her watchfulness.

At last a meeting came about in this way: Next to the king's bed-chamber was a luxuriously furnished little apartment with a well-selected library. Here Brandon and I often went, afternoons, to read, as we were sure to be undisturbed.

Late one day Brandon had gone over to this quiet retreat, and having selected a volume, took his place in a secluded little alcove half hidden in arras draperies. There was a cushioned seat along the wall and a small diamond-shaped window to furnish light.

He had not been there long when in came Mary. I can not say whether she knew Brandon was there or not, but she was there and he was there, which is the only thing to the point, and finding him, she stepped into the alcove before he was aware of her presence.

Brandon was on his feet in an instant, and with a low bow was backing himself out most deferentially, to leave her in sole possession if she wished to rest.

"Master Brandon, you need not go. I will not hurt you. Besides, if this place is not large enough for us both, I will go. I would not disturb you." She spoke with a tremulous voice and a quick, uneasy glance, and started to move backward out of the alcove.

"Lady Mary, how can you speak so? You know—you must know—oh! I beg you—" But she interrupted him by taking his arm and drawing him to a seat beside her on the cushion. She could have drawn down the Colossus of Rhodes with the look she gave Brandon, so full was it of command, entreaty and promise.

"That's it; I don't know, but I want to know; and I want you to sit here beside me and tell me. I am going to be reconciled with you, despite the way you treated me when last we met. I am going to be friends with you whether you will or not. Now what do you say to that, sir?" She spoke with a fluttering little laugh of uneasy non-assurance, which showed that her heart was not nearly so confident nor so bold as her words would make believe. Poor Brandon, usually so ready, had nothing "to say to that," but sat in helpless silence.

Was this the sum total of all his wise determinations made at the cost of so much pain and effort? Was this the answer to all his prayers, "Lead me not into temptation"? He had done his part, for he had done all he could. Heaven had not helped him, since here was temptation thrust upon him when least expected, and when the way was so narrow he could not escape, but must meet it face to face.

Mary soon recovered her self-possession—women are better skilled in this art than men—and continued:

"I am not intending to say one word about your treatment of me that day over in the forest, although it was very bad, and you have acted abominably ever since. Now is not that kind in me?" And she softly laughed as she peeped up at the poor fellow from beneath those sweeping lashes, with the premeditated purpose of tantalizing him, I suppose. She was beginning to know her power over him, and it was never greater than at this moment. Her beauty had its sweetest quality, for the princess was sunk and the woman was dominant, with flushed face and flashing eyes that caught a double luster from the glowing love that made her heart beat so fast. Her gown, too, was the best she could have worn to show her charms. She must have known Brandon was there, and must have dressed especially to go to him. She wore her favorite long flowing outer sleeve, without the close fitting inner one. It was slit to the shoulder, and gave entrancing glimpses of her arms with every movement, leaving them almost bare when she lifted her hands, which was often, for she was as full of gestures as a Frenchwoman. Her bodice was cut low, both back and front, showing her large perfectly molded throat and neck, like an alabaster pillar of beauty and strength, and disclosing her bosom just to its shadowy incurving, white and billowy as drifted snow. Her hair was thrown back in an attempt at a coil, though, like her own rebellious nature, it could not brook restraint, and persistently escaped in a hundred little curls that fringed her face and lay upon the soft white nape of her neck like fluffy shreds of sun-lit floss on new cut ivory.

With the mood that was upon her, I wonder Brandon maintained his self-restraint even for a moment. He felt that his only hope lay in silence, so he sat beside her and said nothing. He told me long afterwards that while sitting there in the intervals between her speech, the oddest, wildest thoughts ran through his brain. He wondered how he could escape. He thought of the window, and that possibly he might break away through it, and then he thought of feigning illness, and a hundred other absurd schemes, but they all came to nothing, and he sat there to let events take their own course as they seemed determined to do in spite of him.

After a short silence, Mary continued, half banteringly: "Answer me, sir! I will have no more of this. You shall treat me at least with the courtesy you would show a bourgeoise girl."

"Oh, that you were only a burgher's daughter."

"Yes, I know all that; but I am not. It can't be helped, and you shall answer me."

"There is no answer, dear lady—I beg you—oh, do you not see—"

"Yes, yes; but answer my question; am I not kind—more than you deserve?"

"Indeed, yes; a thousand times. You have always been so kind, so gracious and so condescending to me that I can only thank you, thank you, thank you," answered Brandon, almost shyly; not daring to lift his eyes to hers.

Mary saw the manner quickly enough—what woman ever missed it, much less so keen-eyed a girl as she—and it gave her confidence, and brought back the easy banter of her old time manner.

"How modest we have become! Where is the boldness of which we used to have so much? Kind? Have I always been so? How about the first time I met you? Was I kind then? And as to condescension, don't—don't use that word between us."

"No," returned Brandon, who, in his turn, was recovering himself, "no, I can't say that you were very kind at first. How you did fly out at me and surprise me. It was so unexpected it almost took me off my feet," and they both laughed in remembering the scene of their first meeting. "No, I can't say your kindness showed itself very strongly in that first interview, but it was there nevertheless, and when Lady Jane led me back, your real nature asserted itself, as it always does, and you were kind to me; kind as only you can be."

That was getting very near to the sentimental; dangerously near, he thought; and he said to himself: "If this does not end quickly I shall have to escape."

"You are easily satisfied if you call that good," laughingly returned Mary. "I can be ever so much better than that if I try."

"Let me see you try," said Brandon.

"Why, I'm trying now," answered Mary with a distracting little pout. "Don't you know genuine out-and-out goodness when you see it? I'm doing my very best now. Can't you tell?"

"Yes, I think I recognize it; but—but—be bad again."

"No, I won't! I will not be bad even to please you; I have determined not to be bad and I will not—not even to be good. This," placing her hand over her heart, "is just full of 'good' to-day," and her lips parted as she laughed at her own pleasantry.

"I am afraid you had better be bad—I give you fair warning," said Brandon huskily. He felt her eyes upon him all the time, and his strength and good resolves were oozing out like wine from an ill-coppered cask. After a short silence Mary continued, regardless of the warning:

"But the position is reversed with us; at first I was unkind to you, and you were kind to me, but now I am kind to you and you are unkind to me."

"I can come back at you with your own words," responded Brandon. "You don't know when I am kind to you. I should be kinder to myself, at least, were I to leave you and take myself to the other side of the world."

"Oh! that is one thing I wanted to ask you about. Jane tells me you are going to New Spain?"

She was anxious to know, but asked the question partly to turn the conversation which was fast becoming perilous. As a girl, she loved Brandon, and knew it only too well, but she knew also that she was a princess, standing next to the throne of the greatest kingdom on earth; in fact, at that time, the heir apparent—Henry having no children—for the people would not have the Scotch king's imp—and the possibility of such a thing as a union with Brandon had never entered her head, however passionate her feelings toward him. She also knew that speaking a thought vitalizes it and gives it force; so, although she could not deny herself the pleasure of being near him, of seeing him, and hearing the tones of his voice, and now and then feeling the thrill of an accidental touch, she had enough good sense to know that a mutual confession, that is, taking it for granted Brandon loved her, as she felt almost sure he did, must be avoided at all hazards. It was not to be thought of between people so far apart as they. The brink was a delightful place, full of all the sweet ecstasies and thrilling joys of a seventh heaven, but over the brink—well! there should be no "over," for who was she? And who was he? Those two dreadfully stubborn facts could not be forgotten, and the gulf between them could not be spanned; she knew that only too well. No one better.

Brandon answered her question: "I do not know about going; I think I shall. I have volunteered with a ship that sails in two or three weeks from Bristol, and I suppose I shall go."

"Oh, no! do you really mean it?" It gave her a pang to hear that he was actually going, and her love pulsed higher; but she also felt a sense of relief, somewhat as a conscientious house-breaker might feel upon finding the door securely locked against him. It would take away a temptation which she could not resist, and yet dared not yield to much longer.

"I think there is no doubt that I mean it," replied Brandon. "I should like to remain in England until I can save enough money out of the king's allowance to pay the debt against my father's estate, so that I may be able to go away and feel that my brother and sisters are secure in their home—my brother is not strong—but I know it is better for me to go now, and I hope to find the money out there. I could have paid it with what I lost to Judson before I discovered him cheating." This was the first time he had ever alluded to the duel, and the thought of it, in Mary's mind, added a faint touch of fear to her feeling toward him.

She looked up with a light in her eyes and asked: "What is the debt? How much? Let me give you the money. I have so much more than I need. Let me pay it. Please tell me how much it is and I will hand it to you. You can come to my rooms and get it or I will send it to you. Now tell me that I may. Quickly." And she was alive with enthusiastic interest.

"There now! you are kind again; as kind as even you can be. Be sure, I thank you, though I say it only once," and he looked into her eyes with a gaze she could not stand even for an instant. This was growing dangerous again, so, catching himself, he turned the conversation back into the bantering vein.

"Ah! you want to pay the debt that I may have no excuse to remain? Is that it? Perhaps you are not so kind after all."

"No! no! you know better. But let me pay the debt. How much is it and to whom is it owing? Tell me at once, I command you."

"No! no! Lady Mary, I cannot."

"Please do. I beg—if I cannot command. Now I know you will; you would not make me *beg* twice for anything?" She drew closer to him as she spoke and put her hand coaxingly upon his arm. With an irresistible impulse he took the hand in his and lifted it to his lips in a lingering caress that could not be mistaken. It was all so quick and so full of fire and meaning that Mary took fright, and the princess, for the moment, came uppermost.

"Master Brandon!" she exclaimed sharply, and drew away her hand. Brandon dropped the hand and moved over on the seat. He did not speak, but turned his face from her and looked out of the window toward the river. Thus they sat in silence, Brandon's hand resting listlessly upon the cushion between them. Mary saw the eloquent movement away from her and his speaking attitude, with averted face; then the princess went into eclipse, and the imperial woman was ascendant once more. She looked at him for a brief space with softening eyes, and, lifting her hand, put it back in his, saying:

"There it is again—if you want it."

Want it? Ah! this was too much! The hand would not satisfy now; it must be all, all! And he caught her to his arms with a violence that frightened her.

"Please don't, please! Not this time. Ah! have mercy, Charl—Well! There! . . . There! . . . Mary mother, forgive me." Then her woman spirit fell before the whirlwind of his passion, and she was on his breast with her white arms around his neck, paying the same tribute to the little blind god that he would have exacted from the lowliest maiden of the land. Just as though it were not the blood of fifty kings and queens that made so red and sweet, aye, sweet as nectar thrice distilled, those lips which now so freely paid their dues in coined bliss.

Brandon held the girl for a moment or two, then fell upon his knees and buried his face in her lap.

"Heaven help me!" he cried.

She pushed the hair back from his forehead with her hand and as she fondled the curls, leaned over him and softly whispered:

"Heaven help us both; for I love you!"

He sprang to his feet. "Don't! don't! I pray you," he said wildly, and almost ran from her.

Mary followed him nearly to the door of the room, but when he turned he saw that she had stopped, and was standing with her hands over her face, as if in tears.

He went back to her and said: "I tried to avoid this, and if you had helped me, it would never—" But he remembered how he had always despised Adam for throwing the blame upon Eve, no matter how much she may have deserved it, and continued: "No; I do not mean that. It is all my fault. I should have gone away long ago. I could not help it; I tried. Oh! I tried."

Mary's eyes were bent upon the floor, and tears were falling over her flushed cheeks, unheeded and unchecked.

"There is no fault in any one; neither could I help it," she murmured.

"No, no; it is not that there is any fault in the ordinary sense; it is like suicide or any other great, self-inflicted injury with me. I am different from other men. I shall never recover."

"I know only too well that you are different from other men, and—and I, too, am different from other women—am I not?"

"Ah, different! There is no other woman in all this wide, long world," and they were in each other's arms again. She turned her shoulder to him and rested with the support of his arms about her. Her eyes were cast down in silence, and she was evidently thinking as she toyed with the lace of his doublet. Brandon knew her varying expressions so well that he saw there was something wanting, so he asked:

"Is there something you wish to say?"

"Not I," she responded with emphasis on the pronoun.

"Then is it something you wish me to say?"

She nodded her head slowly: "Yes."

"What is it? Tell me and I will say it."

She shook her head slowly: "No."

"What is it? I cannot guess."

"Did you not like to hear me say that—that I—loved you?"

"Ah, yes; you know it. But—oh!—do you wish to hear me say it?"

The head nodded rapidly two or three times: "Yes." And the black curving lashes were lifted for a fleeting, luminous instant.

"It is surely not necessary; you have known it so long already, but I am only too glad to say it. I love you."

She nestled closer to him and hid her face on his breast.

"Now that I have said it, what is my reward?" he asked—and the fair face came up, red and rosy, with "rewards," any one of which was worth a king's ransom.

"But this is worse than insanity," cried Brandon, as he almost pushed her from him. "We can never belong to each other; never."

"No," said Mary, with a despairing shake of the head, as the tears began to flow again; "no! never." And falling upon his knees, he caught both her hands in his, sprang to his feet and ran from the room.

Her words showed him the chasm anew. She saw the distance between them even better than he. Evidently it seemed farther looking down than looking up. There was nothing left now but flight.

He sought refuge in his own apartments and wildly walked the floor, exclaiming, "Fool! fool that I am to lay up this store of agony to last me all my days. Why did I ever come to this court? God pity me—pity me!" And he fell upon his knees at the bed, burying his face in his arms, his mighty man's frame shaking as with a palsy.

That same night Brandon told me how he had committed suicide, as he put it, and of his intention to go to Bristol and there await the sailing of the ship, and perhaps find a partial resurrection in New Spain.

Unfortunately, he could not start for Bristol at once, as he had given some challenges for a tournament at Richmond, and could furnish no good excuse to withdraw them; but he would not leave his room, nor again see "that girl who was driving him mad."

It was better, he thought, and wisely too, that there be no leave-taking, but that he should go without meeting her.

"If I see her again," he said, "I shall have to kill some one, even if it is only myself."

I heard him tossing in his bed all night, and when morning came he arose looking haggard enough, but with his determination to run away and see Mary no more, stronger than ever upon him.

But providence, or fate, or some one, ordered it differently, and there was plenty of trouble ahead.

* * * * *

CHAPTER VIII

The Trouble in Billingsgate Ward

About a week after Brandon's memorable interview with Mary an incident occurred which changed everything and came very near terminating his career in the flower of youth. It also brought about a situation of affairs that showed the difference in the quality of these two persons thrown so marvelously together from their far distant stations at each end of the ladder of fortune, in a way that reflected very little credit upon the one from the upper end. But before I tell you of that I will relate briefly one or two other matters that had a bearing upon what was done, and the motives prompting it.

To begin with, Brandon had kept himself entirely away from the princess ever since the afternoon at the king's ante-chamber. The first day or so she sighed, but thought little of his absence; then she wept, and as usual began to grow piqued and irritable.

What was left of her judgment told her it was better for them to remain apart, but her longing to see Brandon grew stronger as the prospect of it grew less, and she became angry that it could not be gratified. Jane was right; an unsatisfied desire with Mary was torture. Even her sense of the great distance between them had begun to fade, and when she so wished for him and he did not come, their positions seemed to be reversed. At the end of the third day she sent for him to come to her rooms, but he, by a mighty effort, sent back a brief note saying that he could not and ought not to go. This, of course, threw Mary into a great passion, for she judged him by herself—a very common but dangerous method of judgment—and thought that if he felt at all as she did, he would throw prudence to the winds and come to her, as she knew she would go to him if she could. It did not occur to her that Brandon knew himself well enough to be sure he would never go to New Spain if he allowed another grain of temptation to fall into the balance against him, but would remain in London to love hopelessly, to try to win a hopeless cause, and end it all by placing his head upon the block.

It required all his strength, even now, to hold fast his determination to go to New Spain. He had reached his limit. He had a fund of that most useful of all wisdom, knowledge of self, and knew his limitations; a little matter concerning which nine men out of ten go all their lives in blissless ignorance.

Mary, who was no more given to self-analysis than her pet linnet, did not appreciate Brandon's potent reasons, and was in a flaming passion when she received his answer. Rage and humiliation completely smothered, for the time, her affection, and she said to herself, over and over again: "I hate the low-born wretch. Oh! to think what I have permitted!" And tears of shame and repentance came in a flood, as they have come from yielding woman's eyes since the world was born. Then she began to doubt his motives. As long as she thought she had given her gift to one who offered a responsive passion, she was glad and proud of what she had done, but she had heard of man's pretense in order to cozen woman out of her favors, and she began to think she had been deceived. To her the logic seemed irresistible; that if the same motive lived in his heart, and prompted him, that burned in her breast, and induced her, who was virgin to her very heart-core, and whose hand had hardly before been touched by the hand of man, to give so much, no power of prudence could keep him away from her. So she concluded she had given her gold for his dross. This conclusion was more easily arrived at owing to the fact that she had never been entirely sure of the state of his heart. There had always been a love-exciting grain of doubt; and when the thought came to her that she had been obliged to ask him to tell her of his affection, and that the advances had really all been made by her, that confirmed her suspicions. It seemed only too clear that she had been too quick to give—no very comforting thought to a proud girl, even though a mistaken one.

As the days went by and Brandon did not come, her anger cooled, as usual, and again her heart began to ache; but her sense of injury grew stronger day by day, and she thought she was, beyond a doubt, the most ill-used of women.

The other matter I wish to tell you is, that the negotiations for Mary's marriage with old Louis XII of France were beginning to be an open secret about the court. The Duc de Longueville, who had been held by Henry for some time as a sort of hostage from the French king, had opened negotiations by inflaming the flickering passions of old Louis with descriptions of Mary's beauty. As there was a prospect of a new emperor soon, and as the imperial bee had of late been making a most vehement buzzing in Henry's bonnet, he encouraged de Longueville, and thought it would be a good time to purchase the help of France at the cost of his beautiful sister and a handsome dower. Mary, of course, had not been consulted, and although she had coaxed her brother out of other marriage projects, Henry had gone about this as if he were in earnest, and it was thought throughout the court that Mary's coaxings would be all in vain—a fear which she herself had begun to share, notwithstanding her usual self-confidence.

She hated the thought of the marriage, and dreaded it as she would death itself, though she said nothing to any one but Jane, and was holding her forces in reserve for the grand attack. She was preparing the way by being very sweet and kind to Henry.

Now, all of this, coming upon the heels of her trouble with Brandon, made her most wretched indeed. For the first time in her life she began to feel suffering; that great broadener, in fact, maker, of human character.

Above all, there was an alarming sense of uncertainty in everything. She could hardly bring herself to believe that Brandon would really go to New Spain, and that she would actually lose him, although she did not want him, as yet; that is, as a prospective husband. Flashes of all sorts of wild schemes had begun to shoot through her anger and grief when she stared in the face the prospect of her double separation from him—her marriage to another, and the countless miles of fathomless sea that would be between them. She could endure anything better than uncertainty. A menacing future is the keenest of all tortures for any of us to bear, but especially for a girl like Mary. Death itself is not so terrible as the fear of it.

Now about this time there lived over in Billingsgate Ward— the worst part of London—a Jewish soothsayer named Grouche. He was also an astrologer, and had of late grown into great fame as prophet of the future—a fortune-teller.

His fame rested on several remarkable predictions which had been fulfilled to the letter, and I really think the man had some wonderful powers. They said he was half Jew, half gypsy, and, if there is alchemy in the mixing of blood, that combination should surely produce something peculiar. The city folk were said to have visited him in great numbers, and, notwithstanding the priests and bishops all condemned him as an imp of Satan and a follower of witchcraft, many fine people, including some court ladies, continued to go there by stealth in order to take a dangerous, inquisitive peep into the future. I say by stealth; because his ostensible occupation of soothsaying and fortune-telling was not his only business. His house was really a place of illicit meeting, and the soothsaying was often but an excuse for going there. Lacking this ostensible occupation, he would not have been allowed to keep his house within the wall, but would have been relegated to his proper place—Bridge Ward Without.

Mary had long wanted to see this Grouche, at first out of mere curiosity; but Henry, who was very moral—with other people's consciences—would not think of permitting it. Two ladies, Lady Chesterfield and Lady Ormond, both good and virtuous women, had been detected in such a visit, and had been disgraced and expelled from court in the most cruel manner by order of the king himself.

Now, added to Mary's old-time desire to see Grouche, came a longing to know the outcome of the present momentous complication of affairs that touched her so closely.

She could not wait for Time to unfold himself, and drop his budget of events as he traveled, but she must plunge ahead of him, and know, beforehand, the stores of the fates—an intrusion they usually resent. I need not tell you that was Mary's only object in going, nor that her heart was as pure as a babe's—quite as chaste and almost as innocent. It is equally true that the large proportion of persons who visited Grouche made his soothsaying an excuse. The thought of how wretched life would be with Louis had put into Mary's mind the thought of how sweet it would be with Brandon. Then came the wish that Brandon had been a prince, or even a great English nobleman; and then leaped up, all rainbow-hued, the hope that he might yet, by reason of his own great virtues, rise to all of these, and she become his wife. But at the threshold of this fair castle came knocking the thought that perhaps he did not care for her, and had deceived her to gain her favors. Then she flushed with anger and swore to herself she hated him, and hoped never to see his face again. And the castle faded and was wafted away to the realms of airy nothingness.

Ah! how people will sometimes lie to themselves; and sensible people at that.

So Mary wanted to see Grouche; first, through curiosity, in itself a stronger motive than we give it credit for; second, to learn if she would be able to dissuade Henry from the French marriage and perhaps catch a hint how to do it; and last, but by no means least, to discover the state of Brandon's heart toward her.

By this time the last-named motive was strong enough to draw her any whither, although she would not acknowledge it, even to herself, and in truth hardly knew it; so full are we of things we know not of.

So she determined to go to see Grouche secretly, and was confident she could arrange the visit in such a way that it would never be discovered.

One morning I met Jane, who told me, with troubled face, that she and Mary were going to London to make some purchases, would lodge at Bridewell House, and go over to Billingsgate that evening to consult Grouche. Mary had taken the whim into her wilful head, and Jane could not dissuade her.

The court was all at Greenwich, and nobody at Bridewell, so Mary thought they could disguise themselves as orange girls and easily make the trip without any one being the wiser.

It was then, as now, no safe matter for even a man to go unattended through the best parts of London after dark, to say nothing of Billingsgate, that nest of water-rats and cut-throats. But Mary did not realize the full danger of the trip, and would, as usual, allow nobody to tell her.

She had threatened Jane with all sorts of vengeance if she divulged her secret, and Jane was miserable enough between her fears on either hand; for Mary, though the younger, held her in complete subjection. Despite her fear of Mary, Jane asked me to go to London and follow them at a distance, unknown to the princess. I was to be on duty that night at a dance given in honor of the French envoys who had just arrived, bringing with them commission of special ambassador to de Longueville to negotiate the treaty of marriage, and it was impossible for me to go. Mary was going partly to avoid this ball, and her wilful persistency made Henry very angry. I regretted that I could not go, but I promised Jane I would send Brandon in my place, and he would answer the purpose of protection far better than I. I suggested that Brandon take with him a man, but Jane, who was in mortal fear of Mary, would not listen to it. So it was agreed that Brandon should meet Jane at a given place and learn the particulars, and this plan was carried out.

Brandon went up to London and saw Jane, and before the appointed time hid himself behind a hedge near the private gate through which the girls intended to take their departure from Bridewell.

They would leave about dusk and return, so Mary said, before it grew dark.

The citizens of London at that time paid very little attention to the law requiring them to hang out their lights, and when it was dark it *was* dark.

Scarcely was Brandon safely ensconced behind a clump of arbor vitæ when whom should he see coming down the path toward the gate but his grace, the Duke of Buckingham. He was met by one of the Bridewell servants who was in attendance upon the princess.

"Yes, your grace, this is the gate," said the girl. "You can hide yourself and watch them as they go. They will pass out on this path. As I said, I do not know where they are going; I only overheard them say they would go out at this gate just before dark. I am sure they go on some errand of gallantry, which your grace will soon learn, I make no doubt."

He replied that he "would take care of that."

Brandon did not see where Buckingham hid himself, but soon the two innocent adventurers came down the path, attired in the short skirts and bonnets of orange girls, and let themselves out at the gate. Buckingham followed them and Brandon quickly followed him. The girls passed through a little postern in the wall opposite Bridewell House, and walked rapidly up Fleet Ditch; climbed Ludgate Hill; passed Paul's church; turned toward the river down Bennett Hill; to the left on Thames street; then on past the Bridge, following Lower Thames street to the neighborhood of Fish-street Hill, where they took an alley leading up toward East Cheap to Grouche's house.

It was a brave thing for the girl to do, and showed the determined spirit that dwelt in her soft white breast. Aside from the real dangers, there was enough to deter any woman, I should think.

Jane wept all the way over, but Mary never flinched.

There were great mud-holes where one sank ankle-deep, for no one paved the street at that time, strangely enough preferring to pay the sixpence fine per square yard for leaving it undone. At one place, Brandon told me, a load of hay blocked the streets, compelling them to squeeze between the houses and the hay. He could hardly believe the girls had passed that way, as he had not always been able to keep them in view, but had sometimes to follow them by watching Buckingham. He, however, kept as close as possible, and presently saw them turn down Grouche's alley and enter his house.

Upon learning where they had stopped, Buckingham hurriedly took himself off, and Brandon waited for the girls to come out. It seemed a very long time that they were in the wretched place, and darkness had well descended upon London when they emerged.

Mary soon noticed that a man was following them, and as she did not know who he was, became greatly alarmed. The object of her journey had been accomplished now, so the spur of a strong motive to keep her courage up was lacking.

"Jane, some one is following us," she whispered.

"Yes," answered Jane, with an unconcern that surprised Mary, for she knew Jane was a coward from the top of her brown head to the tip of her little pink heels.

"Oh, if I had only taken your advice, Jane, and had never come to this wretched place; and to think, too, that I came here only to learn the worst. Shall we ever get home alive, do you think?"

They hurried on, the man behind them taking less care to remain unseen than he did when coming. Mary's fears grew upon her as she heard his step and saw his form persistently following them, and she clutched Jane by the arm.

"It is all over with us, I know. I would give everything I have or ever expect to have on earth for—for Master Brandon at this moment." She thought of him as the one person best able to defend her.

This was only too welcome an opportunity, and Jane said: "That is Master Brandon following us. If we wait a few seconds he will be here," and she called to him before Mary could interpose.

Now this disclosure operated in two ways. Brandon's presence was, it is true, just what Mary had so ardently wished, but the danger, and, therefore, the need, was gone when she found that the man who was following them had no evil intent. Two thoughts quickly flashed through the girl's mind. She was angry with Brandon for having cheated her out of so many favors and for having slighted her love, as she had succeeded in convincing herself was the case, all of which Grouche had confirmed by telling her he was false. Then she had been discovered in doing what she knew she should have left undone, and what she was anxious to conceal from every one; and, worst of all, had been discovered by the very person from whom she was most anxious to hide it.

So she turned upon Jane angrily: "Jane Bolingbroke, you shall leave me as soon as we get back to Greenwich for this betrayal of my confidence."

She was not afraid now that the danger was over, and feared no new danger with Brandon at hand to protect her, for in her heart she felt that to overcome a few fiery dragons and a company or so of giants would be a mere pastime to him; yet see how she treated him. The girls had stopped when Jane called Brandon, and he was at once by their side with uncovered head, hoping for, and, of course, expecting, a warm welcome. But even Brandon, with his fund of worldly philosophy, had not learned not to put his trust in princesses, and his surprise was benumbing when Mary turned angrily upon him.

"Master Brandon, your impudence in following us shall cost you dearly. We do not desire your company, and will thank you to leave us to our own affairs, as we wish you to attend exclusively to yours."

This from the girl who had given him so much within less than a week! Poor Brandon!

Jane, who had called him up, and was the cause of his following them, began to weep.

"Sir," said she, "forgive me; it was not my fault; she had just said—" Slap! came Mary's hand on Jane's mouth; and Jane was marched off, weeping bitterly.

The girls had started up toward East Cheap when they left Grouche's, intending to go home by an upper route, and now they walked rapidly in that direction. Brandon continued to follow them, notwithstanding what Mary had said, and she thanked him and her God ever after that he did.

They had been walking not more than five minutes, when, just as the girls turned a corner into a secluded little street, winding its way among the fish warehouses, four horsemen passed Brandon in evident pursuit of them. Brandon hurried forward, but before he reached the corner heard screams of fright, and as he turned into the street distinctly saw that two of the men had dismounted and were trying to overtake the fleeing girls. Fright lent wings to their feet, and their short skirts affording freedom to their limbs, they were giving the pursuers a warm little race, screaming at every step to the full limit of their voices. How they did run and scream! It was but a moment till Brandon came up with the pursuers, who, all unconscious that they in turn were pursued, did not expect an attack from the rear. The men remaining on horseback shouted an alarm to their comrades, but so intent were the latter in their pursuit that they did not hear. One of the men on foot fell dead, pierced through the back of the neck by Brandon's sword, before either was aware of his presence. The other turned, but was a corpse before he could cry out. The girls had stopped a short distance ahead, exhausted by their flight. Mary had stumbled and fallen, but had risen again, and both were now leaning against a wall, clinging to each other, a picture of abject terror. Brandon ran to the girls, but by the time he reached them the two men on horseback were there also, hacking away at him from their saddles. Brandon did his best to save himself from being cut to pieces and the girls from being trampled under foot by the prancing horses. A narrow jutting of the wall, a foot or two in width, a sort of flying buttress, gave him a little advantage, and up into the slight shelter of the corner thus formed he thrust the girls, and with his back to them, faced his unequal foe with drawn sword. Fortunately the position allowed only one horse to attack them. Two men on foot would have been less in each other's way and much more effective. The men, however, stuck to their horses, and one of them pressed the attack, striking at Brandon most viciously. It being dark, and the distance deceptive, the horseman's sword at last struck the wall, a flash of sparks flying in its trail, and lucky it was, or this story would have ended here. Thereupon Brandon thrust his sword into the horse's throat, causing it to rear backward, plunging and lunging into the street, where it fell, holding its rider by the leg against the cobblestones of a little gutter.

A cry from the fallen horseman brought his companion to his side, and gave Brandon an opportunity to escape with the girls. Of this he took advantage, you may be sure, for one of his mottoes was, that the greatest fool in the world is he who does not early in life learn how and when to run.

In the light of the sparks from the sword-stroke upon the wall, brief as it was, Brandon recognized the face of Buckingham, from which the mask had fallen. Of this he did not speak to any one till long afterward, and his silence was almost his undoing.

How often a word spoken or unspoken may have the very deuce in it either way!

The girls were nearly dead from fright, and in order to make any sort of progress Brandon had to carry the princess and help

Jane until he thought they were out of danger. Jane soon recovered, but Mary did not seem anxious to walk, and lay with her head upon Brandon's shoulder, apparently contented enough.

In a few minutes Jane said, "If you can walk now, my lady, I think you had better. We shall soon be near Fishmonger's Hall, where some one is sure to be standing at this hour."

Mary said nothing in reply to Jane, but, as Brandon fell a step or two behind at a narrow crossing, whispered:

"Forgive me, forgive me; I will do any penance you ask; I am unworthy to speak your name. I owe you my life and more—and more a thousand times." At this she lifted her arm and placed her hand upon his cheek and neck. She then learned for the first time that he was wounded, and the tears came softly as she slipped from his arms to the ground. She walked beside him quietly for a little time, then, taking his hand in both of hers, gently lifted it to her lips and laid it upon her breast. Half an hour afterward Brandon left the girls at Bridewell House, went over to the Bridge where he had left his horse at a hostelry, and rode down to Greenwich.

So Mary had made her trip to Grouche's, but it was labor worse than lost. Grouche had told her nothing she wanted to know, though much that he supposed she would like to learn. He had told her she had many lovers, a fact which her face and form would make easy enough to discover. He informed her also that she had a low-born lover, and in order to put a little evil in with the good fortune, and give what he said an air of truth, he added to Mary's state of unrest more than he thought by telling her that her low-born lover was false. He thought to flatter her by predicting that she would soon marry a very great prince or nobleman, the indications being in favor of the former, and, in place of this making her happy, she wished the wretched soothsayer in the bottomless pit—he and all his prophecies; herself, too, for going to him. His guesses were pretty shrewd; that is, admitting he did not know who Mary was, which she at least supposed was the case. So Mary wept that night and moaned and moaned because she had gone to Grouche's. It had added infinitely to the pain of which her heart was already too full, and made her thoroughly wretched and unhappy. As usual though, with the blunders of stubborn, self-willed people, some one else had to pay the cost of her folly. Brandon was paymaster in this case, and when you see how dearly he paid, and how poorly she requited the debt, I fear you will despise her. Wait, though! Be not hasty. The right of judgment belongs to—you know whom. No man knows another man's heart, much less a woman's, so how can he judge? We shall all have more than enough of judging by and by. So let us put off for as many to-morrows as possible the thing that should be left undone to-day.

* * * * *

CHAPTER IX

Put not your Trust in Princesses

I thought the king's dance that night would never end, so fond were the Frenchmen of our fair ladies, and I was more than anxious to see Brandon and learn the issue of the girls' escapade, as I well knew the danger attending it.

All things, however, must end, so early in the morning I hastened to our rooms, where I found Brandon lying in his clothes, everything saturated with blood from a dozen sword cuts. He was very weak, and I at once had in a barber, who took off his shirt of mail and dressed his wounds. He then dropped into a deep sleep, while I watched the night out. Upon awakening Brandon told me all that had happened, but asked me to say nothing of his illness, as he wished to keep the fact of his wounds secret in order that he might better conceal the cause of them. But, as I told you, he did not speak of Buckingham's part in the affray.

I saw the princess that afternoon, and expected, of course, she would inquire for her defender. One who had given such timely help and who was suffering so much on her account was surely worth a little solicitude; but not a word did she ask. She did not come near me, but made a point of avoidance, as I could plainly see. The next morning she, with Jane, went over to Scotland Palace without so much as a breath of inquiry from either of them. This heartless conduct enraged me; but I was glad to learn afterward that Jane's silence was at Mary's command—that bundle of selfishness fearing that any solicitude, however carefully shown upon her part, might reveal her secret.

It seems that Mary had recent intelligence of the forward state of affairs in the marriage negotiations, and felt that a discovery by her brother of what she had done, especially in view of the disastrous results, would send her to France despite all the coaxing she could do from then till doomsday.

It was a terrible fate hanging over her, doubly so in view of the fact that she loved another man; and looking back at it all from the vantage point of time, I cannot wonder that it drove other things out of her head and made her seem selfish in her frightened desire to save herself.

About twelve o'clock of the following night I was awakened by a knock at my door, and, upon opening, in walked a sergeant of the sheriff of London, with four yeomen at his heels.

The sergeant asked if one Charles Brandon was present, and upon my affirmative answer demanded that he be forthcoming. I told the sergeant that Brandon was confined to his bed with illness, whereupon he asked to be shown to his room.

It was useless to resist or to evade, so I awakened Brandon and took the sergeant in. Here he read his warrant to arrest Charles Brandon, Esquire, for the murder of two citizens of London, perpetrated, done and committed upon the night of such and such a day, of this year of our Lord, 1514. Brandon's hat had been found by the side of the dead men, and the authorities had received information from a high source that Brandon was the guilty person. That high source was evidently Buckingham.

When the sergeant found Brandon covered with wounds there was no longer any doubt, and although hardly able to lift his hand he was forced to dress and go with them. A horse litter was procured and we all started to London.

While Brandon was dressing, I said I would at once go and awaken the king, who I knew would pardon the offense when he heard my story, but Brandon asked the sergeant to leave us to ourselves for a short time, and closed the door.

"Please do nothing of the sort, Caskoden," said he; "if you tell the king I will declare there is not one word of truth in your story. There is only one person in the world who may tell of that night's happenings, and if she does not they shall remain untold. She will make it all right at once, I know. I would not do her the foul wrong to think for one instant that she will fail. You do not know her; she sometimes seems selfish, but it is thoughtlessness fostered by flattery, and her heart is right. I would trust her with my life.

If you breathe a word of what I have told you, you may do more harm than you can ever remedy, and I ask you to say nothing to any one. If the princess would not liberate me . . . but that is not to be thought of. Never doubt that she can and will do it better than you think. She is all gold."

This, of course, silenced me, as I did not know what new danger I might create, nor how I might mar the matter I so much wished to mend. I did not tell Brandon that the girls had left Greenwich, nor of my undefined, and, perhaps, unfounded fear that Mary might not act as he thought she would in a great emergency, but silently helped him to dress and went to London along with him and the sheriff's sergeant.

Brandon was taken to Newgate, the most loathsome prison in London at that time, it being used for felons, while Ludgate was for debtors. Here he was thrown into an underground dungeon foul with water that seeped through the old masonry from the moat, and alive with every noisome thing that creeps. There was no bed, no stool, no floor, not even a wisp of a straw; simply the reeking stone walls, covered with fungus, and the windowless arch overhead. One could hardly conceive a more horrible place in which to spend even a moment. I had a glimpse of it by the light of the keeper's lantern as they put him in, and it seemed to me a single night in that awful place would have killed me or driven me mad. I protested and begged and tried to bribe, but it was all of no avail; the keeper had been bribed before I arrived. Although it could do no possible good, I was glad to stand outside the prison walls in the drenching rain, all the rest of that wretched night, that I might be as near as possible to my friend and suffer a little with him.

Was not I, too, greatly indebted to him? Had he not imperiled his life and given his blood to save the honor of Jane as well as of Mary—Jane, dearer to me a thousand-fold than the breath of my nostrils? And was he not suffering at that moment because of this great service, performed at my request and in my place? If my whole soul had not gone out to him I should have been the most ungrateful wretch on earth; worse even than a pair of selfish, careless girls. But it did go out to him, and I believe I would have bartered my life to have freed him from another hour in that dungeon.

As soon as the prison gates were opened next morning, I again importuned the keeper to give Brandon a more comfortable cell, but his reply was that such crimes had of late become so frequent in London that no favor could be shown those who committed them, and that men like Brandon, who ought to know and act better, deserved the maximum punishment.

I told him he was wrong in this case; that I knew the facts, and everything would be clearly explained that very day and Brandon released.

"That's all very well," responded the stubborn creature; "nobody is guilty who comes here; they can every one prove innocence clearly and at once. Notwithstanding, they nearly all hang, and frequently, for variety's sake, are drawn and quartered."

I waited about Newgate until nine o'clock, and as I passed out met Buckingham and his man Johnson, a sort of lawyer-knight, going in. I went down to the palace at Greenwich, and finding that the girls were still at Scotland Palace, rode over at once to see them.

Upon getting Mary and Jane to myself, I told them of Brandon's arrest on the charge of murder, and of his condition, lying half dead from wounds and loss of blood, in that frightful dungeon. The tale moved them greatly, and they both gave way to tears. I think Mary had heard of the arrest before, as she did not seem surprised.

"Do you think he will tell the cause of the killing?" she asked.

"I know he will not," I answered; "but I also know that he knows you will," and I looked straight into her face.

"Certainly we will," said Jane; "we will go to the king at once," and she was on the *qui vive* to start immediately.

Mary did not at once consent to Jane's proposition, but sat in a reverie, looking with tearful eyes into vacancy, apparently absorbed in thought. After a little pressing from us she said: "I suppose it will have to be done; I can see no other way; but blessed Mother Mary! . . . help me!"

The girls made hasty preparations, and we all started back to Greenwich that Mary might tell the king. On the road over, I stopped at Newgate to tell Brandon that the princess would soon have him out, knowing how welcome liberty would be at her hands; but I was not permitted to see him.

I swallowed my disappointment, and thought it would be only a matter of a few hours' delay—the time spent in riding down to Greenwich and sending back a messenger. So, light-hearted enough at the prospect, I soon joined the girls, and we cantered briskly home.

After waiting a reasonable time for Mary to see the king, I sought her again to learn where and from whom I should receive the order for Brandon's release, and when I should go to London to bring him.

What was my surprise and disgust when Mary told me she had not yet seen the king—that she had waited to "eat, and bathe, and dress," and that "a few moments more or less could make no difference."

"My God! your highness, did I not tell you that the man who saved your life and honor—who is covered with wounds received in your defense, and almost dead from loss of blood, spilled that you might be saved from worse than death—is now lying in a rayless dungeon, a place of frightful filth, such as you would not walk across for all the wealth of London Bridge; is surrounded by loathsome, creeping things that would sicken you but to think of; is resting under a charge whose penalty is that he be hanged, drawn and quartered? And yet you stop to eat and bathe and dress. In God's name, Mary Tudor, of what stuff are you made? If he had waited but one little minute; had stopped for the drawing of a breath; had held back for but one faltering thought from the terrible odds of four swords to one, what would you now be? Think, princess, think!"

I was a little frightened at the length to which my feeling had driven me, but Mary took it all very well, and said slowly and absent-mindedly:

"You are right; I will go at once; I despise my selfish neglect. There is no other way; I have racked my brain—there *is* no other way. It must be done, and I will go at once and do it."

"And I will go with you," said I.

"I do not blame you," she said, "for doubting me, since I have failed once; but you need not doubt me now. It shall be done, and without delay, regardless of the cost to me. I have thought and thought to find some other way to liberate him, but there is none; I will go this instant."

"And I will go with you, Lady Mary," said I, doggedly.

She smiled at my persistency, and took me by the hand, saying, "Come!"

We at once went off to find the king, but the smile had faded from Mary's face, and she looked as if she were going to execution. Every shade of color had fled, and her lips were the hue of ashes.

We found the king in the midst of his council, with the French ambassadors, discussing the all-absorbing topic of the marriage treaty; and Henry, fearing an outbreak, refused to see the princess. As usual, opposition but spurred her determination, so she sat down in the ante-room and said she would not stir until she had seen the king.

After we had waited a few minutes, one of the king's pages came up and said he had been looking all over the palace for me, and that the king desired my presence immediately. I went in with the page to the king, leaving Mary alone and very melancholy in the ante-chamber.

Upon entering the king's presence he asked, "Where have you been, Sir Edwin? I have almost killed a good half-dozen pages hunting you. I want you to prepare immediately to go to Paris with an embassy to his majesty, King Louis. You will be the interpreter. The ambassador you need not know. Make ready at once. The embassy will leave London from the Tabard Inn one hour hence."

Could a command to duty have come at a more inopportune time? I was distracted; and upon leaving the king went at once to seek the Lady Mary where I had left her in the ante-room. She had gone, so I went to her apartments, but could not find her. I went to the queen's salon, but she was not there, and I traversed that old rambling palace from one end to the other without finding her or Lady Jane.

The king had told me the embassy would be a secret one, and that I was to speak of it to nobody, least of all to the Lady Mary. No one was to know that I was leaving England, and I was to communicate with no one at home while in France.

The king's command was not to be disobeyed; to do so would be as much as my life was worth, but besides that, the command of the king I served was my highest duty, and no Caskoden ever failed in that. I may not be as tall as some men, but my fidelity and honor—but you will say I boast.

I was to make ready my bundle and ride six miles to London in one hour; and almost half that time was spent already. I was sure to be late, so I could not waste another minute.

I went to my room and got together a few things necessary for my journey, but did not take much in the way of clothing, preferring to buy that new in Paris, where I could find the latest styles in pattern and fabric.

I tried to assure myself that Mary would see the king at once and tell him all, and not allow my dear friend Brandon to lie in that terrible place another night; yet a persistent fear gnawed at my heart, and a sort of intuition, that seemed to have the very breath of certainty in its foreboding, made me doubt her.

As I could find neither Mary nor Jane, I did the next best thing: I wrote a letter to each of them, urging immediate action, and left them to be delivered by my man Thomas, who was one of those trusty souls that never fail. I did not tell the girls I was about to start for France, but intimated that I was compelled to leave London for a time, and said: "I leave the fate of this man, to whom we all owe so much, in your hands, knowing full well how tender you will be of him."

I was away from home nearly a month, and as I dared not write, and even Jane did not know where I was, I did not receive, nor expect, any letters. The king had ordered secrecy, and if I have mingled with all my faults a single virtue it is that of faithfulness to my trust. So I had no news from England and sent none home.

During all that time the same old fear lived in my heart that Mary might fail to liberate Brandon. She knew of the negotiations concerning the French marriage, as we all did, although only by an indefinite sort of hearsay, and I was sure the half-founded rumors that had reached her ears had long since become certainties, and that her heart was full of trouble and fear of her violent brother. She would certainly be at her coaxing and wheedling again and on her best behavior, and I feared she might refrain from telling Henry of her trip to Grouche's, knowing how severe he was in such matters and how furious he was sure to become at the discovery. I was certain it was this fear which had prevented Mary from going directly to the king on our return to Greenwich from Scotland

Palace, and I knew that her eating, bathing and dressing were but an excuse for a breathing spell before the dreaded interview.

This fear remained with me all the time I was away, but when I reasoned with myself I would smother it as well as I could with argumentative attempts at self-assurance. I would say over and over to myself that Mary could not fail, and that even if she did, there was Jane, dear, sweet, thoughtful, unselfish Jane, who would not allow her to do so. But as far as they go, our intuitions—our "feelings," as we call them—are worth all the logic in the world, and you may say what you will, but my presentiments—I speak for no one else—are well to be minded. There is another sense hidden about us that will develop as the race grows older. I speak to posterity.

In proof of this statement, I now tell you that when I returned to London I found Brandon still in the terrible dungeon; and, worse still, he had been tried for murder, and had been condemned to be hanged, drawn and quartered on the second Friday following. Hanged! Drawn! Quartered! It is time we were doing away with such barbarity.

We will now go back a month for the purpose of looking up the doings of a friend of ours, his grace, the Duke of Buckingham.

On the morning after the fatal battle of Billingsgate, the barber who had treated Brandon's wounds had been called to London to dress a bruised knee for his grace, the duke. In the course of the operation, an immense deal of information oozed out of the barber, one item of which was that he had the night before dressed nine wounds, great and small, for Master Brandon, the king's friend. This established the identity of the man who had rescued the girls, a fact of which Buckingham had had his suspicions all along. So Brandon's arrest followed, as I have already related to you.

I afterward learned from various sources how this nobleman began to avenge his mishap with Brandon at Mary's ball when the latter broke his sword point. First, he went to Newgate and gave orders to the keeper, who was his tool, to allow no communication with the prisoner, and it was by his instructions that Brandon had been confined in the worst dungeon in London. Then he went down to Greenwich to take care of matters there, knowing that the king would learn of Brandon's arrest and probably take steps for his liberation at once.

The king had just heard of the arrest when Buckingham arrived, and the latter found he was right in his surmise that his majesty would at once demand Brandon's release.

When the duke entered the king's room Henry called to him: "My Lord, you are opportunely arrived. So good a friend of the people of London can help us greatly this morning. Our friend Brandon has been arrested for the killing of two men night before last in Billingsgate ward. I am sure there is some mistake, and that the good sheriff has the wrong man; but right or wrong, we want him out, and ask your good offices."

"I shall be most happy to serve your majesty, and will go to London at once to see the lord mayor."

In the afternoon the duke returned and had a private audience with the king.

"I did as your majesty requested in regard to Brandon's release," he said, "but on investigation, I thought it best to consult you again before proceeding further. I fear there is no doubt that Brandon is the right man. It seems he was out with a couple of wenches concerning whom he got into trouble and stabbed two men in the back. It is a very aggravated case and the citizens are much incensed about it, owing partly to the fact that such occurrences have been so frequent of late. I thought, under the circumstances, and in view of the fact that your majesty will soon call upon the city for a loan to make up the Lady Mary's dower, it would be wise not to antagonize them in this matter, but to allow Master Brandon to remain quietly in confinement until the loan is completed and then we can snap our fingers at them."

"We will snap our fingers at the scurvy burghers now and have the loan, too," returned Henry, angrily. "I want Brandon liberated at once, and I shall expect another report from you immediately, my lord."

Buckingham felt that his revenge had slipped through his fingers this time, but he was patient where evil was to be accomplished, and could wait. Then it was that the council was called during the progress of which Mary and I had tried to obtain an audience of the king.

Buckingham had gone to pay his respects to the queen, and on his way back espied Mary waiting for the king in the ante-room, and went to her.

At first she was irritated at the sight of this man, whom she so despised, but a thought came to her that she might make use of him. She knew his power with the citizens and city authorities of London, and also knew, or thought she knew, that a smile from her could accomplish everything with him. She had ample evidence of his infatuation, and she hoped that she could procure Brandon's liberty through Buckingham without revealing her dangerous secret.

Much to the duke's surprise, she smiled upon him and gave a cordial welcome, saying: "My lord, you have been unkind to us of late and have not shown us the light of your countenance. I am glad to see you once more; tell me the news."

"I cannot say there is much of interest. I have learned the new dance from Caskoden, if that is news, and hope for a favor at our next ball from the fairest lady in the world."

"And quite welcome," returned Mary, complacently appropriating the title, "and welcome to more than one, I hope, my lord."

This graciousness would have looked suspicious to one with less vanity than Buckingham, but he saw no craft in it. He did see, however, that Mary did not know who had attacked her in Billingsgate, and he felt greatly relieved.

The duke smiled and smirked, and was enchanted at her kindness. They walked down the corridor, talking and laughing, Mary awaiting an opportunity to put the important question without exciting suspicion. At last it came, when Buckingham, half inquiringly, expressed his surprise that Mary should be found sitting at the king's door.

"I am waiting to see the king," said she. "Little Caskoden's friend, Brandon, has been arrested for a brawl of some sort over in London, and Sir Edwin and Lady Jane have importuned me to obtain his release, which I have promised to do. Perhaps your grace will allow me to petition you in place of carrying my request to the king. You are quite as powerful as his majesty in London, and I should like to ask you to obtain for Master Brandon his liberty at once. I shall hold myself infinitely obliged, if your lordship will do this for me." She smiled upon him her sweetest smile, and assumed an indifference that would have deceived any one but Buckingham. Upon him, under the circumstances, it was worse than wasted.

Buckingham at once consented, and said, that notwithstanding the fact that he did not like Brandon, to oblige her highness, he would undertake to befriend a much more disagreeable person.

"I fear," he said, "it will have to be done secretly—by conniving at his escape rather than by an order for his release. The citizens are greatly aroused over the alarming frequency of such occurrences, and as many of the offenders have lately escaped punishment by reason of court interference, I fear this man Brandon will have to bear the brunt, in the London mind, of all these unpunished crimes. It will be next to impossible to liberate him, except by arranging privately with the keeper for his escape. He could go down into the country and wait in seclusion until it is all blown over, or until London has a new victim, and then an order can be made pardoning him, and he can return."

"Pardoning him! What are you talking of, my lord? He has done nothing to be pardoned for. He should be, and shall be, rewarded." Mary spoke impetuously, but caught herself and tried to remedy her blunder. "That is, if I have heard the straight of it. I have been told that the killing was done in the defense of two—women." Think of this poor unconscious girl, so full of grief and trouble, talking thus to Buckingham, who knew so much more about the affair than even she, who had taken so active a part in it.

"Who told you of it?" asked the duke.

Mary saw she had made a mistake, and, after hesitating for a moment, answered: "Sir Edwin Caskoden. He had it from Master Brandon, I suppose." Rather adroit this was, but equidistant from both truth and effectiveness.

"I will go at once to London and arrange for Brandon's escape," said Buckingham, preparing to leave. "But you must not divulge the fact that I do it. It would cost me all the favor I enjoy with the people of London, though I would willingly lose that favor, a thousand times over, for a smile from you."

She gave the smile, and as he left, followed his retiring figure with her eyes, and thought: "After all, he has a kind heart."

She breathed a sigh of relief, too, for she felt she had accomplished Brandon's release, and still retained her dangerous secret, the divulging of which, she feared, would harden Henry's heart against her blandishments and strand her upon the throne of France.

But she was not entirely satisfied with the arrangement. She knew that her obligation to Brandon was such as to demand of her that she should not leave the matter of his release to any other person, much less to an enemy such as Buckingham. Yet the cost of his freedom by a direct act of her own would be so great that she was tempted to take whatever risk there might be in the way that had opened itself to her. Not that she would not have made the sacrifice willingly, or would not have told Henry all if that were the only chance to save Brandon's life, but the other way, the one she had taken by Buckingham's help, seemed safe, and, though not entirely satisfying, she could not see how it could miscarry. Buckingham was notably jealous of his knightly word, and she had unbounded faith in her influence over him. In short, like many another person, she was as wrong as possible just at the time when she thought she was entirely right, and when the cost of a mistake was at its maximum.

She recoiled also from the thought of Brandon's "escape," and it hurt her that he should be a fugitive from the justice that should reward him, yet she quieted these disturbing suggestions with the thought that it would be only for a short time, and Brandon, she knew, would be only too glad to make the sacrifice if it purchased for her freedom from the worse than damnation that lurked in the French marriage.

All this ran quickly through Mary's mind, and brought relief; but it did not cure the uneasy sense, weighing like lead upon her heart, that she should take up chance with this man's life, and should put no further weight of sacrifice upon him, but should go to the king and tell him a straightforward story, let it hurt where it would. With a little meditation, however, came a thought which decided the question and absolutely made everything bright again for her, so great was her capability for distilling light. She would go at once to Windsor with Jane, and would dispatch a note to Brandon, at Newgate, telling him upon his escape to come to her. He might remain in hiding in the neighborhood of Windsor, and she could see him every day. The time had come to Mary when to "see him every day" would turn Plutonian shades into noonday brightness and weave sunbeams out of utter darkness. With Mary, to resolve was to act; so the note was soon dispatched by a page, and one hour later the girls were on their road to Windsor.

Buckingham went to Newgate, expecting to make a virtue, with Mary, out of the necessity imposed by the king's command, in freeing Brandon. He had hoped to induce Brandon to leave London stealthily and immediately, by representing to him the evil consequences of a break between the citizens and the king, liable to grow out of his release, and relied on Brandon's generosity to help him out; but when he found the note which Mary's page had delivered to the keeper of Newgate, he read it and all his plans were changed.

He caused the keeper to send the note to the king, suppressing the fact that he, Buckingham, had any knowledge of it. The duke then at once started to Greenwich, where he arrived and sought the king a few minutes before the time he knew the messenger with Mary's note would come. The king was soon found, and Buckingham, in apparent anger, told him that the city authorities refused to deliver Brandon except upon an order under the king's seal.

Henry and Buckingham were intensely indignant at the conduct of the scurvy burghers, and an immense amount of self-importance was displayed and shamefully wasted. This manifestation was at its highest when the messenger from Newgate arrived with Mary's poor little note as intended by the duke.

The note was handed to Henry, who read aloud as follows:

"To Master Charles Brandon":

"Greeting—Soon you will be at liberty; perhaps ere this is to your hand. Surely would I not leave you long in prison. I go to Windsor at once, there to live in the hope that I may see you speedily.

"MARY."

"What is this?" cried Henry. "My sister writing to Brandon? God's death! My Lord of Buckingham, the suspicions you whispered in my ear may have some truth. We will let this fellow remain in Newgate, and allow our good people of London to take their own course with him."

Buckingham went to Windsor next day and told Mary that arrangements had been made the night before for Brandon's escape, and that he had heard that Brandon had left for New Spain.

Mary thanked the duke, but had no smiles for any one. Her supply was exhausted.

She remained at Windsor nursing her love for the sake of the very pain it brought her, and dreading the battle for more than life itself which she knew she should soon be called upon to fight.

At times she would fall into one of her old fits of anger because Brandon had not come to see her before he left, but soon the anger melted into tears, and the tears brought a sort of joy when she thought that he had run away from her because he loved her. After Brandon's defense of her in Billingsgate, Mary had begun to see the whole situation differently, and everything was changed. She still saw the same great distance between them as before, but with this difference, she was looking up now. Before that event he had been plain Charles Brandon, and she the Princess Mary. She was the princess still, but he was a demi-god. No mere mortal, thought she, could be so brave and strong and generous and wise; and above all, no mere mortal could vanquish odds of four to one. In the night she would lie on Jane's arm, and amid smothered sobs, would softly talk of her lover, and praise his beauty and perfections, and pour her pathetic little tale over and over again into Jane's receptive ear and warm responsive heart; and Jane answered with soft little kisses that would have consoled Niobe herself. Then Mary would tell how the doors of her life, at the ripe age of eighteen, were closed forever and forever, and that her few remaining years would be but years of waiting for the end. At other times she would brighten, and repeat what Brandon had told her about New Spain; how fortune's door was open there to those who chose to come, and how he, the best and bravest of them all, would surely win glory and fortune, and then return to buy her from her brother Henry with millions of pounds of yellow gold. Ah, she would wait! She would wait! Like Bayard she placed her ransom at a high figure, and honestly thought herself worth it. And so she was—to Brandon, or rather had been. But at this particular time the market was down, as you will shortly hear.

So Mary remained at Windsor and grieved and wept and dreamed, and longed that she might see across the miles of billowy ocean to her love! her love! her love! Meanwhile Brandon had his trial in secret down in London, and had been condemned to be hanged, drawn and quartered for having saved to her more than life itself.

Put not your trust in princesses!

* * * * *

CHAPTER X

Justice, O King!

Such was the state of affairs when I returned from France.

How I hated myself because I had not faced the king's displeasure and had not refused to go until Brandon was safely out of his trouble. It was hard for me to believe that I had left such a matter to two foolish girls, one of them as changeable as the wind, and the other completely under her control. I could but think of the difference between myself and Brandon, and well knew, had I been in his place, he would have liberated me or stormed the very walls of London single-handed and alone.

When I learned that Brandon had been in that dungeon all that long month, I felt that it would surely kill him, and my self-accusation was so strong and bitter, and my mental pain so great, that I resolved if my friend died, either by disease contracted in the dungeon or by execution of his sentence, that I would kill myself. But that is a matter much easier sincerely to resolve upon than to execute when the time comes.

Next to myself, I condemned those wretched girls for leaving Brandon to perish—Brandon, to whom they both owed so much. Their selfishness turned me against all womankind.

I did not dally this time. I trusted to no Lady Jane nor Lady Mary. I determined to go to the king at once and tell him all. I did not care if the wretched Mary and Jane both had to marry the French king, or the devil himself. I did not care if they and all the host of their perfidious sisterhood went to the nether side of the universe, there to remain forever. I would retrieve my fault, in so far as it was retrievable, and save Brandon, who was worth them all put together. I would tell Mary and Jane what I thought of them, and that should end matters between us. I felt as I did toward them not only because of their treatment of Brandon, but because they had made me guilty of a grievous fault, for which I should never, so long as I lived, forgive myself. I determined to go to the king, and go I did within five minutes of the time I heard that Brandon was yet in prison.

I found the king sitting alone at public dinner, and, of course, was denied speech with him. I was in no humor to be balked, so I thrust aside the guards, and, much to everybody's fright, for I was wild with grief, rage and despair, and showed it in every feature, rushed to the king and fell upon my knees at his feet.

"Justice, O king!" I cried, and all the courtiers heard. "Justice, O king! for the worst used man and the bravest, truest soul that ever lived and suffered." Here the tears began to stream down my face and my voice choked in my throat. "Charles Brandon, your majesty's one-time friend, lies in a loathsome, rayless dungeon, condemned to death, as your majesty may know, for the killing of two men in Billingsgate Ward. I will tell you all: I should be thrust out from the society of decent men for not having told you before I left for France, but I trusted it to another who has proved false. I will tell you all. Your sister, the Lady Mary, and Lady Jane Bolingbroke were returning alone, after dark, from a visit to the soothsayer Grouche, of whom your majesty has heard. I had been notified of the Lady Mary's intended visit to him, although she had enjoined absolute secrecy upon my informant. I could not go, being detained upon your majesty's service—it was the night of the ball to the ambassadors—and I asked Brandon to follow them, which he did, without the knowledge of the princess. Upon returning, the ladies were attacked by four ruffians, and would have met with worse than death had not the bravest heart and the best sword in England defended them victoriously against such fearful odds. He left them at Bridewell without hurt or injury, though covered with wounds himself. This man is condemned to be hanged, drawn and quartered, but I know not your majesty's heart if he be not at once reprieved and richly rewarded. Think, my king! He saved the royal honor of your sister, who is so dear to you, and has suffered so terribly for his loyalty and bravery. The day I left so hurriedly for France the Lady Mary promised she would tell you all and liberate this man who had so nobly served her; but she is a woman, and was born to betray."

The king laughed a little at my vehemence.

"What is this you are telling me, Sir Edwin? I know of Brandon's death sentence, but much as I regret it, I cannot interfere with the justice of our good people of London for the murder of two knights in their streets. If Brandon committed such a crime, and, I understand he does not deny it, I cannot help him, however much I should like to do so. But this nonsense about my sister! It cannot be true. It must be trumped up out of your love in order to save your friend. Have a care, good master, how you say such a thing. If it were true, would not Brandon have told it at his trial?"

"It is as true as that God lives, my king! If the Lady Mary and Lady Jane do not bear me out in every word I have said, let my life pay the forfeit. He would not tell of the great reason for killing the men, fearing to compromise the honor of those whom he had saved, for, as your majesty is aware, persons sometimes go to Grouche's for purposes other than to listen to his soothsaying. Not in this case, God knows, but there are slanderous tongues, and Brandon was willing to die with closed lips, rather than set them wagging against one so dear to you. It seems that these ladies, who owe so much to him, are also willing that he should die rather than themselves bear the consequences of their own folly. Do not delay, I beseech your majesty. Eat not another morsel, I pray you, until this brave man, who has so truly served you, be taken from his prison and freed from his sentence of death. Come, come, my king! this moment, and all that I have, my wealth, my life, my honor, are yours for all time."

The king remained a moment in thought with knife in hand.

"Caskoden, I have never detected you in a lie in all the years I have known you; you are not very large in body, but your honor is great enough to stock a Goliath. I believe you are telling the truth. I will go at once to liberate Brandon; and that little hussy, my sister, shall go to France and enjoy life as best she can with her old beauty, King Louis. I know of no greater punishment to inflict upon her. This determines me; she shall coax me out of it no longer. Sir Thomas Brandon, have my horses ready, and I will go to the lord mayor, then to my lord bishop of Lincoln and arrange to close this French treaty at once. Let everybody know that the Princess Mary will, within the month, be queen of France." This was said to the courtiers, and was all over London before night.

I followed closely in the wake of the king, though uninvited, for I had determined to trust to no one, not even his majesty, until Brandon should be free. Henry had said he would go first to the lord mayor and then to Wolsey, but after we crossed the Bridge he passed down Lower Thames street and turned up Fish-street Hill into Grace Church street on toward Bishopsgate. He said he would stop at Mistress Cornwallis's and have a pudding; and then on to Wolsey, who at that time lodged in a house near the wall beyond Bishopsgate.

I well knew if the king once reached Wolsey's, it would be wine and quoits and other games, interspersed now and then with a little blustering talk on statecraft, for the rest of the day. Then the good bishop would have in a few pretty London women and a dance would follow with wine and cards and dice, and Henry would spend the night at Wolsey's, and Brandon lie another night in the mire of his Newgate dungeon.

I resolved to raise heaven and earth, and the other place, too, if necessary, before this should happen. So I rode boldly up to the king, and with uncovered head addressed him: "Your majesty gave me your royal word that you would go to the lord mayor first, and this is the road to my lord bishop of Lincoln. In all the years I have known your majesty, both as gallant prince and puissant king, this is the first request I ever proffered, and now I only ask of you to save your own noble honor, and do your duty as man and king."

These were bold words, but I did not care one little farthing whether they pleased him or not. The king stared at me and said:

"Caskoden, you are a perfect hound at my heels. But you are right; I had forgotten my errand. You disturbed my dinner, and my stomach called loudly for one of Mistress Cornwallis's puddings; but you are right to stick to me. What a friend you are in case of need. Would I had one like you."

"Your majesty has two of whom I know; one riding humbly by your royal side, and the other lying in the worst dungeon in Christendom."

With this the king wheeled about and started west toward Guildhall.

Oh, how I hated Henry for that cold-blooded, selfish forgetfulness worse than crime; and how I hoped the Blessed Virgin would forget him in time to come, and leave his soul an extra thousand years in purging flames, just to show him how it goes to be forgotten—in hell.

To the lord mayor we accordingly went without further delay. He was only too glad to liberate Brandon when he heard my story, which the king had ordered me to repeat. The only hesitancy was from a doubt of its truth.

The lord mayor was kind enough to say that he felt little doubt of my word, but that friendship would often drive a man to any extremity, even falsehood, to save a friend.

Then I offered to go into custody myself and pay the penalty, death, for helping a convicted felon to escape, if I told not the truth, to be confirmed or denied by the princess and her first lady in waiting. I knew Jane and was willing to risk her truthfulness without a doubt—it was so pronounced as to be troublesome at times—and as to Mary—well, I had no doubt of her, either. If she would but stop to think out the right she was sure to do it.

I have often wondered how much of the general fund of evil in this world comes from thoughtlessness. Cultivate thought and you make virtue—I believe. But this is no time to philosophize.

My offer was satisfactory, for what more can a man do than pledge his life for his friend? We have scripture for that, or something like it.

The lord mayor did not require my proffered pledge, but readily consented that the king should write an order for Brandon's pardon and release. This was done at once, and we, that is, I, together with a sheriff's sergeant and his four yeomen, hastened to Newgate, while Henry went over to Wolsey's to settle Mary's fate.

Brandon was brought up with chains and manacles at his ankles and wrists. When he entered the room and saw me, he exclaimed: "Ah! Caskoden, is that you? I thought they had brought me up to hang me, and was glad for the change; but I suppose you would not come to help at that, even if you have left me here to rot; God only knows how long; I have forgotten."

I could not restrain the tears at sight of him.

"Your words are more than just," I said; and, being anxious that he should know at once that my fault had not been so great as it looked, continued hurriedly: "The king sent me to France upon an hour's notice, the day after your arrest. I know only too well I should not have gone without seeing you out of this, but you had enjoined silence upon me, and—and I trusted to the promises of another."

"I thought as much. You are in no way to blame, my friend; all I ask is that you never mention the subject again."

"My friend!" Ah! the words were dear to me as words of love from a sweetheart's lips.

I hardly recognized him, he was so frightfully covered with filth and dirt and creeping things. His hair and beard were unkempt and matted, and his eyes and cheeks were lusterless and sunken; but I will describe him no further. Suffering had well-nigh done its work, and nothing but the hardihood gathered in his years of camp life and war could have saved him from death. I bathed and reclothed him as well as I could at Newgate, and then took him home to Greenwich in a horse litter, where my man and I thoroughly washed, dressed and sheared the poor fellow and put him to bed.

"Ah! this bed is a foretaste of paradise," he said, as he lay upon the mattress.

It was a pitiful sight, and I could hardly refrain from tears. I sent my man to fetch a certain Moor, a learned scholar, though a hated foreigner, who lived just off Cheap and sold small arms, and very soon he was with us. Brandon and I both knew him well, and admired his learning and gentleness, and loved him for his sweet philosophy of life, the leaven of which was charity—a modest little plant too often overshadowed by the rank growth of pompous dogmatism.

The Moor was learned in the healing potions of the east, and insisted, privately, of course, that all the shrines and relics in Christendom put together could not cure an ache in a baby's little finger. This, perhaps, was going too far, for there are some relics that have undoubted potency, but in cases where human agency can cure, the people of the east are unquestionably far in advance of us in knowledge of remedies. The Moor at once gave Brandon a soothing drink, which soon put him into a sweet sleep. He then bathed him as he slept, with some strengthening lotion, made certain learned signs, and spoke a few cabalistic words, and, sure enough, so strong were the healing remedies and incantations that the next morning Brandon was another man, though very far from well and strong. The Moor recommended nutritious food, such as roast beef and generous wine, and, although this advice was contrary to the general belief, which is, with apparent reason, that the evil spirit of disease should be starved and driven out, yet so great was our faith in him that we followed his directions, and in a few days Brandon had almost regained his old-time strength.

I will ask you to go back with me for a moment.

During the week, between Brandon's interview with Mary in the ante-room of the king's bed-chamber and the tragedy at Billingsgate, he and I had many conversations about the extraordinary situation in which he found himself.

At one time, I remember, he said: "I was safe enough before that afternoon. I believe I could have gone away and forgotten her eventually, but our mutual avowal seems to have dazed me and paralyzed every power for effort. I sometimes feel helpless, and, although I have succeeded in keeping away from her since then, I often find myself wavering in my determination to leave England. That was what I feared if I allowed the matter to go to the point of being sure of her love. I only wanted it before, and very easily made myself believe it was impossible, and not for me. But now that I know she loves me it is like holding my breath to live without her. I feel every instant that I can hold it no longer. I know only too well that if I but see her face once more I shall breathe. She is the very breath of life for me. She is mine by the gift of God. Curses upon those who keep us apart." Then musingly and half interrogatively: "She certainly does love me. She could not have treated me as she did unless her love was so strong that she could not resist it."

"Let no doubt of that trouble you," I answered.

"A woman like Mary cannot treat two men as she treated you. Many a woman may love, or think she loves many times, but there is only one man who receives the full measure of her best. Other women, again, have nothing to give but their best, and when they have once given that, they have given all. Unless I have known her in vain, Mary, with all her faults, is such a woman. Again I say, let no doubt of that trouble you."

Brandon answered with a sad little smile from the midst of his reverie. "It is really not so much the doubt as the certainty of it that troubles me." Then, starting to his feet: "If I thought she had lied to me; if I thought she could wantonly lead me on to suffer so for her, I would kill her, so help me God."

"Do not think that. Whatever her faults, and she has enough, there is no man on earth for her but you. Her love has come to her through a struggle against it because it was her master. That is the strongest and best, in fact the only, love; worth all the self-made passions in the world."

"Yes, I believe it. I know she has faults; even my partiality cannot blind me to them, but she is as pure and chaste as a child, and as gentle, strong and true as—as—a woman. I can put it no stronger. She has these, her redeeming virtues, along with her beauty, from her plebeian grandmother, Elizabeth Woodville, who, with them, won a royal husband and elevated herself to the throne beside the chivalrous Edward. This sweet plebeian heritage bubbles up in the heart of Mary, and will not down, but neutralizes the royal poison in her veins and makes a goddess of her." Then with a sigh: "But if her faults were a thousand times as many, and if each fault were a thousand times as great, her beauty would atone for all. Such beauty as hers can afford to have faults. Look at Helen and Cleopatra, and Agnes Sorel. Did their faults make them less attractive? Beauty covereth more sins than charity—and maketh more grief than pestilence."

The last clause was evidently an afterthought.

After his month in Newgate with the hangman's noose about his neck all because of Mary's cruel neglect, I wondered if her beauty would so easily atone for her faults. I may as well tell you that he changed his mind concerning this particular doctrine of atonement.

* * * * *

CHAPTER XI

Louis XII a Suitor

As soon as I could leave Brandon, I had intended to go down to Windsor and give vent to my indignation toward the girls, but the more I thought about it, the surer I felt there had, somehow, been a mistake. I could not bring myself to believe that Mary had deliberately permitted matters to go to such an extreme when it was in her power to prevent it. She might have neglected her duty for a day or two, but, sooner or later, her good impulses always came to her rescue, and, with Jane by her side to urge her on, I was almost sure she would have liberated Brandon long ago—barring a blunder of some sort.

So I did not go to Windsor until a week after Brandon's release, when the king asked me to go down with him, Wolsey and de Longueville, the French ambassador-special, for the purpose of officially offering to Mary the hand of Louis XII, and the honor of becoming queen of France.

The princess had known of the projected arrangement for many weeks, but had no thought of the present forward condition of affairs, or she would have brought her energies to bear upon Henry long before. She could not bring herself to believe that her brother would really force her into such wretchedness, and possibly he would never have done so, much as he desired it from the standpoint of personal ambition, had it not been for the petty excuse of that fatal trip to Grouche's.

All the circumstances of the case were such as to make Mary's marriage a veritable virgin sacrifice. Louis was an old man, and an old Frenchman at that; full of French notions of morality and immorality; and besides, there were objections that cannot be written, but of which Henry and Mary had been fully informed. She might as well marry a leper. Do you wonder she was full of dread and fear, and resisted with the desperation of death?

So Mary, the person most interested, was about the last to learn that the treaty had been signed.

Windsor was nearly eight leagues from London, and at that time was occupied only by the girls and a few old ladies and servants, so that news did not travel fast in that direction from the city. It is also probable that, even if the report of the treaty and Brandon's release had reached Windsor, the persons hearing it would have hesitated to repeat it to Mary. However that may be, she had no knowledge of either until she was informed of the fact that the king and the French ambassador would be at Windsor on a certain day to make the formal request for her hand and to offer the gifts of King Louis.

I had no doubt Mary was in trouble, and felt sure she had been making affairs lively about her. I knew her suffering was keen, but was glad of it in view of her treatment of Brandon.

A day or two after Brandon's liberation I had begun to speak to him of the girls, but he interrupted me with a frightful oath: "Caskoden, you are my friend, but if you ever mention their names again in my hearing you are my friend no longer. I will curse you."

I was frightened, so much stronger did his nature show than mine, and I took good care to remain silent on that subject until— but I am going too fast again; I will tell you of that hereafter.

Upon the morning appointed, the king, Wolsey, de Longueville and myself, with a small retinue, rode over to Windsor, where we found that Mary, anticipating us, had barricaded herself in her bedroom and refused to receive the announcement. The king went up stairs to coax the fair young besieged through two inches of oak door, and to induce her, if possible, to come down. We below could plainly hear the king pleading in the voice of a Bashan bull, and it afforded us some amusement behind our hands. Then his majesty grew angry and threatened to break down the door, but the fair besieged maintained a most persistent and provoking silence throughout it all, and allowed him to carry out his threat without so much as a whimper. He was thoroughly angry, and called to us to come up to see him "compel obedience from the self-willed hussy,"—a task the magnitude of which he underrated.

The door was soon broken down, and the king walked in first, with de Longueville and Wolsey next, and the rest of us following in close procession. But we marched over broken walls to the most laughable defeat ever suffered by besieging army. Our foe, though small, was altogether too fertile in expedients for us. There seemed no way to conquer this girl; her resources were so inexhaustible that in the moment of your expected victory success was turned into defeat; nay, more, ridiculous disaster.

We found Jane crouching on the floor in a corner half dead with fright from the noise and tumult—and where do you think we found her mistress? Frightened? Not at all; she was lying in bed with her face to the wall as cool as a January morning; her clothing in a little heap in the middle of the room.

Without turning her head, she exclaimed: "Come in, brother; you are quite welcome. Bring in your friends; I am ready to receive them, though not in court attire, as you see." And she thrust her bare arm straight up from the bed to prove her words. You should have seen the Frenchman's little black eyes gloat on its beauty.

Mary went on, still looking toward the wall: "I will arise and receive you all informally, if you will but wait."

This disconcerted the imperturbable Henry, who was about at his wit's end.

"Cover that arm, you hussy," he cried in a flaming rage.

"Be not impatient, brother mine! I will jump out in just a moment."

A little scream from Jane startled everybody, and she quickly ran up to the king, saying: "I beg your majesty to go. She will do as she says so sure as you remain; you don't know her; she is very angry. Please go; I will bring her down stairs somehow."

"Ah, indeed! Jane Bolingbroke," came from the bed. "I will receive my guests myself when they are kind enough to come to my room." The cover-lid began to move, and, whether or not she was really going to carry out her threat, I cannot say, but Henry, knowing her too well to risk it, hurried us all out of the room and marched down stairs at the head of his defeated cohorts. He was swearing in a way to make a priest's flesh creep, and protesting by everything holy that Mary should be the wife of Louis or die. He went back to Mary's room at intervals, but there was enough persistence in that one girl to stop the wheels of time, if she but set herself to do it, and the king came away from each visit the victim of another rout.

Finally his anger cooled and he became amused. From the last visit he came down laughing:

"I shall have to give up the fight or else put my armor on with visor down," said he; "it is not safe to go near her without it; she is a very vixen, and but now tried to scratch my eyes out."

Wolsey, who had a wonderful knack for finding the easiest means to a difficult end, took Henry off to a window where they held a whispered conversation.

It was pathetic to see a mighty king and his great minister of state consulting and planning against one poor girl; and, as angry as I felt toward Mary, I could not help pitying her, and admired, beyond the power of pen to write, the valiant and so far impregnable defense she had put up against an array of strength that would have made a king tremble on his throne.

Presently Henry gave one of his loud laughs, and slapped his thigh as if highly satisfied with some proposition of Wolsey's.

"Make ready at once," he said. "We will go back to London."

In a short time we were all at the main stairway ready to mount for the return trip.

The Lady Mary's window was just above, and I saw Jane watching us as we rode away.

After we were well out of Mary's sight the king called me to him, and he, together with de Longueville, Wolsey and myself, turned our horses' heads, rode rapidly by a circuitous path back to another door of the castle and re-entered without the knowledge of any of the inmates.

We four remained in silence, enjoined by the king, and in the course of an hour, the princess, supposing every one had gone, came down stairs and walked into the room where we were waiting.

It was a scurvy trick, and I felt a contempt for the men who had planned it. I could see that Mary's first impulse was to beat a hasty retreat back into her citadel, the bed, but in truth she had in her make-up very little disposition to retreat. She was clear grit. What a man she would have made! But what a crime it would have been in nature to have spoiled so perfect a woman. How beautiful she was! She threw one quick, surprised glance at her brother and his companions, and lifting up her exquisite head carelessly hummed a little tune under her breath as she marched to the other end of the room with a gait that Juno herself could not have improved upon.

I saw the king smile, half in pride of her, and half in amusement, and the Frenchman's little eyes feasted upon her beauty with a relish that could not be mistaken.

Henry and the ambassador spoke a word in whispers, when the latter took a box from a huge side pocket and started across the room toward Mary with the king at his heels.

Her side was toward them when they came up, but she kept her attitude as if she had been of bronze. She had taken up a book that was lying on the table and was examining it as they approached.

De Longueville held the box in his hand, and bowing and scraping said in broken English: "Permit to me, most gracious princess, that I may have the honor to offer on behalf of my august master, this little testament of his high admiration and love." With this he bowed again, smiled like a crack in a piece of old parchment, and held his box toward Mary. It was open, probably in the hope of enticing her with a sight of its contents—a beautiful diamond necklace.

She turned her face ever so little and took it all in with one contemptuous, sneering glance out of the corners of her eyes. Then quietly reaching out her hand she grasped the necklace and deliberately dashed it in poor old de Longueville's face.

"There is my answer, sir! Go home and tell your imbecile old master I scorn his suit and hate him—hate him—hate him!" Then with the tears falling unheeded down her cheeks, "Master Wolsey, you butcher's cur! This trick was of your conception; the others had not brains enough to think of it. Are you not proud to have outwitted one poor heart-broken girl? But beware, sir; I tell you now I will be quits with you yet, or my name is not Mary."

There is a limit to the best of feminine nerve, and at that limit should always be found a flood of healthful tears. Mary had reached it when she threw the necklace and shot her bolt at Wolsey, so she broke down and hastily left the room.

The king, of course, was beside himself with rage.

"By God's soul," he swore, "she shall marry Louis of France, or I will have her whipped to death on the Smithfield pillory." And in his wicked heart—so impervious to a single lasting good impulse—he really meant it.

Immediately after this, the king, de Longueville and Wolsey set out for London.

I remained behind hoping to see the girls, and after a short time a page plucked me by the sleeve, saying the princess wished to see me.

The page conducted me to the same room in which had been fought the battle with Mary in bed. The door had been placed on its hinges again, but the bed was tumbled as Mary had left it, and the room was in great disorder.

"Oh, Sir Edwin," began Mary, who was weeping, "was ever woman in such frightful trouble? My brother is killing me. Can he not see that I could not live through a week of this marriage? And I have been deserted by all my friends, too, excepting Jane. She, poor thing, cannot leave."

"You know I would not go," said Jane, parenthetically. Mary continued: "You, too, have been home an entire week and have not been near me."

I began to soften at the sight of her grief, and concluded, with Brandon, that, after all, her beauty could well cover a multitude of sins; perhaps even this, her great transgression against him.

The princess was trying to check her weeping, and in a moment took up the thread of her unfinished sentence: "And Master Brandon, too, left without so much as sending me one little word—not a line nor a syllable. He did not come near me, but went off as if I did not care—or he did not. Of course *he* did not care, or he would not have behaved so, knowing I was in so much trouble. I did not see him at all after—one afternoon in the king's—about a week before that awful night in London, except that night, when I was so frightened I could not speak one word of all the things I wished to say."

This sounded strange enough, and I began more than ever to suspect something wrong. I, however, kept as firm a grasp as possible upon the stock of indignation I had brought with me.

"How did you expect to see or hear from him," asked I, "when he was lying in a loathsome dungeon without one ray of light, condemned to be hanged, drawn and quartered, because of your selfish neglect to save him who, at the cost of half his blood, and almost his life, had saved so much for you?"

Her eyes grew big, and the tears were checked by genuine surprise.

I continued: "Lady Mary, no one could have made me believe that you would stand back and let the man, to whom you owed so great a debt, lie so long in such misery, and be condemned to such a death for the act that saved you. I could never have believed it!"

"Imp of hell!" screamed Mary; "what tale is this you bring to torture me? Have I not enough already? Tell me it is a lie, or I will have your miserable little tongue torn out by the root."

"It is no lie, princess, but an awful truth, and a frightful shame to you."

I was determined to tell her all and let her see herself as she was.

She gave a hysterical laugh, and throwing up her hands, with her accustomed little gesture, fell upon the bed in utter abandonment, shaking as with a spasm. She did not weep; she could not; she was past that now. Jane went over to the bed and tried to soothe her.

In a moment Mary sprang to her feet, exclaiming: "Master Brandon condemned to death and you and I here talking and moaning and weeping? Come, come, we will go to the king at once. We will start to walk, Edwin—I must be doing something—and Jane can follow with the horses and overtake us. No; I will not dress; just as I am; this will do. Bring me a hat, Jane; any one, any one." While putting on hat and gloves she continued: "I will see the king at once and tell him all! all! I will do anything; I will marry that old king of France, or forty kings, or forty devils; it's all one to me; anything! anything! to save him. Oh! to think that he has been in that dungeon all this time." And the tears came unheeded in a deluge.

She was under such headway, and spoke and moved so rapidly, that I could not stop her until she was nearly ready to go. Then I held her by the arm while I said:

"It is not necessary now; you are too late."

A look of horror came into her face, and I continued slowly: "I procured Brandon's release nearly a week ago; I did what you should have done, and he is now at our rooms in Greenwich."

Mary looked at me a moment, and, turning pale, pressed her hands to her heart and leaned against the door frame.

After a short silence she said: "Edwin Caskoden—fool! Why could you not have told me that at first? I thought my brain would burn and my heart burst."

"I should have told you had you given me time. As to the pain it gave you"—this was the last charge of my large magazine of indignation—"I care very little about that. You deserve it. I do not know what explanation you have to offer, but nothing can excuse you. An explanation, however good, would have been little comfort to you had Brandon failed you in Billingsgate that night."

She had fallen into a chair by this time and sat in reverie, staring at nothing. Then the tears came again, but more softly.

"You are right; nothing can excuse me. I am the most selfish, ungrateful, guilty creature ever born. A whole month in that dungeon!" And she covered her drooping face with her hands.

"Go away for awhile, Edwin, and then return; we shall want to see you again," said Jane.

Upon my return Mary was more composed. Jane had dressed her hair, and she was sitting on the bed in her riding habit, hat in hand. Her fingers were nervously toying at the ribbons and her eyes cast down.

"You are surely right, Sir Edwin. I have no excuse. I can have none; but I will tell you how it was. You remember the day you left me in the waiting-room of the king's council?—when they were discussing my marriage without one thought of me, as if I were but a slave or a dumb brute that could not feel." She began to weep a little, but soon recovered herself. "While waiting for you to return, the Duke of Buckingham came in. I knew Henry was trying to sell me to the French king, and my heart was full of trouble—from more causes than you can know. All the council, especially that butcher's son, were urging him on, and Henry himself was anxious that the marriage should be brought about. He thought it would strengthen him for the imperial crown. He wants everything, and is ambitious to be emperor. Emperor! He would cut a pretty figure! I hoped, though, I should be able to induce him not to sacrifice me to his selfish interests, as I have done before, but I knew only too well it would tax my powers to the utmost this time. I knew that if I did anything to anger or to antagonize him, it would be all at an end with me. You know he is so exacting with other people's conduct, for one who is so careless of his own—so virtuous by proxy. You remember how cruelly he disgraced and crushed poor Lady Chesterfield, who was in such trouble about her husband, and who went to Grouche's only to learn if he were true to her. Henry seems to be particularly sensitive in that direction. One would think it was in the commandments: 'Thou shalt not go to Grouche's.' It may be that some have gone there for other purposes than to have their fortunes told—to meet, to—but I need not say that I—" and she stopped short, blushing to her hair.

"Well, I knew I could do nothing with Henry if he once learned of that visit, especially as it resulted so fatally. Oh! why did I go? Why *did* I go? That was why I hesitated to tell Henry at once. I was hoping some other way would open whereby I might save Charles—Master Brandon. While I was waiting, along came the Duke of Buckingham, and as I knew he was popular in London, and had almost as much influence there as the king, a thought came to me that he might help us.

"I knew that he and Master Brandon had passed a few angry words at one time in my ball-room—you remember—but I also knew that the duke was in—in love with me, you know, or pretended to be—he always said he was—and I felt sure I could, by a little flattery, induce him to do anything. He was always protesting that he would give half his blood to serve me. As if anybody wanted a drop of his wretched blood. Poor Master Brandon! his blood . . ." and the tears came, choking her words for the moment. "So I told the duke I had promised you and Jane to procure Master Brandon's liberty, and asked him to do it for me. He gladly consented, and gave me his knightly word that it should be attended to without an hour's delay. He said it might have to be done secretly in the way of an escape—not officially—as the Londoners were very jealous of their rights and much aroused on account of the killing. Especially, he said that at that time great caution must be used, as the king was anxious to conciliate the city in order to procure a loan for some purpose—my dower, I suppose.

"The duke said it should be as I wished; that Master Brandon should escape, and remain away from London for a few weeks until the king procured his loan, and then be freed by royal proclamation.

"I saw Buckingham the next day, for I was very anxious, you may be sure, and he said the keeper of Newgate had told him it had been arranged the night before as desired. I had come to Windsor because it was more quiet, and my heart was full. It is quite a distance from London, and I thought it might afford a better opportunity to—to see—I thought, perhaps Master Brandon might come—might want to—to—see Jane and me; in fact I wrote him before I left Greenwich that I should be here. Then I heard he had gone to New Spain. Now you see how all my troubles have come upon me at once; and this the greatest of them, because it is my fault. I can ask no forgiveness from any one, for I cannot forgive myself."

She then inquired about Brandon's health and spirits, and I left out no distressing detail you may be sure.

During my recital she sat with downcast eyes and tear-stained face, playing with the ribbons of her hat.

When I was ready to go she said: "Please say to Master Brandon I should like—to—see—him, if he cares to come, if only that I may tell him how it happened."

"I greatly fear, in fact, I know he will not come," said I. "The cruelest blow of all, worse even than the dungeon, or the sentence of death, was your failure to save him. He trusted you so implicitly. At the time of his arrest he refused to allow me to tell the king, saying he knew you would see to it—that you were pure gold."

"Ah, did he say that?" she asked, as a sad little smile lighted her face.

"His faith was so entirely without doubt, that his recoil from you is correspondingly great. He goes to New Spain as soon as his health is recovered sufficiently for him to travel."

This sent the last fleck of color from her face, and with the words almost choking her throat: "Then tell him what I have said to you and perhaps he will not feel so—"

"I cannot do that either, Lady Mary. When I mentioned your name the other day he said he would curse me if I ever spoke it again in his hearing."

"Is it so bad as that?" Then, meditatively: "And at his trial he did not tell the reason for the killing? Would not compromise me, who had served him so ill, even to save his own life? Noble, noble!" And her lips went together as she rose to her feet. No tears now; nothing but glowing, determined womanhood.

"Then I will go to him wherever he may be. He shall forgive me, no matter what my fault."

Soon after this we were on our way to London at a brisk gallop.

We were all very silent, but at one time Mary spoke up from the midst of a reverie: "During the moment when I thought Master Brandon had been executed—when you said it was too late—it seemed that I was born again and all made over; that I was changed in the very texture of my nature by the shock, as they say the grain of the iron cannon is sometimes changed by too violent an explosion." And this proved to be true in some respects.

We rode on rapidly and did not stop in London except to give the horses drink.

After crossing the bridge, Mary said, half to Jane and half to herself: "I will never marry the French king—never." Mary was but a girl pitted against a body of brutal men, two of them rulers of the two greatest nations on earth—rather heavy odds, for one woman.

We rode down to Greenwich and entered the palace without exciting comment, as the princess was in the habit of coming and going at will.

The king and queen and most of the courtiers were in London—at Bridewell House and Baynard's Castle—where Henry was vigorously pushing the loan of five hundred thousand crowns for Mary's dower, the only business of state in which, at that time, he took any active interest. Subsequently, as you know, he became interested in the divorce laws, and the various methods whereby a man, especially a king, might rid himself of a distasteful wife; and after he saw the truth in Anne Boleyn's eyes, he adopted a combined policy of church and state craft that has brought us a deal of senseless trouble ever since—and is like to keep it up.

As to Mary's dower, Henry was to pay Louis only four hundred thousand crowns, but he made the marriage an excuse for an extra hundred thousand, to be devoted to his own private use.

When we arrived at the palace, the girls went to their apartments and I to mine, where I found Brandon reading. There was only one window to our common room—a dormer-window, set into the roof, and reached by a little passage as broad as the window itself, and perhaps a yard and a half long. In the alcove thus formed was a bench along the wall, cushioned by Brandon's great campaign cloak. In this window we often sat and read, and here was Brandon with his book. I had intended to tell him the girls were coming, for when Mary asked me if I thought he would come to her at the palace, and when I had again said no, she reiterated her intention of going to him at once; but my courage failed me and I did not speak of it.

I knew that Mary ought not to come to our room, and that if news of it should reach the king's ears there would be more and worse trouble than ever, and, as usual, Brandon would pay the penalty for all. Then again, if it were discovered it might seriously compromise both Mary and Jane, as the world is full of people who would rather say and believe an evil thing of another than to say their prayers or to believe the holy creed.

I had said as much to the Lady Mary when she expressed her determination to go to Brandon. She had been in the wrong so much of late that she was humbled; and I was brave enough to say whatever I felt; but she said she had thought it all over, and as every one was away from Greenwich it would not be found out if done secretly.

She told Jane she need not go; that she, Mary, did not want to take any risk of compromising her.

You see, trouble was doing a good work in the princess, and had made it possible for a generous thought for another to find spontaneous lodgment in her heart. What a great thing it is, this human suffering, which so sensitizes our sympathy, and makes us tender to another's pain. Nothing else so fits us for earth or prepares us for heaven.

Jane would have gone, though, had she known that all her fair name would go with her. She was right, you see, when she told me, while riding over to Windsor, that should Mary's love blossom into a full-blown passion she would wreck everything and everybody, including herself perhaps, to attain the object of so great a desire.

It looked now as if she were on the high road to that end. Nothing short of chains and fetters could have kept her from going to Brandon that evening. There was an inherent force about her that was irresistible and swept everything before it.

In our garret she was to meet another will, stronger and infinitely better controlled than her own, and I did not know how it would all turn out.

* * * * *

CHAPTER XII

Atonement

I had not been long in the room when a knock at the door announced the girls. I admitted them, and Mary walked to the middle of the floor. It was just growing dark and the room was quite dim, save at the window where Brandon sat reading. Gods! those were exciting moments; my heart beat like a woman's. Brandon saw the girls when they entered, but never so much as looked up from his book. You must remember he had a great grievance. Even looking at it from Mary's side of the case, certainly its best point of view, he had been terribly misused, and it was all the worse that the misuse had come from one who, from his standpoint, had *pretended* to love him, and had wantonly led him on, as he had the best of right to think, to love her, and to suffer the keenest pangs a heart can know. Then you must remember he did not know even the best side of the matter, bad as it was, but saw only the naked fact, that in recompense for his great help in time of need, Mary had deliberately allowed him to lie in that dungeon a long, miserable month, and would have suffered him to die. So it was no wonder his heart was filled with bitterness toward her. Jane and I had remained near the door, and poor Mary was a pitiable princess, standing there so full of doubt in the middle of the room. After a moment she stepped toward the window, and, with quick-coming breath, stopped at the threshold of the little passage.

"Master Brandon, I have come, not to make excuses, for nothing can excuse me, but to tell you how it all happened—by trusting to another."

Brandon arose, and marking the place in his book with his finger, followed Mary, who had stepped backward into the room.

"Your highness is very gracious and kind thus to honor me, but as our ways will hereafter lie as far apart as the world is broad, I think it would have been far better had you refrained from so imprudent a visit; especially as anything one so exalted as yourself may have to say can be no affair of such as I—one just free of the hangman's noose."

"Oh! don't! I pray you. Let me tell you, and it may make a difference. It must pain you, I know, to think of me as you do, after—after—you know; after what has passed between us."

"Yes, that only makes it all the harder. If you could give your kisses"—and she blushed red as blood—"to one for whom you care so little that you could leave him to die like a dog, when a word from you would have saved him, what reason have I to suppose they are not for every man?"

This gave Mary an opening of which she was quick enough to take advantage, for Brandon was in the wrong.

"You know that is not true. You are not honest with me nor with yourself, and that is not like you. You know that no other man ever had, or could have, any favor from me, even the slightest. Wantonness is not among my thousand faults. It is not that which angers you. You are sure enough of me in that respect. In truth, I had almost come to believe you were too sure, that I had grown cheap in your eyes, and you did not care so much as I thought and hoped for what I had to give, for after that day you came not near me at all. I know it was the part of wisdom and prudence that you should remain away; but had you cared as much as I, your prudence would not have held you."

She hung her head a moment in silence; then, looking at him, almost ready for tears, continued: "A man has no right to speak in that way of a woman whose little favors he has taken, and make her regret that she has given a gift only that it may recoil upon her. 'Little,' did I say? Sir, do you know what that—first—kiss was to me? Had I possessed all the crowns of all the earth I would have given them to you as willingly. Now you know the value I placed on it, however worthless it was to you. Yet I was a cheerful giver of that great gift, was I not? And can you find it in your heart to make of it a shame to me—that of which I was so proud?"

She stood there with head inclined a little to one side, looking at him inquiringly as if awaiting an answer. He did not speak, but looked steadily at his book. I felt, however, that he was changing, and I was sure her beauty, never more exquisite than in its present humility, would yet atone for even so great a fault as hers. Err, look beautiful, and receive remission! Such a woman as Mary carries her indulgence in her face.

I now began to realize for the first time the wondrous power of this girl, and ceased to marvel that she had always been able to turn even the king, the most violent, stubborn man on earth, to her own wishes. Her manner made her words eloquent, and already, with true feminine tactics, she had put Brandon in the wrong in everything because he was wrong in part.

Then she quickly went over what she had said to me. She told of her great dread lest the king should learn of the visit to Grouche's and its fatal consequences, knowing full well it would render Henry impervious to her influence and precipitate the French marriage. She told him of how she was going to the king the day after the arrest to ask his release, and of the meeting with Buckingham, and his promise.

Still Brandon said nothing, and stood as if politely waiting for her to withdraw.

She remained silent a little time, waiting for him to speak, when tears, partly of vexation, I think, moistened her eyes.

"Tell me at least," she said, "that you know I speak the truth. I have always believed in you, and now I ask for your faith. I would not lie to you in the faintest shading of a thought—not for heaven itself—not even for your love and forgiveness, much as they are to me, and I want to know that you are sure of my truthfulness, if you doubt all else. You see I speak plainly of what your love is to me, for although, by remaining away, you made me fear I had been too lavish with my favors—that is every woman's fear—I knew in my heart you loved me; that you could not have done and said what you did otherwise. Now you see what faith I have in you, and you a man, whom a woman's instinct prompts to doubt. How does it compare with your faith in me, a woman, whom all the instincts of a manly nature should dispose to trust? It seems to be an unwritten law that a man may lie to a woman concerning the most important thing in life to her, and be proud of it, but you see even now I have all faith in your love for me, else I surely should not be here. You see I trust even your unspoken word, when it might, without much blame to you, be a spoken lie; yet you do not trust me, who have no world-given right to speak falsely about such things, and when that which I now do is full of shame for me, and what I have done full of guilt, if inspired by aught but the purest truth from my heart of hearts. Your words mean so much—so much more, I think, than you realize—and are so cruel in turning to evil the highest, purest impulse a woman can feel—the glowing pride in self-surrender, and the sweet, delightful privilege of giving where she loves. How can you? How can you?"

How eloquent she was! It seemed to me this would have melted the frozen sea, but I think Brandon felt that now his only hope lay in the safeguard of his constantly upheld indignation.

When he spoke he ignored all she had said.

"You did well to employ my Lord of Buckingham. It will make matters more interesting when I tell you it was he who attacked you and was caught by the leg under his wounded horse; he was lame, I am told, for some time afterward. I had watched him following you from the gate at Bridewell, and at once recognized him when his mask fell off during the fight by the wall. You have done well at every step, I see."

"Oh, God; to think of it! Had I but known! Buckingham shall pay for this with his head; but how could I know? I was but a poor, distracted girl, sure to make some fatal error. I was in such agony—your wounds—believe me, I suffered more from them than you could. Every pain you felt was a pang for me—and then that awful marriage! I was being sold like a wretched slave to that old satyr, to be gloated over and feasted upon. No man can know the horror of that thought to a woman—to any woman, good or bad. To have one's beauty turn to curse her and make her desirable only—only as well-fed cattle are prized. No matter how great the manifestation of such so-called love, it all the more repels a woman and adds to her loathing day by day. Then there was something worse than all,"—she was almost weeping now—"I might have been able to bear the thought even of that hideous marriage—others have lived through the like—but—but after—that—that day—when you—it seemed that your touch was a spark dropped into a heart full of tinder, which had been lying there awaiting it all these years. In that one moment the flame grew so intense I could not withstand it. My throat ached; I could scarcely breathe, and it seemed that my heart would burst." Here the tears gushed forth as she took a step toward him with outstretched arms, and said between her sobs: "I wanted you, you! for my husband—for my husband, and I could not bear the torturing thought of losing you or enduring any other man. I could not give you up after that—it was all too late, too late; it had gone too far. I was lost! lost!"

He sprang to where she stood leaning toward him, and caught her to his breast.

She held him from her while she said: "Now you know—now you know that I would not have left you in that terrible place, had I known it. No, not if it had taken my life to buy your freedom."

"I do know; I do know. Be sure of that; I know it and shall know it always, whatever happens; nothing can change me. I will never doubt you again. It is my turn to ask forgiveness now."

"No, no; just forgive me; that is all I ask," and her head was on his breast.

"Let us step out into the passage-way, Edwin," said Jane, and we did. There were times when Jane seemed to be inspired.

When we went back into the room Mary and Brandon were sitting in the window-way on his great cloak. They rose and came to us, holding each other's hands, and Mary asked, looking up to him:

"Shall we tell them?"

"As you like, my lady."

Mary was willing, and looked for Brandon to speak, so he said: "This lady whom I hold by the hand and myself have promised each other before the good God to be husband and wife, if fortune ever so favor us that it be possible."

"No, that is not it," interrupted Mary. "There is no 'if' in it; it shall be, whether it is possible or not. Nothing shall prevent." At this she kissed Jane and told her how she loved her, and gave me her hand, for her love was so great within her that it overflowed upon every one. She, however, always had a plenitude of love for Jane, and though she might scold her and apparently misuse her, Jane was as dear as a sister, and was always sure of her steadfast, tried and lasting affection.

After Mary had said there should be no "if," Brandon replied:

"Very well, Madame Destiny." Then turning to us: "What ought I to do for one who is willing to stoop from so high an estate to honor me and be my wife?"

"Love her, and her alone, with your whole heart, as long as you live. That is all she wants, I am sure," volunteered Jane, sentimentally.

"Jane, you are a Madam Solomon," said Mary, with a tone of her old-time laugh. "Is the course you advise as you would wish to be done by?" And she glanced mischievously from Jane to me, as the laugh bubbled up from her heart, merry and soft as if it had not come from what was but now the home of grief and pain.

"I know nothing about how I should like to be done by," said Jane, with a pout, "but if you have such respect for my wisdom I will offer a little more; I think it is time we should be going."

"Now, Jane, you are growing foolish again; I will not go yet," and Mary made manifest her intention by sitting down. She could not bring herself to forego the pleasure of staying, dangerous as she knew it to be, and could not bear the pain of parting, even for a short time, now that she had Brandon once more. The time was soon coming—but I am too fast again.

After a time Brandon said: "I think Jane's wisdom remains with her, Mary. It is better that you do not stay, much as I wish to have you."

She was ready to obey him at once.

When she arose to go she took both his hands in hers and whispered: "'Mary.' I like the name on your lips," and then glancing hurriedly over her shoulder to see if Jane and I were looking, lifted her face to him and ran after us.

We were a little in advance of the princess, and, as we walked along, Jane said under her breath: "Now look out for trouble; it will come quickly, and I fear for Master Brandon more than any one. He has made a noble fight against her and against himself, and it is no wonder she loves him."

This made me feel a little jealous.

"Jane, you could not love him, could you?" I asked.

"No matter what I could do, Edwin; I do not, and that should satisfy you." Her voice and manner said more than her words. The hall was almost dark, and—I have always considered that occasion one of my lost opportunities; but they are not many.

The next evening Brandon and I, upon Lady Mary's invitation, went up to her apartments, but did not stay long, fearing some one might find us there and cause trouble. We would not have gone at all had not the whole court been absent in London, for discovery would have been a serious matter to one of us at least.

As I told you once before, Henry did not care how much Brandon might love his sister, but Buckingham had whispered suspicions of the state of Mary's heart, and his own observations, together with the intercepted note, had given these suspicions a stronger coloring, so that a very small matter might turn them into certainties.

The king had pardoned Brandon for the killing of the two men in Billingsgate, as he was forced to do under the circumstances, but there his kindness stopped. After a short time he deprived him of his place at court, and all that was left for him of royal favor was permission to remain with me and live at the palace until such time as he should sail for New Spain.

* * * * *

CHAPTER XIII

A Girl's Consent

The treaty had been agreed upon, and as to the international arrangement, at least, the marriage of Louis de Valois and Mary Tudor was a settled fact. All it needed was the consent of an eighteen-year-old girl—a small matter, of course, as marriageable women are but commodities in statecraft, and theoretically, at least, acquiesce in everything their liege lords ordain. Lady Mary's consent had been but theoretical, but it was looked upon by every one as amounting to an actual, vociferated, sonorous "yes;" that is to say, by every one but the princess, who had no more notion of saying "yes" than she had of reciting the Sanscrit vocabulary from the pillory of Smithfield.

Wolsey, whose manner was smooth as an otter's coat, had been sent to fetch the needed "yes"; but he failed.

Jane told me about it.

Wolsey had gone privately to see the princess, and had thrown out a sort of skirmish line by flattering her beauty, but had found her not in the best humor.

"Yes, yes, my lord of Lincoln, I know how beautiful I am; no one knows better; I know all about my hair, eyes, teeth, eyebrows and skin. I tell you I am sick of them. Don't talk to me about them; it won't help you to get my consent to marry that vile old creature. That is what you have come for, of course. I have been expecting you; why did not my brother come?"

"I think he was afraid; and, to tell you the truth, I was afraid myself," answered Wolsey, with a smile. This made Mary smile, too, in spite of herself, and went a long way toward putting her in a good humor. Wolsey continued: "His majesty could not have given me a more disagreeable task. You doubtless think I am in favor of this marriage, but I am not."

This was as great a lie as ever fell whole out of a bishop's mouth. "I have been obliged to fall in with the king's views on the matter, for he has had his mind set on it from the first mention by de Longueville."

"Was it that bead-eyed little mummy who suggested it?"

"Yes, and if you marry the king of France you can repay him with usury."

"'Tis an inducement, by my troth."

"I do not mind saying to you in confidence that I think it an outrage to force a girl like you to marry a man like Louis of France, but how are we to avoid it?"

By the "we" Wolsey put himself in alliance with Mary, and the move was certainly adroit.

"How are we to avoid it? Have no fear of that, my lord; I will show you."

"Oh! but my dear princess; permit me; you do not seem to know your brother; you cannot in any way avoid this marriage. I believe he will imprison you and put you on bread and water to force your consent. I am sure you had better do willingly that which you will eventually be compelled to do anyway; and besides, there is another thought that has come to me; shall I speak plainly before Lady Jane Bolingbroke?"

"I have no secrets from her."

"Very well; it is this: Louis is old and very feeble; he cannot live long, and it may be that you can, by a ready consent now, exact a promise from your brother to allow you your own choice in the event of a second marriage. You might in that way purchase what you could not bring about in any other way."

"How do you know that I want to purchase aught in any way, Master Wolsey? I most certainly do not intend to do so by marrying France."

"I do not know that you wish to purchase anything, but a woman's heart is not always under her full control, and it sometimes goes out to one very far beneath her in station, but the equal of any man on earth in grandeur of soul and nobleness of nature. It might be that there is such a man whom any woman would be amply justified in purchasing at any sacrifice—doubly so if it were buying happiness for two."

His meaning was too plain even to pretend to misunderstand, and Mary's eyes flashed at him, as her face broke into a dimpling smile in spite of her.

Wolsey thought he had won, and to clinch the victory said, in his forceful manner: "Louis XII will not live a year; let me carry to the king your consent, and I guarantee you his promise as to a second marriage."

In an instant Mary's eyes shot fire, and her face was like the blackest storm cloud.

"Carry this to the king: that I will see him and the whole kingdom sunk in hell before I will marry Louis of France. That is my answer once and for all. Good even', Master Wolsey." And she swept out of the room with head up and dilating nostrils, the very picture of defiance.

St. George! She must have looked superb. She was one of the few persons whom anger and disdain and the other passions which we call ungentle seemed to illumine—they were so strong in her, and yet not violent. It seemed that every deep emotion but added to her beauty and brought it out, as the light within a church brings out the exquisite figuring on the windows.

After Wolsey had gone, Jane said to Mary: "Don't you think it would have been better had you sent a softer answer to your brother? I believe you could reach his heart even now if you were to make the effort. You have not tried in this matter as you did in the others."

"Perhaps you are right, Jane. I will go to Henry."

Mary waited until she knew the king was alone, and then went to him.

On entering the room, she said: "Brother, I sent a hasty message to you by the Bishop of Lincoln this morning, and have come to ask your forgiveness."

"Ah! little sister; I thought you would change your mind. Now you are a good girl."

"Oh! do not misunderstand me; I asked your forgiveness for the message; as to the marriage, I came to tell you that it would kill me and that I could not bear it. Oh! brother, you are not a woman—you cannot know." Henry flew into a passion, and with oaths and curses ordered her to leave him unless she was ready to give her consent. She had but two courses to take, so she left with her heart full of hatred for the most brutal wretch who ever sat upon a throne—and that is making an extreme case. As she was going, she turned upon him like a fury, and exclaimed:

"Never, never! Do you hear? Never!"

Preparations went on for the marriage just as if Mary had given her solemn consent. The important work of providing the trousseau began at once, and the more important matter of securing the loan from the London merchants was pushed along rapidly. The good citizens might cling affectionately to their angels, double angels, crowns and pounds sterling, but the fear in which they held the king, and a little patting of the royal hand upon the plebeian head, worked the charm, and out came the yellow gold, never to be seen again, God wot. Under the stimulus of the royal smile they were ready to shout themselves hoarse, and to eat and drink themselves red in the face in celebration of the wedding day. In short, they were ready to be tickled nearly to death for the honor of paying to a wretched old lecher a wagon-load of gold to accept, as a gracious gift, the most beautiful heart-broken girl in the world. That is, she would have been heart-broken had she not been inspired with courage. As it was, she wasted none of her energy in lamentations, but saved it all to fight with. Heavens! how she did fight! If a valiant defense ever deserved victory, it was in her case. When the queen went to her with silks and taffetas and fine cloths, to consult about the trousseau, although the theme was one which would interest almost any woman, she would have none of it, and when Catherine insisted upon her trying on a certain gown, she called her a blackamoor, tore the garment to pieces, and ordered her to leave the room.

Henry sent Wolsey to tell her that the 13th day of August had been fixed upon as the day of the marriage, de Longueville to act as the French king's proxy, and Wolsey was glad to come off with his life.

Matters were getting into a pretty tangle at the palace. Mary would not speak to the king, and poor Catherine was afraid to come within arm's length of her; Wolsey was glad to keep out of her way, and she flew at Buckingham with talons and beak upon first sight. As to the battle with Buckingham, it was short but decisive, and this was the way it came about: There had been a passage between the duke and Brandon, in which the latter had tried to coax the former into a duel, the only way, of course, to settle the weighty matters between them. Buckingham, however, had had a taste of Brandon's nimble sword play, and, bearing in mind Judson's fate, did not care for any more. They had met by accident, and Brandon, full of smiles and as polite as a Frenchman, greeted him.

"Doubtless my lord, having crossed swords twice with me, will do me the great honor to grant that privilege the third time, and will kindly tell me where my friend can wait upon a friend of his grace."

"There is no need for us to meet over that little affair. You had the best of it, and if I am satisfied you should be. I was really in the wrong, but I did not know the princess had invited you to her ball."

"Your lordship is pleased to evade," returned Brandon. "It is not the ball-room matter that I have to complain of; as you have rightly said, if you are satisfied, I certainly should be; but it is that your lordship, in the name of the king, instructed the keeper of Newgate prison to confine me in an underground cell, and prohibited communication with any of my friends. You so arranged it that my trial should be secret, both as to the day thereof and the event, in order that it should not be known to those who might be interested in my release. You promised the Lady Mary that you would procure my liberty, and thereby prevented her going to the king for that purpose, and afterwards told her that it had all been done, as promised, and that I had escaped to New Spain. It is because of this, my Lord Buckingham, that I now denounce you as a liar, a coward and a perjured knight, and demand of you such satisfaction as one man can give to another for mortal injury. If you refuse, I will kill you as I would a cut-throat the next time I meet you."

"I care nothing for your rant, fellow, but out of consideration for the feelings which your fancied injuries have put into your heart, I tell you that I did what I could to liberate you, and received from the keeper a promise that you should be allowed to escape. After that a certain letter addressed to you was discovered and fell into the hands of the king—a matter in which I had no part. As to your confinement and non-communication with your friends, that was at his majesty's command after he had seen the letter, as he will most certainly confirm to you. I say this for my own sake, not that I care what you may say or think."

This offer of confirmation by the king made it all sound like the truth, so much will even a little truth leaven a great lie; and part of Brandon's sails came down against the mast. The whole statement surprised him, and, most of all, the intercepted letter. What letter could it have been? It was puzzling, and yet he dared not ask.

As the duke was about to walk away, Brandon stopped him: "One moment, your grace; I am willing to admit what you have said, for I am not now prepared to contradict it; but there is yet another matter we have to settle. You attacked me on horseback, and tried to murder me in order to abduct two ladies that night over in Billingsgate. That you cannot deny. I watched you follow the ladies from Bridewell to Grouche's, and saw your face when your mask fell off during the mêleé as plainly as I see it now. If other proof is wanting, there is that sprained knee upon which your horse fell, causing you to limp even yet. I am sure now that my lord will meet me like a man; or would he prefer that I should go to the king and tell him and the world the whole shameful story? I have concealed it heretofore, thinking it my personal right and privilege to settle with you."

Buckingham turned a shade paler as he replied: "I do not meet such as you on the field of honor, and have no fear of your slander injuring me."

He felt secure in the thought that the girls did not know who had attacked them, and could not corroborate Brandon in his accusation, or Mary, surely, never would have appealed to him for help.

I was with Brandon—at a little distance, that is—when this occurred, and after Buckingham had left, we went to find the girls in the forest. We knew they would be looking for us, although they would pretend surprise when they saw us. We soon met them, and the very leaves of the trees gave a soft, contented rustle in response to Mary's low, mellow laugh of joy.

After perhaps half an hour, we encountered Buckingham with his lawyer-knight, Johnson. They had evidently walked out to this quiet path to consult about the situation. As they approached, Mary spoke to the duke with a vicious sparkle in her eyes.

"My Lord Buckingham, this shall cost you your head; remember my words when you are on the scaffold, just when your neck fits into the hollow of the block."

He stopped, with an evident desire to explain, but Mary pointed down the path and said: "Go, or I will have Master Brandon spit you on his sword. Two to one would be easy odds compared with the four to one you put against him in Billingsgate. Go!" And the battle was over, the foe never having struck a blow. It hurt me that Mary should speak of the odds being two to one against Brandon when I was at hand. It is true I was not very large, but I could have taken care of a lawyer.

Now it was that the lawyer-knight earned his bread by his wits, for it was he, I know, who instigated the next move—a master stroke in its way, and one which proved a checkmate to us. It was this: the duke went at once to the king, and, in a tone of injured innocence, told him of the charge made by Brandon with Mary's evident approval, and demanded redress for the slander. Thus it seemed that the strength of our position was about to be turned against us. Brandon was at once summoned and promptly appeared before the king, only too anxious to confront the duke. As to the confinement of Brandon and his secret trial, the king did not care to hear; that was a matter of no consequence to him; the important question was, did Buckingham attack the princess?

Brandon told the whole straight story, exactly as it was, which Buckingham as promptly denied, and offered to prove by his almoner that he was at his devotions on the night and at the hour of the attack. So here was a conflict of evidence which called for new witnesses, and Henry asked Brandon if the girls had seen and recognized the duke. To this question, of course, he was compelled to answer no, and the whole accusation, after all, rested upon Brandon's word, against which, on the other hand, was the evidence of the Duke of Buckingham and his convenient almoner.

All this disclosed to the full poor Mary's anxiety to help Brandon, and the duke having adroitly let out the fact that he had just met the princess with Brandon at a certain secluded spot in the forest, Henry's suspicion of her partiality received new force, and he began to look upon the unfortunate Brandon as a partial cause, at least, of Mary's aversion to the French marriage.

Henry grew angry and ordered Brandon to leave the court, with the sullen remark that it was only his services to the Princess Mary that saved him from a day with papers on the pillory.

This was not by any means what Brandon had expected. There seemed to be a fatality for him about everything connected with that unfortunate trip to Grouche's. He had done his duty, and this was his recompense. Virtue is sometimes a pitiful reward for itself, notwithstanding much wisdom to the contrary.

Henry was by no means sure that his suspicions concerning Mary's heart were correct, and in all he had heard he had not one substantial fact upon which to base conviction. He had not seen her with Brandon since their avowal, or he would have had a fact in every look, the truth in every motion, a demonstration in every glance. She seemed powerless even to attempt concealment. In Brandon's handsome manliness and evident superiority, the king thought he saw a very clear possibility for Mary to love, and where there is such a possibility for a girl, she usually fails to fulfill expectations. I suppose there are more wrong guesses as to the sort of man a given woman will fall in love with than on any other subject of equal importance in the whole range of human surmising. It did not, however, strike the king that way, and he, in common with most other sons of Adam, supposing that he knew all about it, marked

Brandon as a very possible and troublesome personage. For once in the history of the world a man had hit upon the truth in this obscure matter, although he had no idea how correct he was.

Now, all this brought Brandon into the deep shadow of the royal frown, and, like many another man, he sank his fortune in the fathomless depths of a woman's heart, and thought himself rich in doing it.

* * * * *

CHAPTER XIV

In the Siren Country

With the king, admiration stood for affection, a mistake frequently made by people not given to self-analysis, and in a day or two a reaction set in toward Brandon which inspired a desire to make some amends for his harsh treatment. This he could not do to any great extent, on Buckingham's account; at least, not until the London loan was in his coffers, but the fact that Brandon was going to New Spain so soon and would be out of the way, both of Mary's eyes and Mary's marriage, stimulated that rare flower in Henry's heart, a good resolve, and Brandon was offered his old quarters with me until such time as he should sail for New Spain.

He had never abandoned this plan, and now that matters had taken this turn with Mary and the king, his resolution was stronger than ever, in that the scheme held two recommendations and a possibility.

The recommendations were, first, it would take him away from Mary, with whom—when out of the inspiring influence of her buoyant hopefulness—he knew marriage to be utterly impossible; and second, admitting and facing that impossibility, he might find at least partial relief from his heartache in the stirring events and adventures of that faraway land of monsters, dragons, savages and gold. The possibility lay in the gold, and a very faintly burning flame of hope held out the still more faintly glimmering chance that fortune, finding him there almost alone, might, for lack of another lover, smile upon him by way of squaring accounts. She might lead him to a cavern of gold, and gold would do anything; even, perhaps, purchase so priceless a treasure as a certain princess of the blood royal. He did not, however, dwell much on this possibility, but kept the delightful hope well neutralized with a constantly present sense of its improbability, in order to save the pain of a long fall when disappointment should come.

Brandon at once accepted the king's offer of lodging in the palace, for now that he felt sure of himself in the matter of New Spain, and his separation from Mary, he longed to see as much as possible of her before the light went out forever, even though it were playing with death itself to do so.

Poor fellow, his suffering was so acute during this period that it affected me like a contagion.

It did not make a mope of him, but came in spasms that almost drove him wild. He would at times pace the room and cry out: "Jesu! Caskoden, what shall I do? She will be the wife of the French king, and I shall sit in the wilderness and try every moment to imagine what she is doing and thinking. I shall find the bearing of Paris, and look in her direction until my brain melts in my effort to see her, and then I shall wander in the woods, a suffering imbecile, feeding on roots and nuts. Would to God one of us might die. If it were not selfish, I should wish I might be the one."

I said nothing in answer to these outbursts, as I had no consolation to offer.

We had two or three of our little meetings of four, dangerous as they were, at which Mary, feeling that each time she saw Brandon might be the last, would sit and look at him with glowing eyes that in turn softened and burned as he spoke. She did not talk much, but devoted all her time and energies to looking with her whole soul. Never before or since was there a girl so much in love. A young girl thoroughly in love is the most beautiful object on earth—beautiful even in ugliness. Imagine, then, what it made of Mary!

Growing partly, perhaps, out of his unattainability—for he was as far out of her reach as she out of his—she had long since begun to worship him. She had learned to know him so well, and his valiant defense of her in Billingsgate, together with his noble self-sacrifice in refusing to compromise her in order to save himself, had presented him to her in so noble a light that she had come to look up to him as her superior. Her surrender had been complete, and she found in it a joy far exceeding that of any victory or triumph she could imagine.

I could not for the life of me tell what would be the outcome of it all. Mary was one woman in ten thousand, so full was she of feminine force and will—a force which we men pretend to despise, but to which in the end we always succumb.

Like most women, the princess was not much given to analysis; and, I think, secretly felt that this matter of so great moment to her would, as everything else always had, eventually turn itself to her desire. She could not see the way, but, to her mind, there could be no doubt about it; fate was her friend; always had been, and surely always would be.

With Brandon it was different; experience as to how the ardently hoped for usually turns out to be the sadly regretted, together with a thorough face-to-face analysis of the situation, showed him the truth, all too clearly, and he longed for the day when he should go, as a sufferer longs for the surgeon's knife that is to relieve him of an aching limb. The hopelessness of the outlook had for the time destroyed nearly all of his combativeness, and had softened his nature almost to apathetic weakness. It would do no good to struggle in a boundless, fathomless sea; so he was ready to sink and was going to New Spain to hope no more.

Mary did not see what was to prevent the separation, but this did not trouble her as much as one would suppose, and she was content to let events take their own way, hoping and believing that in the end it would be hers. Events, however, continued in this wrong course so long and persistently that at last the truth dawned upon her and she began to doubt; and as time flew on and matters evinced a disposition to grow worse instead of better, she gradually, like the sundial in the moonlight, awakened to the fact that there was something wrong; a cog loose somewhere in the complicated machinery of fate—the fate which had always been her tried, trusted and obedient servant.

The trouble began in earnest with the discovery of our meetings in Lady Mary's parlor. There was nothing at all unusual in the fact that small companies of young folk frequently spent their evenings with her, but we knew well enough that the unusual element in our parties was their exceeding smallness. A company of eight or ten young persons was well enough, although it, of course, created jealousy on the part of those who were left out; but four—two of each sex—made a difference in kind, however much we might insist it was only in degree; and this we soon learned was the king's opinion.

You may be sure there was many a jealous person about the court ready to carry tales, and that it was impossible long to keep our meetings secret among such a host as then lived in Greenwich palace.

One day the queen summoned Jane and put her to the question. Now, Jane thought the truth was made only to be told, a fallacy into which many good people have fallen, to their utter destruction; since the truth, like every other good thing, may be abused.

Well! Jane told it all in a moment, and Catherine was so horrified that she was like to faint. She went with her hair-lifting horror to the king, and poured into his ears a tale of imprudence and debauchery well calculated to start his righteous, virtue-prompted indignation into a threatening flame.

Mary, Jane, Brandon and myself were at once summoned to the presence of both their majesties and soundly reprimanded. Three of us were ordered to leave the court before we could speak a word in self-defense, and Jane had enough of her favorite truth for once. Mary, however, came to our rescue with her coaxing eloquence and potent, feminine logic, and soon convinced Henry that the queen, who really counted for little with him, had made a mountain out of a very small mole-hill. Thus the royal wrath was appeased to such an extent that the order for expulsion was modified to a command that there be no more quartette gatherings in Princess Mary's parlor. This leniency was more easy for the princess to bring about, by reason of the fact that she had not spoken to her brother since the day she went to see him after Wolsey's visit, and had been so roughly driven off. At first, upon her refusal to speak to him—after the Wolsey visit—Henry was angry on account of what he called her insolence; but as she did not seem to care for that, and as his anger did nothing toward unsealing her lips, he pretended indifference. Still the same stubborn silence was maintained. This soon began to amuse the king, and of late he had been trying to be on friendly terms again with his sister through a series of elephantine antics and bear-like pleasantries, which were the most dismal failures—that is, in the way of bringing about a reconciliation. They were more successful from a comical point of view. So Henry was really glad for something that would loosen the tongue usually so lively, and for an opportunity to gratify his sister from whom he was demanding such a sacrifice, and for whom he expected to receive no less a price than the help of Louis of France, the most powerful king of Europe, to the imperial crown.

Thus our meetings were broken up, and Brandon knew his dream was over, and that any effort to see the princess would probably result in disaster for them both; for him certainly.

The king upon that same day told Mary of the intercepted letter sent by her to Brandon at Newgate, and accused her of what he was pleased to term an improper feeling for a low-born fellow.

Mary at once sent a full account of the communication in a letter to Brandon, who read it with no small degree of ill comfort as the harbinger of trouble.

"I had better leave here soon, or I may go without my head," he remarked. "When that thought gets to working in the king's brain, he will strike, and I—shall fall."

Letters began to come to our rooms from Mary, at first begging Brandon to come to her, and then upbraiding him because of his coldness and cowardice, and telling him that if he cared for her as she did for him, he would see her, though he had to wade through fire and blood. That was exactly where the trouble lay; it was not fire and blood through which he would have to pass; they were small matters, mere nothings that would really have added zest and interest to the achievement. But the frowning laugh of the tyrant, who could bind him hand and foot, and a vivid remembrance of the Newgate dungeon, with a dangling noose or a hollowed-out block in the near background, were matters that would have taken the adventurous tendency out of even the cracked brain of chivalry itself. Brandon cared only to fight where there was a possible victory or ransom, or a prospect of some sort, at least, of achieving success. Bayard preferred a stone wall, and thought to show his brains by beating them out against it, and in a sense he could do it. * * * What a pity this senseless, stiff-kneed, light-headed chivalry did not beat its brains out several centuries before Bayard put such an absurd price upon himself.

So every phase of the question which his good sense presented told Brandon, whose passion was as ardent though not so impatient as Mary's, that it would be worse than foolhardy to try to see her.

He, however, had determined to see her once more before he left, but as it could, in all probability, be only once, he was reserving the meeting until the last, and had written Mary that it was their best and only chance.

This brought to Mary a stinging realization of the fact that Brandon was about to leave her and that she would lose him if something were not done quickly. Now for Mary, after a life of gratified whims, to lose the very thing she wanted most of all—that for which she would willingly have given up every other desire her heart had ever coined—was a thought hardly to be endured. She felt that the world would surely collapse. It could not, would not, should not be.

Her vigorous young nerves were too strong to be benumbed by an overwhelming agony, as is sometimes the case with those who are fortunate enough to be weaker, so she had to suffer and endure. Life itself, yes, life a thousand times, was slipping away from her. She must be doing something or she would perish. Poor Mary! How a grand soul like hers, full of faults and weakness, can suffer! What an infinite disproportion between her susceptibility to pain and her power to combat it! She had the maximum capacity for one and the minimum strength for the other. No wonder it drove her almost mad—that excruciating pang of love.

She could not endure inaction, so she did the worst thing possible. She went alone, one afternoon, just before dusk, to see Brandon at our rooms. I was not there when she first went in, but, having seen her on the way, suspected something and followed, arriving two or three minutes after her. I knew it was best that I should be present, and was sure Brandon would wish it. When I entered they were holding each other's hands, in silence. They had not yet found their tongues, so full and crowded were their hearts. It was pathetic to see them, especially the girl, who had not Brandon's hopelessness to deaden the pain by partial resignation.

Upon my entrance, she dropped his hands and turned quickly toward me with a frightened look, but was reassured upon seeing who it was. Brandon mechanically walked away from her and seated himself on a stool. Mary, as mechanically, moved to his side and placed her hand on his shoulder. Turning her face toward me, she said: "Sir Edwin, I know you will forgive me when I tell you that we have a great deal to say and wish to be alone."

I was about to go when Brandon stopped me.

"No, no; Caskoden, please stay; it would not do. It would be bad enough, God knows, if the princess should be found here with both of us; but, with me alone, I should be dead before morning. There is danger enough as it is, for they will watch us."

Mary knew he was right, but she could not resist a vicious little glance toward me, who was in no way to blame.

Presently we all moved into the window-way, where Brandon and Mary sat upon the great cloak and I on a camp-stool in front of them, completely filling up the little passage.

"I can bear this no longer," exclaimed Mary. "I will go to my brother to-night and tell him all; I will tell him how I suffer, and that I shall die if you are allowed to go away and leave me forever. He loves me, and I can do anything with him when I try. I know I can obtain his consent to our—our—marriage. He cannot know how I suffer, else he would not treat me so. I will let him see—I will convince him. I have in my mind everything I want to say and do. I will sit on his knee and stroke his hair and kiss him." And she laughed softly as her spirit revived in the breath of a growing hope. "Then I will tell him how handsome he is, and how I hear the ladies sighing for him, and he will come around all right by the third visit. Oh, I know how to do it; I have done it so often. Never fear! I wish I had gone at it long ago."

Her enthusiastic fever of hope was really contagious, but Brandon, whose life was at stake, had his wits quickened by the danger.

"Mary, would you like to see me a corpse before to-morrow noon?" he asked.

"Why! of course not; why do you ask such a dreadful question?"

"Because, if you wish to make sure of it, do what you have just said—go to the king and tell him all. I doubt if he could wait till morning. I believe he would awaken me at midnight to put me to sleep forever—at the end of a rope or on a block pillow."

"Oh! no! you are all wrong; I know what I can do with Henry."

"If that is the case, I say good-bye now, for I shall be out of England, if possible, by midnight. You must promise me that you will not only not go to the king at all about this matter, but that you will guard your tongue, jealous of its slightest word, and remember with every breath that on your prudence hangs my life, which, I know, is dear to you. Do you promise? If you do not, I must fly; so you will lose me one way or the other, if you tell the king; either by my flight or by my death."

"I promise," said Mary, with drooping head; the embodiment of despair; all life and hope having left her again.

After a few minutes her face brightened, and she asked Brandon what ship he would sail in for New Spain, and whence.

"We sail in the Royal Hind, from Bristol," he replied.

"How many go out in her; and are there any women?"

"No! no!" he returned; "no woman could make the trip, and, besides, on ships of that sort, half pirate, half merchant, they do not take women. The sailors are superstitious about it and will not sail with them. They say they bring bad luck—adverse winds, calms, storms, blackness, monsters from the deep and victorious foes."

"The ignorant creatures!" cried Mary.

Brandon continued: "There will be a hundred men, if the captain can induce so many to enlist."

"How does one procure passage?" inquired Mary.

"By enlisting with the captain, a man named Bradhurst, at Bristol, where the ship is now lying. There is where I enlisted by letter. But why do you ask?"

"Oh! I only wanted to know."

We talked awhile on various topics, but Mary always brought the conversation back to the same subject, the Royal Hind and New Spain. After asking many questions, she sat in silence for a time, and then abruptly broke into one of my sentences—she was always interrupting me as if I were a parrot.

"I have been thinking and have made up my mind what I will do, and you shall not dissuade me. I will go to New Spain with you. That will be glorious—far better than the humdrum life of sitting at home—and will solve the whole question."

"But that would be impossible, Mary," said Brandon, into whose face this new evidence of her regard had brought a brightening look; "utterly impossible. To begin with, no woman could stand the voyage; not even you, strong and vigorous as you are."

"Oh, yes I can, and I will not allow you to stop me for that reason. I could bear any hardship better than the torture of the last few weeks. In truth, I cannot bear this at all; it is killing me, so what would it be when you are gone and I am the wife of Louis? Think of that, Charles Brandon; think of that, when I am the wife of Louis. Even if the voyage kills me, I might as well die one way as another; and then I should be with you, where it were sweet to die." And I had to sit there and listen to all this foolish talk!

Brandon insisted: "But no women are going; as I told you, they would not take one; besides, how could you escape? I will answer the first question you ever asked me. You are of 'sufficient consideration about the court' for all your movements to attract notice. It is impossible; we must not think of it; it cannot be done. Why build up hopes only to be cast down?"

"Oh! but it can be done; never doubt it. I will go, not as a woman, but as a man. I have planned all the details while sitting here. To-morrow I will send to Bristol a sum of money asking a separate room in the ship for a young nobleman who wishes to go to New Spain *incognito*, and will go aboard just before they sail. I will buy a man's complete outfit, and will practice being a man before you and Sir Edwin." Here she blushed so that I could see the scarlet even in the gathering gloom. She continued: "As to my escape, I can go to Windsor, and then perhaps on to Berkeley Castle, over by Reading, where there will be no one to watch me. You can leave at once, and there will be no cause for them to spy upon me when you are gone, so it can be done easily enough. That is it; I will go to my sister, who is now at Berkeley Castle, the other side of Reading, you know, and that will make a shorter ride to Bristol when we start."

The thought, of course, could not but please Brandon, to whom, in the warmth of Mary's ardor, it had almost begun to offer hope; and he said musingly: "I wonder if it could be done? If it could—if we could reach New Spain, we might build ourselves a home in the beautiful green mountains and hide ourselves safely away from all the world, in the lap of some cosy valley, rich with nature's bounteous gift of fruit and flowers, shaded from the hot sun and sheltered from the blasts, and live in a little paradise all our own. What a glorious dream! but it is only a dream, and we had better awake from it."

Brandon must have been insane!

"No! no! It is not a dream," interrupted downright, determined Mary; "it is not a dream; it shall be a reality. How glorious it will be! I can see our little house now nestling among the hills, shaded by great spreading trees with flowers and vines and golden fruit all about it, rich plumaged birds and gorgeous butterflies. Oh! I can hardly wait. Who would live in a musty palace when one has within reach such a home, and that, too, with you?"

Here it was again. I thought that interview would be the death of me.

Brandon held his face in his hands, and then looking up said: "It is only a question of your happiness, and hard as the voyage and your life over there would be, yet I believe it would be better than life with Louis of France; nothing could be so terrible as that to both of us. If you wish to go, I will try to take you, though I die in the attempt. There will be ample time to reconsider, so that you can turn back if you wish."

Her reply was inarticulate, though satisfactory; and she took his hand in hers as the tears ran gently down her cheeks; this time tears of joy—the first she had shed for many a day.

In the Siren country again without wax! Overboard and lost!

Yes, Brandon's resolution not to see Mary was well taken, if it could only have been as well kept. Observe, as we progress, into what the breaking of it led him.

He had known that if he should but see her once more, his already toppling will would lose its equipoise, and he would be led to attempt the impossible and invite destruction. At first this scheme appeared to me in its true light, but Mary's subtle feminine logic made it seem such plain and easy sailing that I soon began to draw enthusiasm from her exhaustless store, and our combined attack upon Brandon eventually routed every vestige of caution and common sense that even he had left.

Siren logic has always been irresistible and will continue so, no doubt, despite experience.

I cannot define what it was about Mary that made her little speeches, half argumentative, all-pleading, so wonderfully persuasive. Her facts were mere fancies, and her logic was not even good sophistry. As to real argument and reasoning, there was nothing of either in them. It must have been her native strength of character and intensely vigorous personality; some unknown force of nature, operating through her occultly, that turned the channels of other persons' thoughts and filled them with her own will. There was magic in her power, I am certain, but unconscious magic to Mary, I am equally sure. She never would have used it knowingly.

There was still another obstacle to which Mary administered her favorite remedy, the Gordian knot treatment. Brandon said: "It cannot be; you are not my wife, and we dare not trust a priest here to unite us."

"No," replied Mary, with hanging head, "but we can—can find one over there."

"I do not know how that will be; we shall probably not find one; at least, I fear; I do not know."

After a little hesitation she answered: "I will go with you anyway—and—and risk it. I hope we may find a priest," and she flushed scarlet from her throat to her hair.

Brandon kissed her and said: "You shall go, my brave girl. You make me blush for my faint-heartedness and prudence. I will make you my wife in some way as sure as there is a God."

Soon after this Brandon forced himself to insist on her departure, and I went with her, full of hope and completely blinded to the dangers of our cherished scheme. I think Brandon never really lost sight of the danger, and almost infinite proportion of chance against this wild, reckless venture, but was daring enough to attempt it even in the face of such clearly seen and deadly consequences.

What seems to be bravery, as in Mary's case, for example, is often but a lack of perception of the real danger. True bravery is that which dares a danger fully seeing it. A coward may face an unseen danger, and his act may shine with the luster of genuine heroism. Mary was brave, but it was the feminine bravery that did not see. Show her a danger and she was womanly enough—that is, if you could make her see it. Her wilfulness sometimes extended to her mental vision and she would not see. In common with many others, she needed mental spectacles at times.

* * * * *

CHAPTER XV

To Make a Man of Her

So it was all arranged, and I converted part of Mary's jewels into money. She said she was sorry now she had not taken de Longueville's diamonds, as they would have added to her treasure; I, however, procured quite a large sum, to which I secretly added a goodly portion out of my own store. At Mary's request I sent part to Bradhurst at Bristol, and retained the rest for Brandon to take with him.

A favorable answer soon came from Bristol, giving the young nobleman a separate room in consideration of the large purse he had sent.

The next step was to procure the gentleman's wardrobe for Mary. This was a little troublesome at first, for, of course, she could not be measured in the regular way. We managed to overcome this difficulty by having Jane take the measurements under instructions received from the tailor, which measurements, together with the cloth, I took to the fractional little man who did my work.

He looked at the measurements with twinkling eyes, and remarked: "Sir Edwin, that be the curiousest shaped man ever I see the measures of. Sure it would make a mighty handsome woman, or I know nothing of human dimensions."

"Never you mind about dimensions; make the garments as they are ordered and keep your mouth shut, if you know what is to your interest. Do you hear?"

He delivered himself of a labored wink. "I do hear and understand, too, and my tongue is like the tongue of an obelisk."

In due time I brought the suits to Mary, and they were soon adjusted to her liking.

The days passed rapidly, till it was a matter of less than a fortnight until the Royal Hind would sail, and it really looked as if the adventure might turn out to our desire.

Jane was in tribulation, and thought she ought to be taken along. This, you may be sure, was touching me very closely, and I began to wish the whole infernal mess at the bottom of the sea. If Jane went, his august majesty, King Henry VIII, would be without a Master of the Dance, just as sure as the stars twinkled in the firmament. It was, however, soon decided that Brandon would have his hands more than full to get off with one woman, and that two would surely spoil the plan. So Jane was to be left behind, full of tribulation and indignation, firmly convinced that she was being treated very badly.

Although at first Jane was violently opposed to the scheme, she soon caught the contagious ardor of Mary's enthusiasm, and knowing that her dear lady's every chance of happiness was staked upon the throw, grew more reconciled. To a person of Jane's age, this venture for love offers itself as the last and only cast—the cast for all—and in this particular case there was enough of romance to catch the fancy of any girl. Nothing was lacking to make it truly romantic. The exalted station of at least one of the lovers; the rough road of their true love; the elopement, and, above all, the elopement to a new world, with a cosy hut nestling in fragrant shades and glad with the notes of love from the throats of countless song-birds— what more could a romantic girl desire? So, to my surprise, Jane became more than reconciled, and her fever of anticipation and excitement grew apace with Mary's as the time drew on.

Mary's vanity was delighted with her elopement *trousseau*, for of course it was of the finest. Not that the quality was better than her usual wear, but doublet and hose were so different on her. She paraded for an hour or so before Jane, and as she became accustomed to the new garb, and as the steel reflected a most beautiful image, she determined to show herself to Brandon and me. She said she wanted to become accustomed to being seen in her doublet and hose, and would begin with us. She thought if she could not bear our gaze she would surely make a dismal failure on shipboard among so many strange men. There was some good reasoning in this, and it, together with her vanity, overruled her modesty, and prompted her to come to see us in her character of young nobleman. Jane made one of her mighty protests, so infinitely disproportionate in size to her little ladyship, but the self-willed princess would not listen to her, and was for coming alone if Jane would not come with her. Once having determined, as usual with her, she wasted no time about it, but throwing a long cloak over her shoulders, started for our rooms, with angry, weeping, protesting Jane at her heels.

When I heard the knock I was sure it was the girls, for though Mary had promised Brandon she would not, under any circumstances, attempt another visit, I knew so well her utter inability to combat her desire, and her reckless disregard of danger where there was a motive sufficient to furnish the nerve tension, that I was sure she would come, or try to come, again.

I have spoken before about the quality of bravery. What is it, after all, and how can we analyze it? Women, we say, are cowardly, but I have seen a woman take a risk that the bravest man's nerve would turn on edge against. How is it? Can it be possible that they are braver than we? That our bravery is of the vaunting kind that telleth of itself? My answer, made up from a long life of observation, is: "Yes! Given the motive, and women are the bravest creatures on earth." Yet how foolishly timid they are at times!

I admitted the girls, and when the door was shut Mary unclasped the brooch at her throat and the great cloak fell to her heels. Out she stepped, with a little laugh of delight, clothed in doublet, hose and confusion, the prettiest picture mortal eyes ever rested on. Her hat, something on the broad, flat style with a single white plume encircling the crown, was of purple velvet trimmed in gold braid and touched here and there with precious stones. Her doublet was of the same purple velvet as her hat, trimmed in lace and gold braid. Her short trunks were of heavy black silk slashed by yellow satin, with hose of lavender silk; and her little shoes were of russet French leather. Quite a rainbow, you will say—but such a rainbow!

Brandon and I were struck dumb with admiration and could not keep from showing it. This disconcerted the girl, and increased her embarrassment until we could not tell which was the prettiest—the garments, the girl or the confusion; but this I know, the whole picture was as sweet and beautiful as the eyes of man could behold.

Fine feathers will not make fine birds, and Mary's masculine attire could no more make her look like a man than harness can disguise the graces of a gazelle. Nothing could conceal her intense, exquisite womanhood. With our looks of astonishment and admiration Mary's blushes deepened.

"What is the matter? Is anything wrong?" she asked.

"Nothing is wrong," answered Brandon, smiling in spite of himself; "nothing on earth is wrong with you, you may be sure. You are perfect—that is, for a woman; and one who thinks there is anything wrong about a perfect woman is hard to please. But if you flatter yourself that you, in any way, resemble a man, or that your dress in the faintest degree conceals your sex, you are mistaken. It makes it only more apparent."

"How can that be?" asked Mary, in comical tribulation; "is not this a man's doublet and hose, and this hat—is it not a man's hat? They are all for a man; then why do I not look like one, I ask? Tell me what is wrong. Oh! I thought I looked just like a man; I thought the disguise was perfect."

"Well," returned Brandon, "if you will permit me to say so, you are entirely too symmetrical and shapely ever to pass for a man."

The flaming color was in her cheeks, as Brandon went on: "Your feet are too small, even for a boy's feet. I don't think you could be made to look like a man if you worked from now till doomsday."

Brandon spoke in a troubled tone, for he was beginning to see in Mary's perfect and irrepressible womanhood an insurmountable difficulty right across his path.

"As to your feet, you might find larger shoes, or, better still, jack-boots; and, as to your hose, you might wear longer trunks, but what to do about the doublet I am sure I do not know."

Mary looked up helpless and forlorn, and the hot face went into her bended elbow as a realization of the situation seemed to dawn upon her.

"Oh! I wish I had not come. But I wanted to grow accustomed so that I could wear them before others. I believe I could bear it more easily with any one else. I did not think of it in that way," and she snatched her cloak from where it had fallen on the floor and threw it around her.

"What way, Mary?" asked Brandon gently, and receiving no answer. "But you will have to bear my looking at you all the time if you go with me."

"I don't believe I can do it."

"No, no," answered he, bravely attempting cheerfulness; "we may as well give it up. I have had no hope from the first. I knew it could not be done, and it should not. I was both insane and criminal to think of permitting you to try it."

Brandon's forced cheerfulness died out with his words, and he sank into a chair with his elbows on his knees and his face in his hands. Mary ran to him at once. There had been a little moment of faltering, but there was no real surrender in her.

Dropping on her knee beside him, she said coaxingly: "Don't give up; you are a man; you must not surrender, and let me, a girl, prove the stronger. Shame upon you when I look up to you so much and expect you to help me be brave. I will go. I will arrange myself in some way. Oh! why am I not different; I wish I were as straight as the queen," and for that first time in her life she bewailed her beauty, because it stood between her and Brandon.

She soon coaxed him out of his despondency, and we began again to plan the matter in detail.

The girls sat on Brandon's cloak and he and I on the camp-stool and a box.

Mary's time was well occupied in vain attempts to keep herself covered with the cloak, which seemed to have a right good will toward Brandon and me, but she kept track of our plans, which, in brief, were as follows: As to her costume, we would substitute long trunks and jack-boots for shoes and hose, and as to doublet, Mary laughed and blushingly said she had a plan which she would secretly impart to Jane, but would not tell us. She whispered it to Jane, who, as serious as the Lord Chancellor, gave judgment, and "thought it would do." We hoped so, but were full of doubts.

This is all tame enough to write and read about, but I can tell you it was sufficiently exciting at the time. Three of us at least were playing with that comical old fellow, Death, and he gave the game interest and point to our hearts' content.

Through the thick time-layers of all these years, I can still see the group as we sat there, haloed by a hazy cloud of tear-mist. The figures rise before my eyes, so young and fair and rich in life and yet so pathetic in their troubled earnestness that a great flood of pity wells up in my heart for the poor young souls, so danger-bound and suffering, and withal so daring and so recklessly confident in the might and right of love, and the omnipotence of youth. Ah! If God had seen fit in his infinite wisdom to save just one treasure from the wreck of Eden, what a race of thankful hearts this earth would bear, had he saved us youth alone therewith to compensate us for every other ill.

As to the elopement, it was determined that Brandon should leave London the following day for Bristol, and make all arrangements along the line. He would carry with him two bundles, his own and Mary's clothing, and leave them to be taken up when they should go a-shipboard. Eight horses would be procured; four to be left as a relay at an inn between Berkeley Castle and Bristol, and four to be kept at the rendezvous some two leagues the other side of Berkeley for the use of Brandon, Mary and the two men from Bristol who were to act as an escort on the eventful night. There was one disagreeable little feature that we could not provide against nor entirely eliminate. It was the fact that Jane and I should be suspected as accomplices before the fact of Mary's elopement; and, as you know, to assist in the abduction of a princess is treason—for which there is but one remedy. I thought I had a plan to keep ourselves safe if I could only stifle for the once Jane's troublesome and vigorous tendency to preach the truth to all people, upon all subjects and at all times and places. She promised to tell the story I would drill into her, but I knew the truth would seep out in a thousand ways. She could no more hold it than a sieve can hold water. We were playing for great stakes, which, if I do say it, none but the bravest hearts, bold and daring as the truest knights of chivalry, would think of trying for. Nothing less than the running away with the first princess of the first blood royal of the world. Think of it! It appalls me even now. Discovery meant death to one of us surely—Brandon; possibly to two others—Jane and me; certainly, if Jane's truthfulness should become unmanageable, as it was so apt to do.

After we had settled everything we could think of, the girls took their leave; Mary slyly kissing Brandon at the door. I tried to induce Jane to follow her lady's example, but she was as cool and distant as the new moon.

I saw Jane again that night and told her in plain terms what I thought of her treatment of me. I told her it was selfish and unkind to take advantage of my love for her and treat me so cruelly. I told her that if she had one drop of generous blood she would tell me of her love, if she had any, or let me know it in some way; and if she cared nothing for me she was equally bound to be honest and tell me plainly, so that I should not waste my time and energy in a hopeless cause. I thought it rather clever in me to force her into a position where her refusal to tell me that she did not care for me would drive her to a half avowal. Of course, I had little fear of the former, or perhaps I should not have been so anxious to precipitate the issue.

She did not answer me directly, but said: "From the way you looked at Mary to-day, I was led to think you cared little for any other girl's opinion."

"Ah! Mistress Jane!" cried I joyfully; "I have you at last; you are jealous."

"I give you to understand, sir, that your vanity has led you into a great mistake."

"As to your caring for me, or your jealousy? Which?" I asked seriously. Adroit, wasn't that?

"As to the jealousy, Edwin. There, now; I think that is saying a good deal. Too much," she said pleadingly; but I got something more before she left, even if it was against her will; something that made it almost impossible for me to hold my feet to the ground.

Jane pouted, gave me a sharp little slap and then ran away, but at the door she turned and threw back a rare smile that was priceless to me; for it told me she was not angry; and furthermore shed an illuminating ray upon a fact which I was blind not to have seen long before; that is, that Jane was one of those girls who must be captured *vi et armis*.

Some women cannot be captured at all; they must give themselves; of this class pre-eminently was Mary. Others again will meet you half way and kindly lend a helping hand; while some, like Jane, are always on the run, and are captured only by pursuit. They are usually well worth the trouble though, and make docile captives. After that smile from the door I felt that Jane was mine; all I had to do was to keep off outside enemies, charge upon her defenses when the times were ripe and accept nothing short of her own sweet self as ransom.

The next day Brandon paid his respects to the king and queen, made his adieus to his friends and rode off alone to Bristol. You may be sure the king showed no signs of undue grief at his departure.

* * * * *

CHAPTER XVI

A Hawking Party

A few days after Brandon's departure, Mary, with the king's consent, organized a small party to go over to Windsor for a few weeks during the warm weather.

There were ten or twelve of us, including two chaperons, the old Earl of Hertford and the dowager Duchess of Kent. Henry might as well have sent along a pair of spaniels to act as chaperons—it would have taken an army to guard Mary alone—and to tell you the truth our old chaperons needed watching more than any of us. It was scandalous. Each of them had a touch of gout, and when they made wry faces it was a standing inquiry among us whether they were leering at each other or felt a twinge—whether it was their feet or their hearts, that troubled them.

Mary led them a pretty life at all times, even at home in the palace, and I know they would rather have gone off with a pack of imps than with us. The inducement was that it gave them better opportunities to be together—an arrangement connived at by the queen, I think—and they were satisfied. The earl had a wife, but he fancied the old dowager and she fancied him, and probably the wife fancied somebody else, so they were all happy. It greatly amused the young people, you may be sure, and Mary said, probably without telling the exact truth, that every night she prayed God to pity and forgive their ugliness. One day the princess said she was becoming alarmed; their ugliness was so intense she feared it might be contagious and spread. Then, with a most comical seriousness, she added:

"Mon Dieu! Sir Edwin, what if I should catch it? Master Charles would not take me."

"No danger of that, my lady; he is too devoted to see anything but beauty in you, no matter how much you might change."

"Do you really think so? He says so little about it that sometimes I almost doubt."

Therein she spoke the secret of Brandon's success with her, at least in the beginning; for there is wonderful potency in the stimulus of a healthy little doubt.

We had a delightful canter over to Windsor, I riding with Mary most of the way. I was not averse to this arrangement, as I not only relished Mary's mirth and joyousness, which was at its height, but hoped I might give my little Lady Jane a twinge or two of jealousy perchance to fertilize her sentiments toward me.

Mary talked, and laughed, and sang, for her soul was a fountain of gladness that bubbled up the instant pressure was removed. She spoke of little but our last trip over this same road, and, as we passed objects on the way, told me of what Brandon had said at this place and that. She laughed and dimpled exquisitely in relating how she had deliberately made opportunities for him to flatter her, until, at last, he smiled in her face and told her she was the most beautiful creature living, but that "after all, 'beauty was as beauty did!'"

"That made me angry," said she. "I pouted for a while, and, two or three times, was on the point of dismissing him, but thought better of it and asked him plainly wherein I did so much amiss. Then what do you think the impudent fellow said?"

"I cannot guess."

"He said: 'Oh, there is so much it would take a lifetime to tell it.'

"This made me furious, but I could not answer, and a moment later he said: 'Nevertheless I should be only too glad to undertake the task.'

"The thought never occurred to either of us then that he would be taken at his word. Bold? I should think he was; I never saw anything like it! I have not told you a tenth part of what he said to me that day; he said anything he wished, and it seemed that I could neither stop him nor retaliate. Half the time I was angry and half the time amused, but by the time we reached Windsor there never was a girl more hopelessly and desperately in love than Mary Tudor." And she laughed as if it were a huge joke on Mary.

She continued: "That day settled matters with me for all time. I don't know how he did it. Yes I do . . ." and she launched forth into an account of Brandon's perfections, which I found somewhat dull, and so would you.

We remained a day or two at Windsor, and then, over the objections of our chaperons, moved on to Berkeley Castle, where Margaret of Scotland was spending the summer.

We had another beautiful ride up the dear old Thames to Berkeley, but Mary had grown serious and saw none of it.

On the afternoon of the appointed day, the princess suggested a hawking party, and we set out in the direction of the rendezvous. Our party consisted of myself, three other gentlemen and three ladies besides Mary. Jane did not go; I was afraid to trust her. She wept, and, with difficulty, forced herself to say something about a headache, but the rest of the inmates of the castle of course had no thought that possibly they were taking their last look upon Mary Tudor.

Think who this girl was we were running away with! What reckless fools we were not to have seen the utter hopelessness, certain failure, and deadly peril of our act; treason black as Plutonian midnight. But Providence seems to have an especial care for fools, while wise men are left to care for themselves, and it does look as if safety lies in folly.

We rode on and on, and although I took two occasions, in the presence of others, to urge Mary to return, owing to the approach of night and threatened rain, she took her own head, as everybody knew she always would, and continued the hunt.

Just before dark, as we neared the rendezvous, Mary and I managed to ride ahead of the party quite a distance. At last we saw a heron rise, and the princess uncapped her hawk.

"This is my chance," she said; "I will run away from you now and lose myself; keep them off my track for five minutes and I shall be safe. Good-bye, Edwin; you and Jane are the only persons I regret to leave. I love you as my brother and sister. When we are settled in New Spain we will have you both come to us. Now, Edwin, I shall tell you something: don't let Jane put you off any longer. She loves you; she told me so. There! Good-bye, my friend; kiss her a thousand times for me." And she flew her bird and galloped after it at headlong speed.

As I saw the beautiful young form receding from me, perhaps forever, the tears stood in my eyes, while I thought of the strong heart that so unfalteringly braved such dangers and was so loyal to itself and daring for its love. She had shown a little feverish excitement for a day or two, but it was the fever of anticipation, not of fear or hesitancy.

Soon the princess was out of sight, and I waited for the others to overtake me. When they came up I was greeted in chorus: "Where is the princess?" I said she had gone off with her hawk, and had left me to bring them after her. I held them talking while I could, and when we started to follow took up the wrong scent. A short ride made this apparent, when I came in for my full share of abuse and ridicule, for I had led them against their judgment. I was credited with being a blockhead, when in fact they were the dupes.

We rode hurriedly back to the point of Mary's departure and wound our horns lustily, but my object had been accomplished, and I knew that within twenty minutes from the time I last saw her, she would be with Brandon, on the road to Bristol, gaining on any pursuit we could make at the rate of three miles for two. We scoured the forest far and near, but of course found no trace. After a time rain set in and one of the gentlemen escorted the ladies home, while three of us remained to prowl about the woods and roads all night in a soaking drizzle. The task was tiresome enough for me, as it lacked motive; and when we rode into Berkeley Castle next day, a sorrier set of bedraggled, rain-stained, mud-covered knights you never saw. You may know the castle was wild with excitement. There were all sorts of conjectures, but soon we unanimously concluded it had been the work of highwaymen, of whom the country was full, and by whom the princess had certainly been abducted.

The chaperons forgot their gout and each other, and Jane, who was the most affected of all, had a genuine excuse for giving vent to her grief and went to bed—by far the safest place for her.

What was to be done? First we sent a message to the king, who would probably have us all flayed alive—a fear which the chaperons shared to the fullest extent. Next, an armed party rode back to look again for Mary, and, if possible, rescue her.

The fact that I had been out the entire night before, together with the small repute in which I was held for deeds of arms, excused me from taking part in this bootless errand, so again I profited by the small esteem in which I was held. I say I profited, for I stayed at the castle with Jane, hoping to find my opportunity in the absence of everybody else. All the ladies but Jane had ridden out, and the knights who had been with me scouring the forest were sleeping, since they had not my incentive to remain awake. They had no message to deliver; no duty to perform for an absent friend. A thousand! Only think of it! I wished it had been a million, and so faithful was I to my trust that I swore in my soul I would deliver them, every one.

And Jane loved me! No more walking on the hard, prosaic earth now; from this time forth I would fly; that was the only sensible method of locomotion. Mary had said: "She told me so." Could it really be true? You will at once see what an advantage this bit of information was to me.

I hoped that Jane would wish to see me to talk over Mary's escape—so I sent word to her that I was waiting, and she quickly enough recovered her health and came down. I suggested that we walk out to a secluded little summer-house by the river, and Jane was willing. Ah! my opportunity was here at last.

She found her bonnet, and out we went. What an enchanting walk was that, and how rich is a man who has laid up such treasures of memory to grow the sweeter as he feeds upon them. A rich memory is better than hope, for it lasts after fruition, and serves us at a time when hope has failed and fruition is but—a memory. Ah! how we cherish it in our hearts, and how it comes at our beck and call to thrill us through and through and make us thank God that we have lived, and wonder in our hearts why he has given poor undeserving us so much.

After we arrived at the summer-house, Jane listened, half the time in tears, while I told her all about Mary's flight.

Shall I ever forget that summer day? A sweet briar entwined our enchanted bower, and, when I catch its scent even now, time-vaulting memory carries me back, making years seem as days, and I see it all as I saw the light of noon that moment—and all was Jane. The softly lapping river, as it gently sought the sea, sang in soothing cadence of naught but Jane; the south wind from his flowery home breathed zephyr-voiced her name again, and, as it stirred the rustling leaves on bush and tree, they whispered back the same sweet strain; and every fairy voice found its echo in my soul; for there it was as 'twas with me, "Jane! Jane! Jane!" I have heard men say they would not live their lives over and take its meager grains of happiness, in such infinite disproportion to its grief and pain, but, as for me, thanks to one woman, I almost have the minutes numbered all along the way, and know them one from the other; and when I sit alone to dream, and live again some portion of the happy past, I hardly know what time to choose or incident to dwell upon, my life is so much crowded with them all. Would I live again my life? Aye, every moment except perhaps when Jane was ill—and therein even was happiness, for what a joy there was at her recovery. I do not even regret that it is closing; it would be ungrateful; I have had so much more than my share that I simply fall upon my knees and thank God for what He has given.

Jane's whole attitude toward me was changed, and she seemed to cling to me in a shy, unconscious manner, that was sweet beyond the naming, as the one solace for all her grief.

After I had answered all her questions, and had told her over and over again every detail of Mary's flight, and had assured her that the princess was, at that hour, breasting the waves with Brandon, on their high road to paradise, I thought it time to start myself in the same direction and to say a word in my own behalf. So I spoke very freely and told Jane what I felt and what I wanted.

"Oh! Sir Edwin," she responded, "let us not think of anything but my mistress. Think of the trouble she is in."

"No! no! Jane; Lady Mary is out of her trouble by now, and is as happy as a lark, you may be sure. Has she not won everything her heart longed for? Then let us make our own paradise, since we have helped them make theirs. You have it, Jane, just within your lips; speak the word and it will change everything—if you love me, and I know you do."

Jane's head was bowed and she remained silent.

Then I told her of Lady Mary's message, and begged, if she would not speak in words what I so longed to hear, she would at least tell it by allowing me to deliver only one little thousandth part of the message Mary had sent; but she drew away and said she would return to the castle if I continued to behave in that manner. I begged hard, and tried to argue the point, but logic seems to lose its force in such a situation, and all I said availed nothing. Jane was obdurate, and was for going back at once. Her persistence was beginning to look like obstinacy, and I soon grew so angry that I asked no permission, but delivered Mary's message, or a good part of it, at least, whether she would or no, and then sat back and asked her what she was going to do about it.

Poor little Jane thought she was undone for life. She sat there half pouting, half weeping, and said she could do nothing about it; that she was alone now, and if I, her only friend, would treat her that way, she did not know where to look.

"Where to look?" I demanded. "Look *here*, Jane, here; you might as well understand, first as last, that I will not be trifled with longer, and that I intend to continue treating you that way as long as we both live. I have determined not to permit you to behave as you have for so long; for I know you love me. You have half told me so a dozen times, and even your half words are whole truths; there is not a fraction of a lie in you. Besides, Mary told me that you told her so."

"She did not tell you that?"

"Yes; upon my knightly honor." Of course there was but one answer to this—tears. I then brought the battle to close quarters at once, and, with my arm uninterrupted at my lady's waist, asked:

"Did you not tell her so? I know you will speak nothing but the truth. Did you not tell her? Answer me, Jane." The fair head nodded as she whispered between the hands that covered her face:

"Yes; I—I—d-did;" and I—well, I delivered the rest of Mary's message, and that, too, without a protest from Jane.

Truthfulness is a pretty good thing after all.

So Jane was conquered at last, and I heaved a sigh as the battle ended, for it had been a long, hard struggle.

I asked Jane when we should be married, but she said she could not think of that now—not until she knew that Mary was safe; but she would promise to be my wife sometime. I told her that her word was as good as gold to me; and so it was and always has been; as good as fine gold thrice refined. I then told her I would bother her no more about it, now that I was sure of her, but when she was ready she should tell me of her own accord and make my happiness complete. She said she would, and I told her I believed her and was satisfied. I did, however, suggest that the intervening time would be worse than wasted—happiness thrown right in the face of Providence, as it were—and begged her not to waste any more than necessary; to which she seriously and honestly answered that she would not.

We went back to the castle, and as we parted Jane said timidly: "I am glad I told you, Edwin; glad it is over."

She had evidently dreaded it; but—I was glad, too; very glad. Then I went to bed.

* * * * *

CHAPTER XVII

The Elopement

Whatever the king might think, I knew Lord Wolsey would quickly enough guess the truth when he heard that the princess was missing, and would have a party in pursuit. The runaways, however, would have at least twenty-four hours the start, and a ship leaves no tracks. When Mary left me she was perhaps two-thirds of a league from the rendezvous, and night was rapidly falling. As her road lay through a dense forest all the way, she would have a dark, lonely ride of a few minutes, and I was somewhat uneasy for that part of the journey. It had been agreed that if everything was all right at the rendezvous, Mary should turn loose her horse, which had always been stabled at Berkeley Castle and would quickly trot home. To further emphasize her safety a thread would be tied in his forelock. The horse took his time in returning, and did not arrive until the second morning after the flight, but when he came I found the thread, and, unobserved, removed it. I quickly took it to Jane, who has it yet, and cherishes it for the mute message of comfort it brought her. In case the horse should not return, I was to find a token in a hollow tree near the place of meeting; but the thread in the forelock told us our friends had found each other.

When we left the castle, Mary wore under her riding habit a suit of man's attire, and, as we rode along, she would shrug her shoulders and laugh as if it were a huge joke; and by the most comical little pantomime, call my attention to her unusual bulk. So when she found Brandon, the only change necessary to make a man of her was to throw off the riding habit and pull on the jackboots and slouch hat, both of which Brandon had with him.

They wasted no time you may be sure, and were soon under way. In a few minutes they picked up the two Bristol men who were to accompany them, and, when night had fairly fallen, left the by-paths and took to the main road leading from London to Bath and Bristol. The road was a fair one; that is, it was well defined and there was no danger of losing it; in fact, there was more danger of losing one's self in its fathomless mud-holes and quagmires. Brandon had recently passed over it twice, and had made mental note of the worst places, so he hoped to avoid them.

Soon the rain began to fall in a soaking drizzle; then the lamps of twilight went out, and even the shadows of the night were lost among themselves in blinding darkness. It was one of those black nights fit for witch traveling; and, no doubt, every witch in England was out brewing mischief. The horses' hoofs sucked and splashed in the mud with a sound that Mary thought might be heard at Land's End; and the hoot of an owl, now and then disturbed by a witch, would strike upon her ear with a volume of sound infinitely disproportionate to the size of any owl she had ever seen or dreamed of before.

Brandon wore our cushion, the great cloak, and had provided a like one of suitable proportions for the princess. This came in good play, as her fine gentleman's attire would be but poor stuff to turn the water. The wind, which had arisen with just enough force to set up a dismal wail, gave the rain a horizontal slant and drove it in at every opening. The flaps of the comfortable great cloak blew back from Mary's knees, and she felt many a chilling drop through her fine new silk trunks that made her wish for buckram in their place. Soon the water began to trickle down her legs and find lodgment in the jack-boots, and as the rain and wind came in tremulous little whirs, she felt wretched enough—she who had always been so well sheltered from every blast. Now and then mud and water would fly up into her face—striking usually in the eyes or mouth—and then again her horse would stumble and almost throw her over his head, as he sank, knee deep, into some unexpected hole. All of this, with the thousand and one noises that broke the still worse silence of the inky night soon began to work upon her nerves and make her fearful. The road was full of dangers aside from stumbling horses and broken necks, for many were the stories of murder and robbery committed along the route they were traveling. It is true they had two stout men, and all were armed, yet they might easily come upon a party too strong for them; and no one could tell what might happen, thought the princess. There was that pitchy darkness through which she could hardly see her horse's head—a thing of itself that seemed to have infinite powers for mischief, and which no amount of argument ever induced any normally constituted woman to believe was the mere negative absence of light, and not a terrible entity potent for all sorts of mischief. Then that wailing howl that rose and fell betimes; no wind ever made such a noise she felt sure. There were those shining white gleams which came from the little pools of water on the road, looking like dead men's faces upturned and pale; perhaps they were water and perhaps they were not. Mary had all confidence in Brandon, but that very fact operated against her. Having that confidence and trust in him, she felt no need to waste her own energy in being brave; so she relaxed completely, and had the feminine satisfaction of allowing herself to be thoroughly frightened.

Is it any wonder Mary's gallant but womanly spirit sank low in the face of all those terrors? She held out bravely, however, and an occasional clasp from Brandon's hand under cover of the darkness comforted her. When all those terrors would not suggest even a thought of turning back, you may judge of the character of this girl and her motive.

They traveled on, galloping when they could, trotting when they could not gallop, and walking when they must.

At one time they thought they heard the sound of following horses, and hastened on as fast as they dared go, until, stopping to listen and hearing nothing, they concluded they were wrong. About eleven o'clock, however, right out of the black bank of night in front of them they heard, in earnest, the sucking splash of horses' hoofs. In an instant the sound ceased and the silence was worse than the noise. The cry "Hollo!" brought them all to a stand, and Mary thought her time had come.

Both sides shouted, "Who comes there?" to which there was a simultaneous and eager answer, "A friend," and each party passed its own way, only too glad to be rid of the other. Mary's sigh of relief could be heard above even the wind and the owls, and her heart beat as if it had a task to finish within a certain time.

After this they rode on as rapidly as they dared, and about midnight arrived at the inn where the relay of horses was awaiting them.

The inn was a rambling old thatched-roofed structure, half mud, half wood, and all filth. There are many inns in England that are tidy enough, but this one was a little off the main road—selected for that reason—and the uncleanness was not the least of Mary's trials that hard night. She had not tasted food since noon, and felt the keen hunger natural to youth and health such as hers, after twelve hours of fasting and eight hours of riding. Her appetite soon overcame her repugnance, and she ate, with a zest that was new to her, the humblest fare that had ever passed her lips. One often misses the zest of life's joys by having too much of them. One must want a thing before it can be appreciated.

A hard ride of five hours brought our travelers to Bath, which place they rode around just as the sun began to gild the tile roofs and steeples, and another hour brought them to Bristol.

The ship was to sail at sunrise, but as the wind had died out with the night, there was no danger of its sailing without them. Soon the gates opened, and the party rode to the Bow and String, where Brandon had left their chests. The men were then paid off; quick sale was made of the horses; breakfast was served, and they started for the wharf, with their chests following in the hands of four porters.

A boat soon took them aboard the Royal Hind, and now it looked as if their daring scheme, so full of improbability as to seem impossible, had really come to a successful issue.

From the beginning, I think, it had never occurred to Mary to doubt the result. There had never been with her even a suggestion of possible failure, unless it was that evening in our room, when, prompted by her startled modesty, she had said she could not bear for us to see her in the trunk hose. Now that fruition seemed about to crown her hopes she was happy to her heart's core; and when once to herself wept for sheer joy. It is little wonder she was happy. She was leaving behind no one whom she loved excepting Jane, and perhaps, me. No father nor mother; only a sister whom she barely knew, and a brother whose treatment of her had turned her heart against him. She was also fleeing with the one man in all the world for her, and from a marriage that was literally worse than death.

Brandon, on the other hand, had always had more desire than hope. The many chances against success had forced upon him a haunting sense of certain failure, which, one would think, should have left him now. It did not, however, and even when on shipboard, with a score of men at the windlass ready to heave anchor at the first breath of wind, it was as strong as when Mary first proposed their flight, sitting in the window on his great cloak. Such were their opposite positions. Both were without doubt, but with this difference; Mary had never doubted success; Brandon never doubted failure. He had a keen analytical faculty that gave him truthfully the chances for and against, and, in this case, they were overwhelmingly unfavorable. Such hope as he had been able to distil out of his desire was sadly dampened by an ever-present premonition of failure, which he could not entirely throw off. Too keen an insight for the truth often stands in a man's way, and too clear a view of an overwhelming obstacle is apt to paralyze effort. Hope must always be behind a hearty endeavor.

Our travelers were, of course, greatly in need of rest; so Mary went to her room, and Brandon took a berth in the cabin set apart for the gentlemen.

They had both paid for their passage, although they had enlisted and were part of the ship's company. They were not expected to do sailor's work, but would be called upon in case of fighting to do their part at that. Mary was probably as good a fighter, in her own way, as one could find in a long journey, but how she was to do her part with sword and buckler Brandon did not know. That, however, was a bridge to be crossed when they should come to it.

They had gone aboard about seven o'clock, and Brandon hoped the ship would be well down Bristol channel before he should leave his berth. But the wind that had filled Mary's jack-boots with rain and had howled so dismally all night long would not stir, now that it was wanted. Noon came, yet no wind, and the sun shone as placidly as if Captain Charles Brandon were not fuming with impatience on the poop of the Royal Hind. Three o'clock and no wind. The captain said it would come with night, but sundown was almost at hand and no wind yet. Brandon knew this meant failure if it held a little longer, for he was certain the king, with Wolsey's help, would long since have guessed the truth.

Brandon had not seen the princess since morning, and the delicacy he felt about going to her cabin made the situation somewhat difficult. After putting it off from hour to hour in hope that she would appear of her own accord, he at last knocked at her door, and, of course, found the lady in trouble.

The thought of the princess going on deck caused a sinking at his heart every time it came, as he felt that it was almost impossible to conceal her identity. He had not seen her in her new male attire, for when she threw off her riding habit on meeting him the night before, he had intentionally busied himself about the horses, and saw her only after the great cloak covered her as a gown. He felt that however well her garments might conceal her form, no man on earth ever had such beauty in his face as her transcendent eyes, rose-tinted cheeks, and coral lips, with their cluster of dimples; and his heart sank at the prospect. She might hold out for a while with a straight face, but when the smiles should come—it were just as well to hang a placard about her neck: "This is a woman." The tell-tale dimples would be worse than Jane for outspoken, untimely truthfulness and trouble-provoking candor.

Upon entering, Brandon found Mary wrestling with the problem of her complicated male attire; the most beautiful picture of puzzled distress imaginable. The port was open and showed her rosy as the morn when she looked up at him. The jack-boots were in a corner, and her little feet seemed to put up a protest all their own, against going into them, that ought to have softened every peg. She looked up at Brandon with a half-hearted smile, and then threw her arms about his neck and sobbed like the child that she was.

"Do you regret coming, Lady Mary?" asked Brandon, who, now that she was alone with him, felt that he must take no advantage of the fact to be familiar.

"No! no! not for one moment; I am glad—only too glad. But why do you call me 'Lady'? You used to call me 'Mary.'"

"I don't know; perhaps because you are alone."

"Ah! that is good of you; but you need not be quite so respectful."

The matter was settled by mute but satisfactory arbitration, and Brandon continued: "You must make yourself ready to go on deck. It will be hard, but it must be done."

He helped her with the heavy jack-boots and handed her the rain-stained slouch hat which she put on, and stood a complete man ready for the deck—that is, as complete as could be evolved from her utter femininity.

When Brandon looked her over, all hope went out of him. It seemed that every change of dress only added to her bewitching beauty by showing it in a new phase.

"It will never do; there is no disguising you. What is it that despite everything shows so unmistakably feminine? What shall we do? I have it; you shall remain here under the pretense of illness until we are well at sea, and then I will tell the captain all. It is too bad; and yet I would not have you one whit less a woman for all the world. A man loves a woman who is so thoroughly womanly that nothing can hide it."

Mary was pleased at his flattery, but disappointed at the failure in herself. She had thought that surely these garments would make a man of her in which the keenest eye could not detect a flaw.

They were discussing the matter when a knock came at the door with the cry, "All hands on deck for inspection." Inspection! Jesu! Mary would not safely endure it a minute. Brandon left her at once and went to the captain.

"My lord is ill, and begs to be excused from deck inspection," he said.

Bradhurst, a surly old half pirate of the saltiest pattern, answered: "Ill? Then he had better go ashore as soon as possible. I will refund his money. We cannot make a hospital out of the ship. If his lordship is too ill to stand inspection, see that he goes ashore at once."

This last was addressed to one of the ship's officers, who answered with the usual "Aye, aye, sir," and started for Mary's cabin.

That was worse than ever; and Brandon quickly said he would have his lordship up at once. He then returned to Mary, and after buckling on her sword and belt they went on deck and climbed up the poop ladder to take their places with those entitled to stand aft.

Brandon has often told me since that it was as much as he could do to keep back the tears when he saw Mary's wonderful effort to appear manly. It was both comical and pathetic. She was a princess to whom all the world bowed down, yet that did not help her here. After all she was only a girl, timid and fearful, following at Brandon's heels; frightened lest she should get out of arm's reach of him among those rough men, and longing with all her heart to take his hand for moral as well as physical support. It must have been both laughable and pathetic in the extreme. That miserable sword persisted in tripping her, and the jack-boots, so much too large, evinced an alarming tendency to slip off with every step. How insane we all were not to have foreseen this from the very beginning. It must have been a unique figure she presented climbing up the steps at Brandon's heels, jack-boots and all. So unique was it that the sailors working in the ship's waist stopped their tasks to stare in wonderment, and the gentlemen on the poop made no effort to hide their amusement. Old Bradhurst stepped up to her.

"I hope your lordship is feeling better;" and then, surveying her from head to foot, with a broad grin on his features, "I declare, you look the picture of health, if I ever saw it. How old are you?"

Mary quickly responded, "Fourteen years."

"Fourteen," returned Bradhurst: "well, I don't think you will shed much blood. You look more like a deuced handsome girl than any man I ever saw." At this the men all laughed, and were very impertinent in the free and easy manner of such gentry, most of whom were professional adventurers, with every finer sense dulled and debased by years of vice.

These fellows, half of them tipsy, now gathered about Mary to inspect her personally, each on his own account. Their looks and conduct were very disconcerting, but they did nothing insulting until one fellow gave her a slap on the back, accompanying it by an indecent remark. Brandon tried to pay no attention to them, but this was too much, so he lifted his arm and knocked the fellow off the poop into the waist. The man was back in a moment, and swords were soon drawn and clicking away at a great rate. The contest was brief, however, as the fellow was no sort of match for Brandon, who, with his old trick, quickly twisted his adversary's sword out of his grasp, and with a flash of his own blade flung it into the sea. The other men were now talking together at a little distance in whispers, and in a moment one drunken brute shouted: "It is no man; it is a woman; let us see more of her."

Before Brandon could interfere, the fellow had unbuckled Mary's doublet at the throat, and with a jerk, had torn it half off, carrying away the sleeve and exposing Mary's shoulder, almost throwing her to the deck.

He waved his trophy on high, but his triumph was short-lived, for almost instantly it fell to the deck, and with it the offending hand severed at the wrist by Brandon's sword. Three or four friends of the wounded man rushed upon Brandon; whereupon Mary screamed and began to weep, which of course told the whole story.

A great laugh went up, and instantly a general fight began. Several of the gentlemen, seeing Brandon attacked by such odds, took up his defense, and within twenty seconds all were on one side or the other, every mother's son of them fighting away like mad.

You see how quickly and completely one woman without the slightest act on her part, except a modest effort to be let alone, had set the whole company by the ears, cutting and slashing away at each other like very devils. The sex must generate mischief in some unknown manner, and throw it off, as the sun throws off its heat. However, Jane is an exception to that rule—if it is a rule.

The officers soon put a stop to this lively little fight, and took Brandon and Mary, who was weeping as any right-minded woman would, down into the cabin for consultation.

With a great oath Bradhurst exclaimed: "It is plain enough that you have brought a girl on board under false colors, and you may as well make ready to put her ashore. You see what she has already done—a hand lost to one man and wounds for twenty others—and she was on deck less than five minutes. Heart of God! At that rate she would have the ship at the bottom of Davy Jones's locker before we could sail half down the channel."

"It was not my fault," sobbed Mary, her eyes flashing fire; "I did nothing; all I wanted was to be left alone; but those brutes of men—you shall pay for this; remember what I say. Did you expect Captain Brandon to stand back and not defend me, when that wretch was tearing my garments off?"

"Captain Brandon, did you say?" asked Bradhurst, with his hat off instantly.

"Yes," answered that individual. "I shipped under an assumed name, for various reasons, and desire not to be known. You will do well to keep my secret."

"Do I understand that you are Master Charles Brandon, the king's friend?" asked Bradhurst.

"I am," was the answer.

"Then, sir, I must ask your pardon for the way you have been treated. We, of course, could not know it, but a man must expect trouble when he attaches himself to a woman." It is a wonder the flashes from Mary's eyes did not strike the old sea-dog dead. He, however, did not see them, and went on: "We are more than anxious that so valiant a knight as Sir Charles Brandon should go with us, and hope your reception will not drive you back, but as to the lady—you see already the result of her presence, and much as we want you, we cannot take her. Aside from the general trouble which a woman takes with her everywhere"—Mary would not even look at the creature—"on shipboard there is another and greater objection. It is said, you know, among sailors, that a woman on board draws bad luck to certain sorts of ships, and every sailor would desert, before we could weigh anchor, if it were known this lady was to go with us. Should they find it out in mid-ocean, a mutiny would be sure to follow, and God only knows what would happen. For her sake, if for no other reason, take her ashore at once."

Brandon saw only too plainly the truth that he had really seen all the time, but to which he had shut his eyes, and throwing Mary's cloak over her shoulders, prepared to go ashore. As they went over the side and pulled off, a great shout went up from the ship far more derisive than cheering, and the men at the oars looked at each other askance and smiled. What a predicament for a princess! Brandon cursed himself for having been such a knave and fool as to allow this to happen. He had known the danger all the time, and his act could not be chargeable to ignorance or a failure to see the probable consequences. Temptation, and selfish desire, had given him temerity in place of judgment. He had attempted what none but an insane man would have tried, without even the pitiable excuse of insanity. He had seen it all only too clearly from the very beginning, and he had deliberately and with open eyes brought disgrace, ruin, and death—unless he could escape—upon himself, and utter humiliation to her whom his love should have prompted him to save at all cost. If Mary could only have disguised herself to look like a man they might have succeeded, but that little "if" was larger than Paul's church, and blocked the road as completely as if it had been a word of twenty syllables.

When the princess stepped ashore it seemed to her as if the heart in her breast was a different and separate organ from the one she had carried aboard.

As the boat put off again for the ship, its crew gave a cheer coupled with some vile advice, for which Brandon would gladly have run them through, each and every one. He had to swallow his chagrin and anger, and really blamed no one but himself, though it was torture to him that this girl should be subjected to such insults, and he powerless to avenge them. The news had spread from the wharf like wildfire, and on their way back to the Bow and String, there came from small boys and hidden voices such exclamations as: "Look at the woman in man's clothing;" "Isn't he a beautiful man?" "Look at him blush;" and others too coarse to be repeated. Imagine the humiliating situation, from which there was no escape.

At last they reached the inn, whither their chests soon followed them, sent by Bradhurst, together with their passage money, which he very honestly refunded.

Mary soon donned her woman's attire, of which she had a supply in her chest, and at least felt more comfortable without the jack-boots. She had made her toilet alone for the first time in her life, having no maid to help her, and wept as she dressed, for this disappointment was like plucking the very heart out of her. Her hope had been so high that the fall was all the harder. Nay, even more; hope had become fruition to her when they were once a-shipboard, and failure right at the door of success made it doubly hard to bear. It crushed her, and, where before had been hope and confidence, was nothing now but despair. Like all people with a great capacity for elation, when she sank she touched the bottom. Alas! Mary, the unconquerable, was down at last.

This failure meant so much to her; it meant that she would never be Brandon's wife, but would go to France to endure the dreaded old Frenchman. At that thought a recoil came. Her spirit asserted itself, and she stamped her foot and swore upon her soul it should never be; never! never! so long as she had strength to fight or voice to cry, "No." The thought of this marriage and of the loss of Brandon was painful enough, but there came another, entirely new to her and infinitely worse.

Hastily arranging her dress, she went in search of Brandon, whom she quickly found and took to her room.

After closing the door she said: "I thought I had reached the pinnacle of disappointment and pain when compelled to leave the ship, for it meant that I should lose you and have to marry Louis of France. But I have found that there is still a possible pain more poignant than either, and I cannot bear it; so I come to you—you who are the great cure for all my troubles. Oh! that I could lay them here all my life long," and she put her head upon his breast, forgetting what she had intended to say.

"What is the trouble, Mary?"

"Oh! yes! I thought of that marriage and of losing you, and then, oh! Mary Mother! I thought of some other woman having you to herself. I could see her with you, and I was jealous—I think they call it. I have heard of the pangs of jealousy, and if the fear of a rival is so great what would the reality be? It would kill me; I could not endure it. I cannot endure even this, and I want you to swear that—"

Brandon took her in his arms as she began to weep.

"I will gladly swear by everything I hold sacred that no other woman than you shall ever be my wife. If I cannot have you, be sure you have spoiled every other woman for me. There is but one in all the world—but one. I can at least save you that pain."

She then stood on tip-toes to lift her lips to him, and said: "I give you the same promise. How you must have suffered when you thought I was to wed another."

After a pause she went on: "But it might have been worse— that is, it would be worse if you should marry some other woman; but that is all settled now and I feel easier. Then I might have married the old French king, but that, too, is settled; and we can endure the lesser pain. It always helps us when we are able to think it might have been worse."

Her unquestioning faith in Brandon was beautiful, and she never doubted that he spoke the unalterable truth when he said he would never marry any other woman. She had faith in herself, too, and was confident that her promise to marry no man but Brandon ended that important matter likewise, and put the French marriage totally out of the question for all time to come.

As for Brandon, he was safe enough in his part of the contract. He knew only too well that no woman could approach Mary in her inimitable perfections, and he had tested his love closely enough, in his struggle against it, to feel that it had taken up its abode in his heart to stay, whether he wanted it or not. He knew that he was safe in making her a promise which he was powerless to break. All this he fully explained to Mary, as they sat looking out of the window at the dreary rain which had come on again with the gathering gloom of night.

Brandon did not tell her that his faith in her ultimate ability to keep her promise was as small as it was great in his own. Neither did he dampen her spirits by telling her that there was a reason, outside of himself, which in all probability would help him in keeping his word, and save her from the pangs of that jealousy she so much feared; namely, that he would most certainly wed the block and ax should the king get possession of him. He might have escaped from England in the Royal Hind, for the wind had come up shortly after they left the ship, and they could see the sails indistinctly through the gloom as she got under way. But he could not leave Mary alone, and had made up his mind to take her back to London and march straight into the jaws of death with her, if the king's men did not soon come.

He knew that a debt to folly bears no grace, and was ready with his principal and usance.

* * * * *

CHAPTER XVIII

To the Tower

Whether or not Brandon would have found some way to deliver the princess safely home, and still make his escape, I cannot say, as he soon had no choice in the matter. At midnight a body of yeomen from the tower took possession of the Bow and String, and carried Brandon off to London without communication with Mary. She did, not know of his arrest until next morning, when she was informed that she was to follow immediately, and her heart was nearly broken.

Here again was trouble for Mary. She felt, however, that the two great questions, the marriage of herself to Louis, and Brandon to any other person, were, as she called it, "settled"; and was almost content to endure this as a mere putting off of her desires—a meddlesome and impertinent interference of the Fates, who would soon learn with whom they were dealing, and amend their conduct.

She did not understand the consequences for Brandon, nor that the Fates would have to change their purpose very quickly or something would happen worse, even, than his marriage to another woman.

On the second morning after leaving Bristol, Brandon reached London, and, as he expected, was sent to the Tower. The next evening Lady Mary arrived and was taken down to Greenwich.

The girl's fair name was, of course, lost—but, fortunately, that goes for little with a princess—since no one would believe that Brandon had protected her against himself as valiantly and honorably as he would against another. The princess being much more unsophisticated than the courtiers were ready to believe, never thought of saying anything to establish her innocence or virtue, and her silence was put down to shame and taken as evidence against her.

Jane met Mary at Windsor, and, of course, there was a great flood of tears.

Upon arriving at the palace, the girls were left to themselves, upon Mary's promise not to leave her room; but, by the next afternoon, she, having been unable to learn anything concerning Brandon, broke her parole and went out to see the king.

It never occurred to Mary that Brandon might suffer death for attempting to run away with her. She knew only too well that she alone was to blame, not only for that, but for all that had taken place between them, and never for one moment thought that he might be punished for her fault, even admitting there was fault in any one, which she was by no means ready to do.

The trouble in her mind, growing out of a lack of news from Brandon, was of a general nature, and the possibility of his death had no place in her thoughts. Nevertheless, for the second time, Brandon had been condemned to die for her sake. The king's seal had stamped the warrant for the execution, and the headsman had sharpened his ax and could almost count the golden fee for his butchery.

Mary found the king playing cards with de Longueville. There was a roomful of courtiers, and as she entered she was the target for every eye; but she was on familiar ground now, and did not care for the glances nor the observers, most of whom she despised. She was the princess again and full of self-confidence; so she went straight to the object of her visit, the king. She had not made up her mind just what to say first, there was so much; but Henry saved her the trouble. He, of course, was in a great rage, and denounced Mary's conduct as unnatural and treasonable; the latter, in Henry's mind, being a crime many times greater than the breaking of all the commandments put together, in one fell, composite act. All this the king had communicated to Mary by the lips of Wolsey the evening before, and Mary had received it with a silent scorn that would have withered any one but the worthy bishop of York. As I said, when Mary approached her brother, he saved her the trouble of deciding where to begin by speaking first himself, and his words were of a part with his nature—violent, cruel and vulgar. He abused her and called her all the vile names in his ample vocabulary of billingsgate. The queen was present and aided and abetted with a word now and then, until Henry, with her help, at last succeeded in working himself into a towering passion, and wound up by calling Mary a vile wanton in plainer terms than I like to write. This aroused all the antagonism in the girl, and there was plenty of it. She feared Henry no more than she feared me. Her eyes flashed a fire that made even the king draw back as she exclaimed: "You give me that name and expect me to remember you are my brother? There are words that make a mother hate her first-born, and that is one. Tell me what I have done to deserve it? I expected to hear of ingratitude and disobedience and all that, but supposed you had at least some traces of brotherly feeling—for ties of blood are hard to break—even if you have of late lost all semblance to man or king."

This was hitting Henry hard, for it was beginning to be the talk in every mouth that he was leaving all the affairs of state to Wolsey and spending his time in puerile amusement. "The toward hope which at all poyntes appeared in the younge Kynge" was beginning to look, after all, like nothing more than the old-time royal cold fire, made to consume but not to warm the nation.

Henry looked at Mary with the stare of a baited bull.

"If running off in male attire, and stopping at inns and boarding ships with a common Captain of the guard doesn't justify my accusation and stamp you what you are, I do not know what would."

Even Henry saw her innocence in her genuine surprise. She was silent for a little time, and I, standing close to her, could plainly see that this phase of the question had never before presented itself.

She hung her head for a moment and then spoke: "It may be true, as you say, that what I have done will lose me my fair name—I had never thought of it in that light—but it is also true that I am innocent and have done no wrong. You may not believe me, but you can ask Master Brandon"—here the king gave a great laugh, and of course the courtiers joined in.

"It is all very well for you to laugh, but Master Brandon would not tell you a lie for your crown—" Gods! I could have fallen on my knees to a faith like that—"What I tell you is true. I trusted him so completely that the fear of dishonor at his hands never suggested itself to me. I knew he would care for and respect me. I trusted him, and my trust was not misplaced. Of how many of these creatures who laugh when the king laughs could I say as much?" And Henry knew she spoke the truth, both concerning herself and the courtiers.

With downcast eyes she continued: "I suppose, after all, you are partly right in regard to me; for it was his honor that saved me, not my own; and if I am not what you called me I have Master Brandon to thank—not myself."

"We will thank him publicly on Tower Hill, day after to-morrow, at noon," said the king, with his accustomed delicacy, breaking the news of Brandon's sentence as abruptly as possible.

With a look of terror in her eyes, Mary screamed: "What! Charles Brandon . . . Tower Hill? . . . You are going to kill him?"

"I think we will," responded Henry; "it usually has that effect, to separate the head from the body and quarter the remains to decorate the four gates. We will take you up to London in a day or two and let you see his beautiful head on the bridge."

"Behead—quarter—bridge! Lord Jesu!" She could not grasp the thought; she tried to speak, but the words would not come. In a moment she became more coherent, and the words rolled from her lips as a mighty flood tide pours back through the arches of London Bridge.

"You shall not kill him; he is blameless; you do not know. Drive these gawking fools out of the room, and I will tell you all."

The king ordered the room cleared of everybody but Wolsey, Jane and myself, who remained at Mary's request. When all were gone, the princess continued: "Brother, this man is in no way to blame; it is all my fault—my fault that he loves me; my fault that he tried to run away to New Spain with me. It may be that I have done wrong and that my conduct has been unmaidenly, but I could not help it. From the first time I ever saw him in the lists with you at Windsor there was a gnawing hunger in my heart beyond my control. I supposed, of course, that day he would contrive some way to be presented to me . . ."

"You did?"

"Yes, but he made no effort at all, and when we met he treated me as if I were an ordinary girl."

"He did?"

"Yes."

"Horrible."

Mary was too intent on her story to heed the sarcasm, and continued: "That made me all the more interested in him since it showed that he was different from the wretches who beset you and me with their flattery, and I soon began to seek him on every occasion. This is an unmaidenly history I am giving, I know, but it is the truth, and must be told. I was satisfied at first if I could only be in the same room with him, and see his face, and hear his voice. The very air he breathed was like an elixir for me. I made every excuse to have him near me; I asked him to my parlor—you know about that—and—and did all I could to be with him. At first he was gentle and kind, but soon, I think, he saw the dawning danger in both our hearts, as I too saw it, and he avoided me in every way he could, knowing the trouble it held for us both. Oh! he was the wiser—and to think to what I have brought him. Brother, let me die for him—I who alone am to blame; take my life and spare him—spare him! He was the wiser, but I doubt if all the wisdom in the world could have saved us. He almost insulted me once in the park—told me to leave him—when it hurt him more than me, I am now sure; but he did it to keep matters from growing worse between us. I tried to remember the affront, but could not, and had he struck me I believe I should have gone back to him sooner or later. Oh! it was all my fault; I would not let him save himself. So strong was my feeling that I could bear his silence no longer, and one day I went to him in your bed-chamber ante-room and fairly thrust myself and my love upon him. Then, after he was liberated from Newgate, I could not induce him to come to me, so I went to him and begged for his love. Then I coaxed him into taking me to New Spain, and would listen to no excuse and hear no reason. Now lives there another man who would have taken so much coaxing?"

"No! by heaven! your majesty," said Wolsey, who really had a kindly feeling for Brandon and would gladly save his life, if, by so doing, he would not interfere with any of his own plans and interests. Wolsey's heart was naturally kind when it cost him nothing, and much has been related of him, which, to say the least, tells a great deal more than the truth. Ingratitude always recoils upon the ingrate, and Henry's loss was greater than Wolsey's when Wolsey fell.

Henry really liked, or, rather, admired, Brandon, as had often been shown, but his nature was incapable of real affection. The highest point he ever reached was admiration, often quite extravagant for a time, but usually short-lived, as naked admiration is apt to be. If he had affection for any one it was for Mary. He could not but see the justice of his sister's position, but he had no intention of allowing justice, in the sense of right, to interfere with justice in the sense of the king's will.

"You have been playing the devil at a great rate," he said, "You have disobeyed your brother and your king; have disgraced yourself; have probably made trouble between us and France, for if Louis refuses to take you now I will cram you down his throat; and by your own story have led a good man to the block. Quite a budget of evils for one woman to open. But I have noticed that the trouble a woman can make is in proportion to her beauty, and no wonder my little sister has made so much disturbance. It is strange, though, that he should so affect you. Master Wolsey, surely there has been witchery here. He must have used it abundantly to cast such a spell over my sister." Then turning to the princess: "Was it at any time possible for him to have given you a love powder; or did he ever make any signs or passes over you?"

"Oh, no! nothing of that sort. I never ate or drank anything which he could possibly have touched. And as to signs and passes, I know he never made any. Sir Edwin, you were always present when I was with him until after we left for Bristol; did you ever see anything of the sort?"

I answered "No," and she went on. "Besides, I do not believe much in signs and passes. No one can affect others unless he can induce them to eat or drink something in which he has placed a love powder or potion. Then again, Master Brandon did not want me to love him, and surely would not have used such a method to gain what he could have had freely without it."

I noticed that Henry's mind had wandered from what Mary was saying, and that his eyes were fixed upon me with a thoughtful, half vicious, inquiring stare that I did not like. I wondered what was coming next, but my curiosity was more than satisfied when the king asked: "So Caskoden was present at all your interviews?"

Ah! Holy Mother! I knew what was coming now, and actually began to shrivel with fright. The king continued: "I suppose he helped you to escape?"

I thought my day had come, but Mary's wit was equal to the occasion. With an expression on her face of the most dove-like innocence, she quickly said:

"Oh! no! neither he nor Jane knew anything of it. We were afraid they might divulge it."

Shade of Sapphira!

A lie is a pretty good thing, too, now and then, and the man who says that word of Mary's was not a blessed lie, must fight me with lance, battle-ax, sword and dagger till one or the other of us bites the dust in death, be he great or small.

"I am glad to learn that you knew nothing of it," said Henry, addressing me; and I was glad, too, for him to learn it, you may be sure.

Then spoke Wolsey: "If your majesty will permit, I would say that I quite agree with you; there has been witchery here—witchery of the most potent kind; the witchery of lustrous eyes, of fair skin and rosy lips; the witchery of all that is sweet and intoxicating in womanhood, but Master Brandon has been the victim of this potent spell, not the user of it. One look upon your sister standing there, and I know your majesty will agree that Brandon had no choice against her."

"Perhaps you are right," returned Henry.

Then spoke Mary, all unconscious of her girlish egotism: "Of course he had not. Master Brandon could not help it." Which was true beyond all doubt.

Henry laughed at her naïveté, and Wolsey's lips wore a smile, as he plucked the king by the sleeve and took him over to the window, out of our hearing.

Mary began to weep and show signs of increasing agitation.

After a short whispered conversation, the king and Wolsey came back and the former said: "Sister, if I promise to give Brandon his life, will you consent decently and like a good girl to marry Louis of France?"

Mary almost screamed, "Yes, yes; gladly; I will do anything you ask," and fell at his feet hysterically embracing his knees.

As the king stooped and lifted her to her feet, he kissed her, saying: "His life shall be spared, my sweet sister." After this, Henry felt that he had done a wonderfully gracious act and was the kindest-hearted prince in all Christendom.

Poor Mary! Two mighty kings and their great ministers of state had at last conquered you, but they had to strike you through your love—the vulnerable spot in every woman.

Jane and I led Mary away through a side door and the king called for de Longueville to finish the interrupted game of cards.

Before the play was resumed Wolsey stepped softly around to the king and asked: "Shall I affix your majesty's seal to Brandon's pardon?"

"Yes, but keep him in the Tower until Mary is off for France."

Wolsey had certainly been a friend to Brandon in time of need, but, as usual, he had value received for his friendliness. He was an ardent advocate of the French marriage, notwithstanding the fact he had told Mary he was not; having no doubt been bribed thereto by the French king.

The good bishop had, with the help of de Longueville, secretly sent Mary's miniature to the French court in order that it might, as if by accident, fall into the hands of Louis, and that worthy's little, old, shriveled heart began to flutter, just as if there could be kindled in it a genuine flame.

Louis had sent to de Longueville, who was then in England, for confirmation of Mary's beauty, and de Longueville grew so eloquent on the theme that his French majesty at once authorized negotiations.

As reports came in Louis grew more and more impatient. This did not, however, stand in the way of his driving a hard bargain in the matter of dower, for "The Father of the People" had the characteristics of his race, and was intensely practical as well as inflammable. They never lose sight of the *dot*—but I do not find fault.

Louis little knew what thorns this lovely rose had underneath her velvet leaves, and what a veritable Tartar she would be, linked to the man she did not love; or he would have given Henry four hundred thousand crowns to keep her at home.

* * * * *

CHAPTER XIX

Proserpina

So the value received for Wolsey's friendship to Brandon was Mary's promise to marry Louis.

Mary wanted to send a message at once to Brandon, telling him his life would be spared, and that she had made no delay this time—a fact of which she was very proud—but the Tower gates would not open until morning, so she had to wait. She compensated herself as well as she could by writing a letter, which I should like to give you here, but it is too long. She told him of his pardon, but not one word upon the theme he so wished yet feared to hear of—her promise never to wed any other man. Mary had not told him of her final surrender in the matter of the French marriage, for the reason that she dreaded to pain him, and feared he might refuse the sacrifice.

"It will almost kill him, I know," she said to Jane that night, "and I fear it is a false kindness I do him. He would, probably, rather die than that I should marry another; I know that I should rather die, or have anything else terrible to happen, than for another woman to possess him. He promised me he never would; but suppose he should fail in his word, as I have to-day failed in mine? The thought of it absolutely burns me." And she threw herself into Jane's arms, and that little comforter tried to soothe her by making light of her fears.

"Oh! but suppose he should?"

"Well! there is no need to borrow trouble. You said he promised you, and you know he is one who keeps his word."

"But I promised, too, and think of what I am about to do. Mary in heaven, help me! But he is made of different stuff from me. I can and do trust his word, and when I think of all my troubles, and when it seems that I cannot bear them, the one comforting thought comes that no other woman will ever possess him; no other woman; no other woman. I am glad that my only comfort comes from him."

"I hoped that I might have been some comfort to you; I have tried hard enough," said Jane, who was jealous.

"Oh! yes! my sweet Jane; you do comfort me; you are like a soothing balm to an aching pain," and she kissed the hands that held hers. This was all that modest little Jane required. She was content to be an humble balm and did not aspire to the dignity of an elixir.

The girls then said their prayers in concert and Mary gently wept herself to sleep. She lay dreaming and tossing nervously until sunrise, when she got up and added more pages to her letter, until I called to take it.

I was on hand soon after the Tower gates had opened and was permitted to see Brandon at once. He read Mary's letter and acted like every other lover, since love-letters first began. He was quick to note the absence of the longed for, but not expected assurance, and when he did not see it went straight to the point.

"She has promised to marry the French king to purchase my life. Is that not true?"

"I hope not," I answered, evasively; "I have seen very little of her, and she has said nothing about it."

"You are evading my question, I see. Do you know nothing of it?"

"Nothing," I replied, telling an unnecessary lie.

"Caskoden, you are either a liar or a blockhead."

"Make it a liar, Brandon," said I, laughingly, for I was sure of my place in his heart and knew that he meant no offense.

I never doubt a friend; one would better be trustful of ninety-nine friends who are false than doubtful of one who is true. Suspicion and super-sensitiveness are at once the badge and the bane of a little soul.

I did not leave the Tower until noon, and Brandon's pardon had been delivered to him before I left. He was glad that the first news of it had come from Mary.

He naturally expected his liberty at once, and when told that he was to be honorably detained for a short time, turned to me and said: "I suppose they are afraid to let me out until she is off for France. King Henry flatters me."

I looked out of the window up Tower street and said nothing.

When I left I took a letter to Mary, which plainly told her he had divined it all, and she wrote a tear-stained answer, begging him to forgive her for having saved his life at a cost greater than her own.

For several days I was kept busy carrying letters from Greenwich to the Tower and back again, but soon letters ceased to satisfy Mary, and she made up her mind that she must see him. Nothing else would do. She must not, could not, and, in short, would not go another day without seeing him; no, not another hour. Jane and I opposed her all we could, but the best we could accomplish was to induce her for Brandon's sake—for she was beginning to see that he was the one who had to suffer for her indiscretions—to ask Henry's permission, and if he refused, then try some other way. To determine was to act with Mary, so off she went without delay to hunt the king, taking Jane and me along as escort. How full we were of important business, as we scurried along the corridors, one on each side of Mary, all talking excitedly at once. When anything was to be done, it always required three of us to do it.

We found the king, and without any prelude, Mary proffered her request. Of course it was refused. Mary pouted, and was getting ready for an outburst, when Wolsey spoke up: "With your majesty's gracious permission, I would subscribe to the petition of the princess. She has been good enough to give her promise in the matter of so much importance to us, and in so small a thing as this I hope you may see your way clear toward favoring her. The interview will be the last and may help to make her duty easier." Mary gave the cardinal a fleeting glance from her lustrous eyes full of surprise and gratitude, and as speaking as a book.

Henry looked from one to the other of us for a moment, and broke into a boisterous laugh.

"Oh, I don't care, so that you keep it a secret. The old king will never know. We can hurry up the marriage. He is getting too much already; four hundred thousand crowns and a girl like you; he cannot complain if he have an heir. It would be a good joke on the miserly old dotard, but better on '*Ce Gros Garçon.*'"

Mary sprang from her chair with a cry of rage. "You brute! Do you think I am as vile as you because I have the misfortune to be your sister, or that Charles Brandon is like you simply because he is a man?" Henry laughed, his health at that time being too good for him to be ill-natured. He had all he wanted out of his sister, so her outbursts amused him.

Mary hurriedly left the king and walked back to her room, filled with shame and rage; feelings actively stimulated by Jane, who was equally indignant.

Henry had noticed Jane's frown, but had laughed at her, and had tried to catch and kiss her as she left; but she struggled away from him and fled with a speed worthy of the cause.

This insulting suggestion put a stop to Mary's visit to the Tower more effectually than any refusal could have done, and she sat down to pour forth her soul's indignation in a letter.

She remained at home then, but saw Brandon later, and to good purpose, as I believe, although I am not sure about it, even to this day.

I took this letter to Brandon, along with Mary's miniature—the one that had been painted for Charles of Germany, but had never been given—and a curl of her hair, and it looked as if this was all he would ever possess of her.

De Longueville heard of Henry's brutal consent that Mary might see Brandon, and, with a Frenchman's belief in woman's depravity, was exceedingly anxious to keep them apart. To this end he requested that a member of his own retinue be placed near Brandon. To this Henry readily consented, and there was an end to even the letter-writing. Opportunities increase in value doubly fast as they drift behind us, and now that the princess could not see Brandon, or even write to him, she regretted with her whole soul that she had not gone to the Tower when she had permission, regardless of what any one would say or think.

Mary was imperious and impatient, by nature, but upon rare and urgent occasions could employ the very smoothest sort of finesse.

Her promise to marry Louis of France had been given under the stress of a frantic fear for Brandon, and without the slightest mental reservation, for it was given to save his life, as she would have given her hands or her eyes, her life or her very soul itself; but now that the imminent danger was passed she began to revolve schemes to evade her promise and save Brandon notwithstanding. She knew that under the present arrangement his life depended upon her marriage, but she had never lost faith in her ability to handle the king if she had but a little time in which to operate, and had secretly regretted that she had not, in place of flight, opened up her campaign along the line of feminine diplomacy at the very beginning.

Henry was a dullard mentally, while Mary's mind was keen and alert—two facts of which the girl was perfectly aware—so it was no wonder she had such confidence in herself. When she first heard of Brandon's sentence her fear for him was so great, and the need for action so urgent, that she could not resort to her usual methods for turning matters her way, but eagerly applied the first and quickest remedy offered. Now, however, that she had a breathing spell, and time in which to operate her more slowly moving, but, as she thought, equally sure forces of cajolery and persuasion, she determined to marshal the legions of her wit and carry war into the enemy's country at once.

Henry's brutal selfishness in forcing upon her the French marriage, together with his cruel condemnation of Brandon, and his vile insinuations against herself, had driven nearly every spark of affection for her brother from her heart. But she felt that she might feign an affection she did not feel, and that what she so wanted would be cheap at the price. Cheap? It would be cheap at the cost of her immortal soul. Cheap? What she wanted was life's condensed sweets—the man she loved; and what she wanted to escape was life's distilled bitterness—marriage with a man she loathed. None but a pure woman can know the torture of that. I saw this whole disastrous campaign from start to finish. Mary began with a wide flank movement conducted under masked batteries and skilfully executed. She sighed over her troubles and cried a great deal, but told the king he had been such a dear, kind brother to her that she would gladly do anything to please him and advance his interests. She said it would be torture to live with that old creature, King Louis, but she would do it willingly to help her handsome brother, no matter how much she might suffer.

The king laughed and said: "Poor old Louis! What about him? What about his suffering? He thinks he is making such a fine bargain, but the Lord pity him, when he has my little sister in his side for a thorn. He had better employ some energetic soul to prick him with needles and bodkins, for I think there is more power for disturbance in this little body than in any other equal amount of space in all the universe. You will furnish him all the trouble he wants, won't you, sister?"

"I shall try," said the princess demurely, perfectly willing to obey in everything.

"Devil a doubt of that, and you will succeed, too, or my crown's a stew-pan," and he laughed at the huge joke he was about to perpetrate on his poor, old royal brother.

It would seem that the tremendous dose of flattery administered by Mary would have been so plainly self-interested as to alarm the dullest perception, but Henry's vanity was so dense, and his appetite for flattery so great, that he accepted it all without suspicion, and it made him quite affable and gracious.

Mary kept up her show of affection and docile obedience for a week or two until she thought Henry's suspicions were allayed; and then, after having done enough petting and fondling, as she thought, to start the earth itself a-moving—as some men are foolish enough to say it really does—she began the attack direct by putting her arms about the king's neck, and piteously begging him not to sacrifice her whole life by sending her to France.

Her pathetic, soul-charged appeal might have softened the heart of Caligula himself; but Henry was not even cruel. He was simply an animal so absorbed in himself that he could not feel for others.

"Oh! it is out at last," he said, with a laugh. "I thought all this sweetness must have been for something. So the lady wants her Brandon, and doesn't want her Louis, yet is willing to obey her dear, kind brother? Well, we'll take her at her word and let her obey. You may as well understand, once and for all, that you are to go to France. You promised to go decently if I would not cut off that fellow's head, and now I tell you that if I hear another whimper from you off it comes, and you will go to France, too."

This brought Mary to terms quickly enough. It touched her one vulnerable spot—her love.

217

"I will go; I promise it again. You shall never hear another word of complaint from me if you give me your royal word that no harm shall come to him—to him," and she put her hands over her face to conceal her tears as she softly wept.

"The day you sail for France, Brandon shall go free and shall again have his old post at court. I like the fellow as a good companion, and really believe you are more to blame than he."

"I am all to blame, and am ready this day to pay the penalty. I am at your disposal to go when and where you choose," answered Mary, most pathetically.

Poor, fair Proserpina, with no kind mother Demeter to help her. The ground will soon open, and Pluto will have his bride.

That evening Cavendish took me aside and said his master, Wolsey, wished to speak to me privately at a convenient opportunity. So, when the bishop left his card-table, an hour later, I threw myself in his way. He spoke gayly to me, and we walked down the corridor arm in arm. I could not imagine what was wanted, but presently it came out: "My dear Caskoden"—had I been one for whom he could have had any use, I should have grown suspicious—"My dear Caskoden, I know I can trust you; especially when that which I have to say is for the happiness of your friends. I am sure you will never name me in connection with the suggestion I am about to make, and will use the thought only as your own."

I did not know what was coming, but gave him the strongest assurance of my trustworthiness.

"It is this: Louis of France is little better than a dead man. King Henry, perhaps, is not fully aware of this, and, if he is, he has never considered the probability of his speedy death. The thought occurred to me that although the princess cannot dissuade her brother from this marriage, she may be able, in view of her ready and cheerful compliance, to extract some virtue out of her sore necessity and induce him to promise that, in case of the death of Louis, she herself shall choose her second husband."

"My lord," I replied, quickly grasping the point, "it is small wonder you rule this land. You have both brain and heart."

"I thank you, Sir Edwin, and hope that both may always be at the service of you and your friends."

I gave the suggestion to Mary as my own, recommending that she proffer her request to the king in the presence of Wolsey, and, although she had little faith or hope, she determined to try.

Within a day or two an opportunity offered, and she said to Henry: "I am ready to go to France any time you wish, and shall do it decently and willingly; but if I do so much for you, brother, you might at least promise me that when King Louis is dead I may marry whomsoever I wish. He will probably live forever, but let me have at least that hope to give me what cheer it may while I suffer."

The ever-present Wolsey, who was standing near and heard Mary's petition, interposed: "Let me add my prayer to that of her highness. We must give her her own way in something."

Mary was such a complete picture of wretchedness that I thought at the time she had really found a tender spot in Henry's heart, for he gave the promise. Since then I have learned, as you will shortly, that it was given simply to pacify the girl, and without any intention whatever of its being kept; but that, in case of the death of King Louis, Henry intended again to use his sister to his own advantage.

To be a beautiful princess is not to enjoy the bliss some people imagine. The earth is apt to open at any time, and Pluto to snatch her away to—the Lord knows where.

Mary again poured out her soul on paper—a libation intended for Brandon. I made a dozen attempts, in as many different ways, to deliver her letters, but every effort was a failure, and this missive met the fate of the others. De Longueville kept close watch on his master's rival, and complained to Henry about these attempts at communication. Henry laughed and said he would see that they were stopped, but paid no more attention to the matter.

If Mary, before her interview with Henry, had been averse to the French marriage, she was now equally anxious to hurry it on, and longed to go upon the rack in order that Brandon might be free. He, of course, objected as strenuously as possible to the purchase of his life by her marriage to Louis, but his better judgment told him—in fact, had told him from the first—that she would be compelled eventually to marry the French king, and common sense told him if it must be, she might as well save his life at the same time. Furthermore, he felt a certain sense of delight in owing his life to her, and knew that the fact that she had saved him—that her sacrifice had not all been in vain—would make it easier for her to bear.

The most beautiful feature of the relations between these two lovers was their entire faith in each other. The way of their true love was at least not roughened by cobble-stones of doubt, however impassable it was from mountains of opposition.

My inability to deliver Mary's letters did not deter her from writing them; and as she was to be married in a few days—de Longueville to act as proxy—she devoted her entire time to her letters, and wrote pages upon pages, which she left with me to be delivered "after death," as she called her marriage.

At this time I was called away from court for a day or two, and when I returned and called upon Brandon at the Tower, I found him whistling and singing, apparently as happy as a lark. "You heartless dog," thought I, at first; but I soon found that he felt more than happiness—exaltation.

"Have you seen her?" I asked.

"Who?" As if there were more than one woman in all the world for him.

"The princess."

"Not since I left her at Bristol."

I believed then, and believe now, that this was a point blank falsehood—a very unusual thing for Brandon—but for some reason probably necessary in this case.

There was an expression in his face which I could not interpret, but he wrote, as if carelessly scribbling on a scrap of paper that lay upon the table, the words, "Be careful," and I took the hint—we were watched. There is an unpleasant sensation when one feels that he is watched by unseen eyes, and after talking for awhile on common topics I left and took a boat for Greenwich.

When I arrived at the palace and saw Mary, what was my surprise to find her as bright and jubilant as I had left Brandon. She, too, laughed and sang, and was so happy that she lighted the whole room. What did it all mean? There was but one explanation; they had met, and there was some new plan on foot—with a fatal ending. The next failure would mean death to Brandon, as certainly as the sun rises in the east. What the plan was I could not guess. With Brandon in the Tower under guard both day and night, and

Mary as closely guarded in the palace, I could not see any way of escape for either of them, nor how they could possibly have come together.

Brandon had not told me, I supposed, for fear of being overheard, and Mary, although she had the opportunity, was equally non-communicative, so I had recourse to Jane upon the first occasion. She, by the way, was as blue and sad-faced as Mary was joyous. I asked her if the princess and Brandon had met, and she sadly said: "I do not know. We went down to London yesterday, and as we returned stopped at Bridewell House, where we found the king and Wolsey. The princess left the room, saying she would return in a few minutes, and then Wolsey went out, leaving me alone with the king. Mary did not return for half an hour, and she may have seen Master Brandon during that time. I do not understand how the meeting could have occurred, but that is the only time she has been away from me." Here Jane deliberately put her head on my shoulder and began to weep piteously.

"What is the trouble?" I asked.

She shook her head: "I cannot, dare not tell you."

"Oh! but you must, you must," and I insisted so emphatically that she at length said:

"The king!"

"The king! God in heaven, Jane, tell me quickly." I had noticed Henry of late casting glances at my beautiful little Jane, and had seen him try to kiss her a few days before, as I have told you. This annoyed me very much, but I thought little of it, as it was his habit to ogle every pretty face. When urged, Jane said between her sobs: "He tried to kiss me and to—mistreat me when Wolsey left the room at Bridewell House. I may have been used to detain him, while Mary met Master Brandon, but if so, I am sure she knew nothing of it."

"And what did you do?"

"I struggled away from him and snatched this dagger from my breast, telling him that if he took but one step toward me I would plunge it in my heart; and he said I was a fool."

"God keep you always a fool," said I, prayerfully. "How long has this been going on?"

"A month or two; but I have always been able to run away from him. He has been growing more importunate of late, so I bought a dagger that very day, and had it not one hour too soon." With this she drew out a gleaming little weapon that flashed in the rays of the candle.

This was trouble in earnest for me, and I showed it very plainly. Then Jane timidly put her hand in mine, for the first time in her life, and murmured:

"We will be married, Edwin, if you wish, before we return from France." She was glad to fly to me to save herself from Henry, and I was glad even to be the lesser of two evils.

As to whether my two friends met or not that day at Bridewell I cannot say; but I think they did. They had in some way come to an understanding that lightened both their hearts before Mary left for France, and this had been their only possible opportunity. Jane and I were always taken into their confidence on other occasions, but as to this meeting, if any there was, we have never been told a word. My belief is that the meeting was contrived by Wolsey upon a solemn promise from Brandon and Mary never to reveal it, and if so, they have sacredly kept their word.

On the 13th of August, 1514, Mary Tudor, with her golden hair falling over her shoulders, was married at Greenwich to Louis de Valois; de Longueville acting as his French majesty's proxy. Poor, fair Proserpina! . . .

* * * * *

Note.—Maidens only were married with their hair down. It was "the sacred token of maidenhood."—Editor.

* * * * *

CHAPTER XX

Down into France

So it came to pass that Mary was married unto Louis and went down into France.

* * * * *

[Again the editor takes the liberty of substituting Hall's quaint account of Mary's journey to France.]

Then when all things were redy for the conueyaunce of this noble Ladye, the kyng her brother in the moneth of Auguste, and the xV daye, with the quene his wife and his sayde sister and al the court came to Douer and there taryed, for the wynde was troblous and the wether fowle, in so muche that shippe of the kynges called the Libeck of IXC. tonne was dryuen a shore before Sangate and there brase & of VI C. men scantely escaped iiiC and yet the most part of them were hurt with the wrecke. When the wether was fayre, then al her wardrobe, stable, and riches was shipped, and such as were appoyncted to geue their attendaunce on her as the duke of Norfolke, the Marques of Dorset, the Bysshop of Durham, the Earle of Surrey, the lorde Delawar, sir Thomas Bulleyn and many other knights, Squyers, getlemen & ladies, al these went to shippe and the sayde ladye toke her leaue of the quene in the castell of Douer, and the king brought her to the sea syde, and kissed her, and betoke her to GOD and the fortune of the see and to the gouernaunce of the French king her husband. Thus at the hower of foure of the clock in the morenynge thys fayre ladye toke her shippe with al her noble compaignie: and when they had sayled a quarter of the see, the wynde rose and seuered some of the shippes to Cayles, and some in Flaunders and her shippe with greate difficultie to Bulleyn, and with greate ieopardy at the entrying of the hauen, for the master ran the shippe hard on shore, but the botes were redy and receyued this noble ladye, and at the landyng Sir Christopher Garnysha stode in the water and toke her in his armes, and so caryed her to land, where the Duke of Vandosme and a Cardynall with many estates receyued her, and her ladies, and welcommed all the noble men into the countrey, and so the quene and all her trayne came to Bulleyn and ther rested, and from thence she remoued by dyuerse lodgynges tyll she came all most within iii miles of Abuylé besyde the forrest of Arders, and ther kynge Loyes vppon a greate courser met her, (which he so longe desired) but she toke her way righte on, not stopping to conurse. Then he returned to Abuyle by a secret waye, & she was with greate triumphe, procession & pagiantes receyued into the toune of Abuyle the VIII day of October by the Dolphin, which receyued her with greate honor. She was appeareilled in cloth of siluer, her horse was trapped in goldsmythes work very rychly. After her followed xxxvi ladies al ther palfreys trapped with crymsyn veluet, embraudered: after the folowed one charyott of cloth of tyssue, the seconde clothe of golde and the third Crymsyn veluet embraudered with the kynges armes & hers, full of roses. After them folowed a greate nomber of archers and then wagons laden with their stuf. Greate was the riches in plate, iuels, money, and hangynges that this ladye brought into France. The Moday beyng the daye of Sayncte Denyce, the same kynge Leyes maried the lady Mary in the greate church of Abuyle, bothe appareled in goldesmythes woorke. After the masse was done ther was a greate banket and fest and the ladyes of England highly entreteyned.

The Tewesdaye beyng the x daye of October all the Englishmen except a fewe that wer officers with the sayde quene were discharged whiche was a greate sorowe for theim, for some had serued her longe in the hope of preferment and some that had honest romes left them to serue her and now they wer out of seruice, which caused the to take thought in so much, some dyed by way returning, and some fell mad, but ther was no remedy. After the English lordes had done ther commission the French kynge wylled the to take no lenger payne & so gaue to theim good rewardes and they toke ther leaue of the quene and returned.

Then the Dolphyn of Fraunce called Frauncys duke of Valoys, or Fraunceys d'Angouleme, caused a solempne iustes to be proclaymed, which shoulde be kept in Parys in the moneth of Noueber next ensuyng, and while al these thinges were prepearyng, the Ladye Mary, the V. daye of Noueber, then beying Sondaye was with greate solempnitee crowned Queen of Fraunce in the monasterye of Saynct Denyce, and the Lorde Dolphyn, who was young, but very toward, al the season held the crowune ouer her hed, because it was of greate waight, to her greuaunce.

* * * * *

Madame Mary took her time, since a more deliberate journey bride never made to waiting bride-groom. She was a study during this whole period—weeping and angry by turns. She, who had never known a moment's illness in all her days, took to her bed upon two occasions from sheer antipathetic nervousness, and would rest her head upon Jane's breast and cry out little, half-articulate prayers to God that she might not kill the man who was her husband, when they should meet.

When we met the king about a league this side of Abbeville, and when Mary beheld him with the shadow of death upon his brow, she took hope, for she knew he would be but putty in her hands, so manifestly weak was he, mentally and physically. As he came up she whipped her horse and rode by him at a gallop, sending me back with word that he must not be so ardent; that he frightened her, poor, timid little thing, so afraid of—nothing in the world. This shocked the French courtiers, and one would think would have offended Louis, but he simply grinned from ear to ear, showing his yellow fangs, and said whimperingly: "Oh, the game is worth the trouble. Tell her majesty I wait at Abbeville."

The old king had ridden a horse to meet his bride in order that he might appear more gallant before her, but a litter was waiting to take him back to Abbeville by a shorter route, and they were married again in person.

* * * * *

[Again a quotation from Hall is substituted]:

> Mondaye the .vi daye of Noueber, ther the sayde quene was receyued into the cytee of Parys after the order thar foloweth. First the garde of the cytee met her with oute Sayncte Denyce al in coates of goldsmythes woorke with shippes gylt, and after them mett her al the prestes and religious whiche were estemed to be. iiiM. The quene was in a chyre coured about (but not her ouer person) in white clothe of golde, the horses that drewe it couered in clothe of golde, on her bed a coronall, al of greate perles, her necke and brest full of Iuels, before her wente a garde of Almaynes after ther fascion, and after them al noblemen, as the Dolphyn, the Duke of Burbon, Cardynalles, and a greate nomber of estates. Aboute her person rode the kynge's garde the whiche wer Scottes. On the morowe bega the iustes, and the quene stode so that al men might see her, and wonder at her beautie, and the kynge was feble and lay on a couche for weakenes.

* * * * *

So Mary was twice married to Louis, and, although she was his queen fast and sure enough, she was not his wife.

You may say what you will, but I like a fighting woman; one with a touch of the savage in her when the occasion arises; one who can fight for what she loves as well as against what she hates. She usually loves as she fights—with all her heart.

So Mary was crowned, and was now a queen, hedged about by the tinseled divinity that hedgeth royalty.

It seemed that she was climbing higher and higher all the time from Brandon, but in her heart every day she was brought nearer to him.

There was one thing that troubled her greatly, and all the time. Henry had given his word that Brandon should be liberated as soon as Mary had left the shores of England, but we had heard nothing of this matter, although we had received several letters from home. A doubt of her brother, in whom she had little faith at best, made an ache at her heart, which seemed at times likely to break it—so she said. One night she dreamed that she had witnessed Brandon's execution, her brother standing by in excellent humor at the prank he was playing her, and it so worked upon her waking hours that by evening she was ill. At last I received a letter from Brandon— which had been delayed along the road—containing one for Mary. It told of his full pardon and restoration to favor, greater even than before; and her joy was so sweet and quiet, and yet so softly delirious, that I tell you plainly it brought tears to my eyes and I could not hold them back.

The marriage, when once determined upon, had not cast her down nearly so deep as I had expected, and soon she grew to be quite cheerful and happy. This filled me with regret, for I thought of how Brandon must suffer, and felt that her heart was a poor, flimsy thing to take this trouble so lightly.

I spoke to Jane about it, but she only laughed. "Mary is all right," said she; "do not fear. Matters will turn out better than you think, perhaps. You know she generally manages to have her own way in the end."

"If you have any comfort to give, please give it, Jane. I feel most keenly for Brandon, heart-tied to such a wilful, changeable creature as Mary."

"Sir Edwin Caskoden, you need not take the trouble to speak to me at all unless you can use language more respectful concerning my mistress. The queen knows what she is about, but it appears that you cannot see it. I see it plainly enough, although no word has ever been spoken to me on the subject. As to Brandon being tied to her, it seems to me she is tied to him, and that he holds the reins. He could drive her into the mouth of purgatory."

"Do you think so?"

"I know it."

I remained in thought a moment or two, and concluded that she was right. In truth, the time had come to me when I believed that Jane, with her good sense and acute discernment, could not be wrong in anything, and I think so yet. So I took comfort on faith from her, and asked: "Do you remember what you said should happen before we return to England?"

Jane hung her head. "I remember."

"Well?"

She then put her hand in mine and murmured, "I am ready any time you wish."

Great heaven! I thought I should go out of my senses. She should have told me gradually. I had to do something to express my exultation, so I walked over to a bronze statue of Bacchus, about my size—that is, height—put my hat—which I had been carrying under my arm—on his head, cut a few capers in an entirely new and equally antic step, and then drew back and knocked that Bacchus down. Jane thought I had gone stark mad, and her eyes grew big with wonder, but I walked proudly back to her after my victory over Bacchus, and reassured her—with a few of Mary's messages that I had still left over, if the truth must be told. Then we made arrangements that resulted in our marriage next morning.

Accordingly, Queen Mary and one or two others went with us down to a little church, where, as fortune would have it, there was a little priest ready to join together in the holy bonds of wedlock little Jane and little me. Everything so appropriate, you see; I suppose in the whole world we couldn't have found another set of conditions so harmonious. Mary laughed and cried, and laughed again, and clapped her hands over and over, and said it was "like a play wedding"; and, as she kissed Jane, quietly slipped over her head a beautiful diamond necklace that was worth full ten thousand pounds—aside, that is, from the millions of actual value, because it came from Mary. "A play wedding" it was; and a play life it has been ever since.

We were barely settled at court in Paris when Mary began to put her plans in motion and unsettle things generally. I could not but recall Henry's sympathy toward Louis, for the young queen soon took it upon herself to make life a burden to the Father of his People; and, in that particular line, I suppose she had no equal in all the length and breadth of Christendom.

I heartily detested King Louis, largely, I think, because of prejudice absorbed from Mary, but he was, in fact, a fairly good old man, and at times I could but pity him. He was always soft in heart and softer in head, especially where women were concerned. Take his crazy attempt to seize the Countess of Croy while he was yet Duke of Orleans; and his infatuation for the Italian woman, for whom he built the elaborate burial vault—much it must have comforted her. Then his marriage to dictatorial little Anne of Brittany, for whom he had induced Pope Alexander to divorce him from the poor little crippled owlet, Joan. In consideration of this divorce he had put Cæsar Borgia, Pope Alexander's son, on his feet, financially and politically. I think he must have wanted the owlet back again before he was done with Anne, because Anne was a termagant—and ruled him with the heaviest rod of iron she could lift. But this last passion—the flickering, sputtering flame of his dotage—was the worst of all, both subjectively and objectively; both as to his senile fondness for the English princess and her impish tormenting of him. From the first he evinced the most violent delight in Mary, who repaid it by holding him off and evading him in a manner so cool, audacious and adroit that it stamped her queen of all the arts feminine and demoniac. Pardon me, ladies, if I couple these two arts, but you must admit they are at times somewhat akin. Soon she eluded him so completely that for days he would not have a glimpse of her, while she was perhaps riding, walking or coquetting with some of the court gallants, who aided and abetted her in every way they could. He became almost frantic in pursuit of his elusive bride, and would expostulate with her, when he could catch her, and smile uneasily, like a man who is the victim of a practical joke of which he does not see, or enjoy, the point. On such occasions she would laugh in his face, then grow angry—which was so easy for her to do—and, I grieve to say, would sometimes almost swear at him in a manner to make the pious, though ofttimes lax-virtued, court ladies shudder with horror. She would at other times make sport of his youthful ardor, and tell him in all seriousness that it was indecorous for him to behave so and frighten her, a poor, timid little child, with his impetuosities. Then she would manage to give him the slip; and he would go off and play a game of cards with himself, firmly convinced in his own feeble way that woman's nature had a tincture of the devil in it. He was the soul of conciliatory kindness to the young vixen, but at times she would break violently into tears, accuse him of cruelly mistreating her, a helpless woman and a stranger in his court, and threaten to go home to dear old England and tell her brother, King Henry, all about it, and have him put things to right and redress her wrongs generally. In fact, she acted the part of injured innocence so perfectly that the poor old man would apologize for the wrongs she invented, and try to coax her into a good humor. Thereupon she would weep more bitterly than ever, grow hysterical, and require to be carried off by her women, when recovery and composure were usually instantaneous. Of course the court gossips soon carried stories of the quick recoveries to the king, and, when he spoke to Mary of them, she put on her injured air again and turned the tables by upbraiding him for believing such calumnies about her, who was so good to him and loved him so dearly.

I tell you it is a waste of time to fight against that assumption of injured innocence—that impregnable feminine redoubt—and when the enemy once gets fairly behind it one might as well raise the siege. I think it the most amusing, exasperating and successful defense and counter attack in the whole science of war, and every woman has it at her finger-tips, ready for immediate use upon occasion.

Mary would often pout for days together and pretend illness. Upon one occasion she kept the king waiting at her door all the morning, while she, having slipped through the window, was riding with some of the young people in the forest. When she returned— through the window—she went to the door and scolded the poor old king for keeping her waiting penned up in her room all the morning. And he apologized.

She changed the dinner hour to noon in accordance with the English custom, and had a heavy supper at night, when she would make the king gorge himself with unhealthful food and coax him "to drink as much as brother Henry," which invariably resulted in Louis de Valois finding lodgment under the table. This amused the whole court, except a few old cronies and physicians, who, of course, were scandalized beyond measure. She took the king on long rides with her on cold days, and would jolt him almost to death, and freeze him until the cold tears streamed down his poor pinched nose, making him feel like a half animated icicle, and wish that he were one in fact.

At night she would have her balls, and keep him up till morning drinking and dancing, or trying to dance, with her, until his poor old heels, and his head, too, for that matter, were like to fall off; then she would slip away from him and lock herself in her room. December, say I, let May alone; she certainly will kill you. Despite which sound advice, I doubt not December will go on coveting May up to the end of the chapter; each old fellow—being such a fine man for his age, you understand—fondly believing himself an exception. Age in a fool is damnable.

Mary was killing Louis as certainly and deliberately as if she were feeding him slow poison. He was very weak and decrepit at best, being compelled frequently, upon public occasions, such, for example, as the coronation tournament of which I have spoken, to lie upon a couch.

Mary's conduct was really cruel! but then, remember her provocation and that she was acting in self-defense. All this was easier for her than you might suppose, for the king's grasp of power, never very strong, was beginning to relax even what little grip it had. All faces were turned toward the rising sun, young Francis, duke of Angouleme, the king's distant cousin, who would soon be king in Louis's place. As this young rising sun, himself vastly smitten with Mary, openly encouraged her in what she did, the courtiers of course followed suit, and the old king found himself surrounded by a court only too ready to be amused by his lively young queen at his expense.

This condition of affairs Mary welcomed with her whole soul, and to accent it and nail assurance, I fear, played ever so lightly and coyly upon the heart-strings of the young duke, which responded all too loudly to her velvet touch, and almost frightened her to death with their volume of sound later on. This Francis d'Angouleme, the dauphin, had fallen desperately in love with Mary at first sight, something against which the fact that he was married to Claude, daughter of Louis, in no way militated. He was a very distant relative of Louis, going away back to St. Louis for his heirship to the French crown. The king had daughters in plenty, but as you know, the gallant Frenchmen say, according to their Law Salic: "The realm of France is so great and glorious a heritage that it may not be taken by a woman." Too great and glorious to be taken by woman, forsooth! France would have been vastly better off had she been governed by a woman now and then, for a country always prospers under a queen.

Francis had for many years lived at court as the recognized heir, and as the custom was, called his distant cousin Louis, "Uncle." "Uncle" Louis in turn called Francis "*Ce Gros Garçon*," and Queen

Mary called him "*Monsieur, mon beau fils,*" in a mock-motherly manner that was very laughable. A mother of eighteen to a "good boy" of twenty-two! Dangerous relationship! And dangerous, indeed, it would have been for Mary, had she not been as pure and true as she was wilful and impetuous. "Mon beau fils" allowed neither his wife nor the respect he owed the king to stand in the way of his very marked attention to the queen. His position as heir, and his long residence at court, almost as son to Louis, gave him ample opportunities for pressing his unseemly suit. He was the first to see Mary at the meeting place this side of Abbeville, and was the king's representative on all occasions.

"Beau fils" was rather a handsome fellow, but thought himself vastly handsomer than he was; and had some talents, which he was likewise careful to estimate at their full value, to say the least. He was very well liked by women, and in turn considered himself irresistible. He was very impressionable to feminine charms, was at heart a libertine, and, as he grew older, became a debauchee whose memory will taint France for centuries to come.

Mary saw his weakness more clearly than his wickedness, being blinded to the latter by the veil of her own innocence. She laughed at, and with him, and permitted herself a great deal of his company; so much, in fact, that I grew a little jealous for Brandon's sake, and, if the truth must be told, for the first time began to have doubts of her. I seriously feared that when Louis should die, Brandon might find a much more dangerous rival in the new king, who, although married, would probably try to keep Mary at his court, even should he be driven to the extreme of divorcing Claude, as Claude's father had divorced Joan.

I believed, in case Mary should voluntarily prove false and remain in France, either as the wife or the mistress of Francis, that Brandon would quietly but surely contrive some means to take her life, and I hoped he would. I spoke to my wife, Jane, about the queen's conduct, and she finally admitted that she did not like it; so I, unable to remain silent any longer, determined to put Mary on her guard, and for that purpose spoke very freely to her on the subject.

"Oh! you goose!" she said, laughingly. "He is almost as great a fool as Henry." Then the tears came to her eyes, and half angrily, half hysterically, shaking me by the arm, she continued: "Do you not know? Can you not see that I would give this hand, or my eyes, almost my life, just to fall upon my face in front of Charles Brandon at this moment? Do you not know that a woman with a love in her heart such as I have for him is safe from every one and everything? That it is her sheet anchor, sure and fast? Have you not wit enough to know that?"

"Yes, I have," I responded, for the time completely silenced. With her favorite tactics, she had, as usual, put me in the wrong, though I soon came again to the attack.

"But he is so base that I grieve to see you with him."

"I suppose he is not very good," she responded, "but it seems to be the way of these people among whom I have fallen, and he cannot harm me."

"Oh! but he can. One does not go near smallpox, and there is a moral contagion quite as dangerous, if not so perceptible, and equally to be avoided. It must be a wonderfully healthy moral nature, pure and chaste to the core, that will be entirely contagion-proof and safe from it."

She hung her head in thought, and then lifted her eyes appealingly to me. "Am I not that, Edwin? Tell me! Tell me frankly; am I not? It is the one thing of good I have always striven for. I am so full of other faults that if I have not that there is no good in me." Her eyes and voice were full of tears, and I knew in my heart that I stood before as pure a soul as ever came from the hand of God.

"You are, your majesty; never doubt," I answered. "It is pre-eminently the one thing in womanhood to which all mankind kneels." And I fell upon my knee and kissed her hand with a sense of reverence, faith and trust that has never left me from that day to this. As to my estimate of how Francis would act when Louis should die, you will see that I was right.

Not long after this Lady Caskoden and I were given permission to return to England, and immediately prepared for our homeward journey.

Ah! it was pretty to see Jane bustling about, making ready for our departure—superintending the packing of our boxes and also superintending me. That was her great task. I never was so thankful for riches as when they enabled me to allow Jane full sway among the Paris shops. But at last, all the fine things being packed, and Mary having kissed us both—mind you, both—we got our little retinue together and out we went, through St. Denis, then ho! for dear old England.

As we left, Mary placed in my hands a letter for Brandon, whose bulk was so reassuring that I knew he had never been out of her thoughts. I looked at the letter a moment and said, in all seriousness: "Your majesty, had I not better provide an extra box for it?"

She gave a nervous little laugh, and the tears filled her eyes, as she whispered huskily: "I fancy there is one who will not think it too large. Good-bye! good-bye!" So we left Mary, fair, sweet girl-queen, all alone among those terrible strangers; alone with one little English maiden, seven years of age—Anne Boleyn.

* * * * *

CHAPTER XXI

Letters from a Queen

Upon our return to England I left Jane down in Suffolk with her uncle, Lord Bolingbroke, having determined never to permit her to come within sight of King Henry again, if I could prevent it. I then went up to London with the twofold purpose of seeing Brandon and resigning my place as Master of the Dance.

When I presented myself to the king and told him of my marriage, he flew into a great passion because we had not asked his consent. One of his whims was that everyone must ask his permission to do anything; to eat, or sleep, or say one's prayers; especially to marry, if the lady was of a degree entitled to be a king's ward. Jane, fortunately, had no estate, the king's father having stolen it from her when she was an infant; so all the king could do about our marriage was to grumble, which I let him do to his heart's content.

"I wish also to thank your majesty for the thousand kindnesses you have shown me," I said, "and, although it grieves me to the heart to separate from you, circumstances compel me to tender my resignation as your Master of Dance." Upon this he was kind enough to express regret, and ask me to reconsider; but I stood my ground firmly, and then and there ended my official relations with Henry Tudor forever.

Upon taking my leave of the king I sought Brandon, whom I found comfortably ensconced in our old quarters, he preferring them to much more pretentious apartments offered him in another part of the palace. The king had given him some new furnishings for them, and as I was to remain a few days to attend to some matters of business, he invited me to share his comfort with him, and I gladly did so.

Those few days with Brandon were my farewell to individuality. Thereafter I was to be so mysteriously intermingled with Jane that I was only a part—and a small part at that I fear—of two. I did not, of course, regret the change, since it was the one thing in life I most longed for, yet the period was tinged with a faint sentiment of pathos at parting from the old life that had been so kind to me, and which I was leaving forever. I say I did not regret it, and though I was leaving my old haunts and companions and friends so dear to me, I was finding them all again in Jane, who was friend as well as wife.

Mary's letter was in one of my boxes which had been delayed, and Jane was to forward it to me when it should come. When I told Brandon of it, I dwelt with emphasis upon its bulk, and he, of course, was delighted, and impatient to have it. I had put the letter in the box, but there was something else which Mary had sent to him that I had carried with me. It was a sum of money sufficient to pay the debt against his father's estate, and in addition, to buy some large tracts of land adjoining. Brandon did not hesitate to accept the money, and seemed glad that it had come from Mary, she, doubtless, being the only person from whom he would have taken it.

One of Brandon's sisters had married a rich merchant at Ipswich, and another was soon to marry a Scotch gentleman. The brother would probably never marry, so Brandon would eventually have to take charge of the estates. In fact, he afterwards lived there many years, and as Jane and I had purchased a little estate near by, which had been generously added to by Jane's uncle, we saw a great deal of him. But I am getting ahead of my story again.

The d'Angouleme complication troubled me greatly, notwithstanding my faith in Mary, and although I had resolved to say nothing to Brandon about it, I soon told him plainly what I thought and feared.

He replied with a low, contented little laugh.

"Do not fear for Mary, I do not. That young fellow is of different stuff, I know, from the old king, but I have all faith in her purity and ability to take care of herself. Before she left she promised to be true to me, whatever befell, and I trust her entirely. I am not so unhappy by any means as one would expect. Am I?" And I was compelled to admit that he certainly was not.

So it seems they had met, as Jane and I suspected, but how Mary managed it I am sure I cannot tell; she beat the very deuce for having her own way, by hook or by crook. Then came the bulky letter, which Brandon pounced upon and eagerly devoured. I leave out most of the sentimental passages, which, like effervescent wine, lose flavor quickly. She said—in part:

"To Master Brandon:

"Sir and Dear Friend, Greeting—After leaving thee, long time had I that mighty grief and dole within my heart that it was like to break; for my separation from thee was so much harder to bear even than I had taken thought of, and I also doubted me that I could live in Paris, as I did wish. Sleep rested not upon my weary eyes, and of a very deed could I neither eat nor drink, since food distasted me like a nausea, and wine did strangle in my throat. This lasted through my journey hither, which I did prolong upon many pretexts, nearly two months, but when I did at last rest mine eyes for the first time upon this King Louis's face, I well knew that I could rule him, and when I did arrive, and had adjusted myself in this Paris, I found it so easy that my heart leaped for very joy. Beauty goeth so far with this inflammable people that easily do I rule them all, and truly doth a servile subject make a sharp, capricious tyrant. Thereby the misfortune which hath come upon us is of so much less evil, and is so like to be of such short duration, that I am almost happy—but for lack of thee— and sometimes think that after all it may verily be a blessing unseen.

"This new, unexpected face upon our trouble hath so driven the old gnawing ache out of my heart that I love to be alone, and dream, open-eyed, of the time, of a surety not far off, when I shall be with thee . . . It is ofttimes sore hard for me, who have never waited, to have to wait, like a patient Griselda, which of a truth I am not, for this which I do so want; but I try to make myself content with the thought that full sure it will not be for long, and that when this tedious time hath spent itself, we shall look back upon it as a very soul-school, and shall rather joy that we did not purchase our heaven too cheaply.

"I said I find it easy to live here as I wish, and did begin to tell thee how it was, when I ran off into telling of how I long for thee; so I will try again. This Louis, to begin with, is but the veriest shadow of a man, of whom thou needst have not one jealous thought. He is on a bed of sickness most of the time, of his own accord, and if, perchance, he be but fairly well a day or so, I do straightway make him ill again in one way or another, and, please God, hope to wear him out entirely ere long time. Of a deed, brother Henry was right; better had it been for Louis to have married a human devil than me, for it maketh a very one out of me if mine eyes but rest upon him, and thou knowest full well what kind of a devil I make—brother Henry knoweth, at any rate. For all this do I grieve, but have no remedy, nor want one. I sometimes do almost compassionate the old king, but I cannot forbear, for he turneth my very blood to biting gall, and must e'en take the consequences of his own folly. Truly is he wild for love of me, this poor old man, and the more I hold him at a distance the more he fondly dotes. I do verily believe he would try to stand upon his foolish old head, did I but insist. I sometimes have a thought to make him try it. He doeth enough that is senseless and absurd, in all conscience, as it is. At all of this do the courtiers smile, and laugh, and put me forward to other pranks; that is, all but a few of the elders, who shake their heads, but dare do nothing else for fear of the dauphin, who will soon be king, and who stands first in urging and abetting me. So it is easy for me to do what I wish, and above all to leave undone that which I wish not, for I do easily rule them all, as good Sir Edwin and dear Jane will testify. I have a ball every night, wherein I do make a deal of amusement for every one by dancing La Volta with his majesty until his heels, and his poor old head, too, are like to fall off. Others importune me for those dances, especially the dauphin, but I laugh and shake my head and say that I will dance with no one but the king, because he dances so well. This pleases his majesty mightily, and maketh an opening for me to avoid the touch of other men, for I am jealous of myself for thy sake, and save and garner every little touch for thee . . . Sir Edwin will tell you I dance with no one else and surely never will. You remember well, I doubt not, when thou first didst teach me this new dance. Ah! how delightful it was! and yet how at first it did frighten and anger me. Thou canst not know how my heart beat during all the time of that first dance. I thought, of a surety, it would burst; and then the wild thrill of frightened ecstasy that made my blood run like fire! I knew it must be wrong, for it was, in truth, too sweet a thing to be right. And then I grew angry at thee as the cause of my wrong-doing and scolded thee, and repented it, as usual. Truly didst thou conquer, not win me. Then afterwards, withal it so frightened me, how I longed to dance again, and could in no way stay myself from asking. At times could I hardly wait till evening fell, and when upon occasion thou didst not come, I was so angry I said I hated thee. What must thou have thought of me, so forward and bold! And that afternoon! Ah! I think of it every hour, and see and hear it all, and live it o'er and o'er, as it sweeter grows with memory's ripening touch. Some moments there are, that send their glad ripple down through life's stream to the verge of the grave, and truly blest is one who can smile upon and kiss these memory waves, and draw from thence a bliss that never fails. But thou knowest full well my heart, and I need not tease thee with its outpourings.

"There is yet another matter of which I wish to write in very earnestness. Sir Edwin spoke to me thereof, and what he said hath given me serious thought. I thank him for his words, of which he will tell thee in full if thou but importune him thereto. It is this: the Dauphin, Francis d'Angouleme, hath fallen desperately fond of me, and is quite as importunate, and almost as foolish as the elder lover. This people, in this strange land of France, have, in sooth, some curious notions. For an example thereto: no one thinks to find anything unseeming in the dauphin's conduct, by reason of his having already a wife, and more, that wife the Princess Claude, daughter to the king. I laugh at him and let him say what he will, for in truth I am powerless to prevent it. Words cannot scar even a rose leaf, and will not harm me. Then, by his help and example I am justified in the eyes of the court in that I so treat the king, which otherwise it were impossible for me to do and live here. So, however much I may loathe them, yet I am driven to tolerate his words, which I turn off with a laugh, making sure, thou mayest know, that it come to nothing more than words.

And thus it is, however much I wish it not, that I do use him to help me treat the king as I like, and do then use the poor old king as my buckler against this duke's too great familiarity. But my friend, when the king comes to die then shall I have my fears of this young Francis d'Angouleme. He is desperate for me, and I know not to what length he might go. The king cannot live long, as the thread of his life is like rotten flax, and when he dies thou must come without delay, since I shall be in deadly peril. I have a messenger waiting at all hours ready to send to thee upon a moment's notice, and when he comes waste not a precious instant; it may mean all to thee and me. I could write on and on forever, but it would be only to tell thee o'er and o'er that my heart is full of thee to overflowing. I thank thee that thou hast never doubted me, and will see that thou hast hereafter only good cause for better faith.

"MARY, Regina."

"Regina!" That was all. Only a queen! Surely no one could charge Brandon with possessing too modest tastes.

It was, I think, during the second week in December that I gave this letter to Brandon, and about a fortnight later there came to him a messenger from Paris, bringing another from Mary, as follows:

"*Master Charles Brandon*:

"Sir and Dear Friend, Greeting—I have but time to write that the king is so ill he cannot but die ere morning. Thou knowest that which I last wrote to thee, and in addition thereto I would say that although I have, as thou likewise knowest, my brother's permission to marry whom I wish, yet as I have his one consent it is safer that we act upon that rather than be so scrupulous as to ask for another. So it were better that thou take me to wife upon the old one, rather than risk the necessity of having to do it without any. I say no more, but come with all the speed thou knowest.

"MARY."

It is needless to say that Brandon started in haste for Paris. He left court for the ostensible purpose of paying me a visit and came to Ipswich, whence we sailed.

The French king was dead before Mary's message reached London, and when we arrived at Paris, Francis I reigned on the throne of his father-in-law. I had guessed only too accurately. As soon as the restraint of the old king's presence, light as it had been, was removed, the young king opened his attack upon Mary in dreadful earnest. He begged and pleaded and swore his love, which was surely manifest enough, and within three days after the old king's death offered to divorce Claude and make Mary his queen. When she refused this flattering offer his surprise was genuine.

"Do you know what you refuse?" he asked in a temper. "I offer to make you my wife—queen of fifteen millions of the greatest subjects on earth—and are you such a fool as to refuse a gift like that, and a man like me for a husband?"

"That I am, your majesty, and with a good grace. I am Queen of France without your help, and care not so much as one penny for the honor. It is greater to be a princess of England. As for this love you avow, I would make so bold as to suggest that you have a good, true wife to whom you would do well to give it all. To me it is nothing, even were you a thousand times the king you are. My heart is another's, and I have my brother's permission to marry him."

"Another's? God's soul! Tell me who this fellow is that I may spit him on my sword."

"No! no! you would not; even were you as valiant and grand as you think yourself, you would be but a child in his hands."

Francis was furious, and had Mary's apartments guarded to prevent her escape, swearing he would have his way.

As soon as Brandon and I arrived in Paris we took private lodgings, and well it was that we did. I at once went out to reconnoiter, and found the widowed queen a prisoner in the old palace des Tournelles. With the help of Queen Claude I secretly obtained an interview, and learned the true state of affairs.

Had Brandon been recognized and his mission known in Paris, he would certainly have been assassinated by order of Francis.

When I saw the whole situation, with Mary nothing less than a prisoner in the palace, I was ready to give up without a struggle, but not so Mary. Her brain was worth having, so fertile was it in expedients, and while I was ready to despair, she was only getting herself in good fighting order.

After Mary's refusal of Francis, and after he had learned that the sacrifice of Claude would not help him, he grew desperate, and determined to keep the English girl in his court at any price and by any means. So he hit upon the scheme of marrying her to his weak-minded cousin, the Count of Savoy. To that end he sent a hurried embassy to Henry VIII, offering, in case of the Savoy marriage, to pay back Mary's dower of four hundred thousand crowns. He offered to help Henry in the matter of the imperial crown in case of Maximilian's death—a help much greater than any King Louis could have given. He also offered to confirm Henry in all his French possessions, and to relinquish all claims of his own thereto—all as the price of one eighteen-year-old girl. Do you wonder she had an exalted estimate of her own value?

As to Henry, it, of course, need not be said, that half the price offered would have bought him to break an oath made upon the true cross itself. The promise he had made to Mary, broken in intent before it was given, stood not for an instant in the way of the French king's wishes; and Henry, with a promptitude begotten of greed, was as hasty in sending an embassy to accept the offer as Francis had been to make it. It mattered not to him what new torture he put upon his sister; the price, I believe, was sufficient to have induced him to cut off her head with his own hands.

If Francis and Henry were quick in their movements, Mary was quicker. Her plan was made in the twinkling of an eye. Immediately upon seeing me at the palace she sent for Queen Claude, with whom she had become fast friends, and told her all she knew. She did not know of the scheme for the Savoy marriage, though Queen Claude did, and fully explained it to Mary. Naturally enough, Claude would be glad to get Mary as far away from France and her husband as possible, and was only too willing to lend a helping hand to our purpose, or Mary's, rather, for she was the leader.

We quickly agreed among ourselves that Mary and Queen Claude should within an hour go out in Claude's new coach for the ostensible purpose of hearing mass. Brandon and I were to go to the same little chapel in which Jane and I had been married, where Mary said the little priest could administer the sacrament of marriage and perform the ceremony as well as if he were thrice as large.

I hurriedly found Brandon and repaired to the little chapel, where we waited for a very long time, we thought. At last the two queens entered as if to make their devotions. As soon as Brandon and Mary caught sight of each other, Queen Claude and I began to examine the shrines and decipher the Latin inscriptions. If these two had not married soon they would have been the death of me. I was compelled at length to remind them that time was very precious just at that juncture, whereupon Mary, who was half laughing, half crying, lifted her hands to her hair and let it fall in all its lustrous wealth down over her shoulders. When Brandon saw this, he fell upon his knee and kissed the hem of her gown, and she, stooping over him, raised him to his feet and placed her hand in his.

Thus Mary was married to the man to save whose life she had four months before married the French king.

She and Queen Claude had forgotten nothing, and all arrangements were completed for the flight. A messenger had been dispatched two hours before with an order from Queen Claude that a ship should be waiting at Dieppe, ready to sail immediately upon our arrival.

After the ceremony Claude quickly bound up Mary's hair, and the queens departed from the chapel in their coach. We soon followed, meeting them again at St. Denis gate, where we found the best of horses and four sturdy men awaiting us. The messenger to Dieppe who had preceded us would arrange for relays, and as Mary, according to her wont when she had another to rely upon, had taken the opportunity to become thoroughly frightened, no time was lost. We made these forty leagues in less than twenty-four hours from the time of starting; having paused only for a short rest at a little town near Rouen, which city we carefully passed around.

We had little fear of being overtaken at the rate we were riding, but Mary said she supposed the wind would die down for a month immediately upon our arrival at Dieppe. Fortunately no one pursued us, thanks to Queen Claude, who had spread the report that Mary was ill, and fortunately, also, much to Mary's surprise and delight, when we arrived at Dieppe, as fair a wind as a sailor's heart could wish was blowing right up the channel. It was a part of the system of relays—horses, ship, and wind.

"When the very wind blows for our special use, we may surely dismiss fear," said Mary, laughing and clapping her hands, but nearly ready for tears, notwithstanding.

The ship was a fine new one, well fitted to breast any sea, and learning this, we at once agreed that upon landing in England, Mary and I should go to London and win over the king if possible. We felt some confidence in being able to do this, as we counted upon Wolsey's help, but in case of failure we still had our plans. Brandon was to take the ship to a certain island off the Suffolk coast and there await us the period of a year if need be, as Mary might, in case of Henry's obstinacy, be detained; then re-victual and re-man the ship and out through the North Sea for their former haven, New Spain.

In case of Henry's consent, how they were to live in a style fit for a princess, Brandon did not know, unless Henry should open his heart and provide for them—a doubtful contingency upon which they did not base much hope. At a pinch, they might go down into Suffolk and live next to Jane and me on Brandon's estates. To this Mary readily agreed, and said it was what she wanted above all else.

There was one thing now in favor of the king's acquiescence: during the last three months Brandon had become very necessary to his amusement, and amusement was his greatest need and aim in life.

Mary and I went to London to see the king, having landed at Southampton for the purpose of throwing off the scent any one who might seek the ship. The king was delighted to see his sister, and kissed her over and over again.

Mary had as hard a game to play as ever fell to the lot of woman, but she was equal to the emergency if any woman ever was. She did not give Henry the slightest hint that she knew anything of the Count of Savoy episode, but calmly assumed that of course her brother had meant literally what he said when he made the promise as to the second marriage.

The king soon asked: "But what are you doing here? They have hardly buried Louis as yet, have they?"

"I am sure I do not know," answered Mary, "and I certainly care less. I married him only during his life, and not for one moment afterwards, so I came away and left them to bury him or keep him, as they choose; I care not which."

"But——" began Henry, when Mary interrupted him, saying: "I will tell you——"

I had taken good care that Wolsey should be present at this interview; so we four, the king, Wolsey, Mary and myself, quietly stepped into a little alcove away from the others, and prepared to listen to Mary's tale, which was told with all her dramatic eloquence and feminine persuasiveness. She told of the ignoble insults of Francis, of his vile proposals—insisted upon, almost to the point of force—carefully concealing, however, the offer to divorce Claude and make her queen, which proposition might have had its attractions for Henry. She told of her imprisonment in the palace des Tournelles, and of her deadly peril and many indignities, and the tale lost nothing in the telling. Then she finished by throwing her arms around Henry's neck in a passionate flood of tears and begging him to protect her—to save her! save her! save her! his little sister.

It was all such perfect acting that for the time I forgot it was acting, and a great lump swelled up in my throat. It was, however, only for the instant, and when Mary, whose face was hidden from all the others, on Henry's breast, smiled slyly at me from the midst of her tears and sobs, I burst into a laugh that was like to have spoiled everything. Henry turned quickly upon me, and I tried to cover it by pretending that I was sobbing. Wolsey helped me out by putting a corner of his gown to his eyes, when Henry, seeing us all so affected, began to catch the fever and swell with indignation. He put Mary away from him, and striding up and down the room exclaimed, in a voice that all could hear, "The dog! the dog! to treat my sister so. My sister! My father's daughter! My sister! The first princess of England and queen of France for his mistress! By every god that ever breathed, I'll chastise this scurvy cur until he howls again. I swear it by my crown, if it cost me my kingdom," and so on until words failed him. But see how he kept his oath, and see how he and Francis hobnobbed not long afterward at the Field of the Cloth of Gold.

Henry came back to Mary and began to question her, when she repeated the story for him. Then it was she told of my timely arrival, and how, in order to escape and protect herself from Francis, she had been compelled to marry Brandon and flee with us.

She said: "I so wanted to come home to England and be married where my dear brother could give me away, but I was in such mortal dread of Francis, and there was no other means of escape, so—"

"God's death! If I had but one other sister like you, I swear before heaven I'd have myself hanged. Married to Brandon? Fool! idiot! what do you mean? Married to Brandon! Jesu! You'll drive me mad! Just one other like you in England, and the whole damned kingdom might sink; I'd have none of it. Married to Brandon without my consent!"

"No! no! brother," answered Mary softly, leaning affectionately against his bulky form; "do you suppose I would do that? Now don't be unkind to me when I have been away from you so long! You gave your consent four months ago. Do you not remember? You know I would never have done it otherwise."

"Yes, I know! You would not do anything—you did not want; and it seems equally certain that in the end you always manage to do everything you do want. Hell and furies!"

"Why! brother, I will leave it to my Lord Bishop of York if you did not promise me that day, in this very room, and almost on this very spot, that if I would marry Louis of France I might marry whomsoever I wished when he should die. Of course you knew, after what I had said, whom I should choose, so I went to a little church in company with Queen Claude, and took my hair down and married him, and I am his wife, and no power on earth can make it otherwise," and she looked up into his face with a defiant little pout, as much as to say, "Now, what are you going to do about it?"

Henry looked at her in surprise and then burst out laughing. "Married to Brandon with your hair down?" And he roared again, holding his sides. "Well, you do beat the devil; there's no denying that. Poor old Louis! That was a good joke on him. I'll stake my crown he was glad to die! You kept it warm enough for him, I make no doubt."

"Well," said Mary, with a little shrug of her shoulders, "he would marry me."

"Yes, and now poor Brandon doesn't know the trouble ahead of him, either. He has my pity, by Jove!"

"Oh, that is different," returned Mary, and her eyes burned softly, and her whole person fairly radiated, so expressive was she of the fact that "it was different."

Different? Yes, as light from darkness; as love from loathing; as heaven from the other place; as Brandon from Louis; and that tells it all.

Henry turned to Wolsey: "Have you ever heard anything equal to it, my Lord Bishop?"

My Lord Bishop, of course, never had; nothing that even approached it.

"What are we to do about it?" continued Henry, still addressing Wolsey.

The bishop assumed a thoughtful expression, as if to appear deliberate in so great a matter, and said: "I see but one thing that can be done," and then he threw in a few soft, oily words upon the troubled waters that made Mary wish she had never called him "thou butcher's cur," and Henry, after a pause, asked: "Where is Brandon? He is a good fellow, after all, and what we can't help we must endure. He'll find punishment enough in you. Tell him to come home—I suppose you have him hid around some place—and we'll try to do something for him."

"What will you do for him, brother?" said Mary, not wanting to give the king's friendly impulse time to weaken.

"Oh! don't bother about that now," but she held him fast by the hand and would not let go.

"Well, what do you want? Out with it. I suppose I might as well give it up easily, you will have it sooner or later. Out with it and be done."

"Could you make him Duke of Suffolk?"

"Eh? I suppose so. What say you, my Lord of York?"

York was willing—thought it would be just the thing.

"So be it then," said Henry. "Now I am going out to hunt and will not listen to another word. You will coax me out of my kingdom for that fellow yet." He was about to leave the room when he turned to Mary, saying: "By the way, sister, can you have Brandon here by Sunday next? I am to have a joust."

Mary thought she could, ... and the great event was accomplished.

One false word, one false syllable, one false tone would have spoiled it all, had not Mary—but I fear you are weary with hearing so much of Mary.

So after all, Mary, though a queen, came portionless to Brandon. He got the title, but never received the estates of Suffolk; all he received with her was the money I carried to him from France. Nevertheless, Brandon thought himself the richest man in all the earth, and surely he was one of the happiest. Such a woman as Mary is dangerous, except in a state of complete subjection—but she was bound hand and foot in the silken meshes of her own weaving, and her power for bliss-making was almost infinite.

And now it was, as all who read may know, that this fair, sweet, wilful Mary dropped out of history; a sure token that her heart was her husband's throne; her soul his empire; her every wish his subject, and her will, so masterful with others, the meek and lowly servant of her strong but gentle lord and master, Charles Brandon, Duke of Suffolk.

* * * * *

NOTE BY THE EDITOR

Sir Edwin Caskoden's history differs in some minor details from other authorities of the time. Hall's chronicle says Sir William Brandon, father of Charles, had the honor of being killed by the hand of Richard III himself, at Bosworth Field, and the points wherein his account of Charles Brandon's life differs from that of Sir Edwin may be gathered from the index to the 1548 edition of that work, which is as follows:

Charles Brandon, Esquire,

> Is made knight,
> Created Viscount Lysle,
> Made duke of Suffolke,
> Goeth to Paris to the Iustes,
> Doeth valiantly there,
> Returneth into England,
> He is sent into Fraunce to fetch home the French quene
>   into England,
> He maryeth her,

and so on until

> "He dyeth and is buryed at Wyndesore."

No mention is made in any of the chronicles of the office of Master of Dance. In all other essential respects Sir Edwin is corroborated by his contemporaries.

* * * * *

THE AUTHOR AND THE BOOK

By Maurice Thompson

When a man does something by which the world is attracted, we immediately feel a curiosity to know all about him personally. Mr. Charles Major, of Shelbyville, Indiana, wrote the wonderfully popular historical romance, When Knighthood was in Flower, which has already sold over a quarter million copies.

It is not mere luck that makes a piece of fiction acceptable to the public. The old saying, "Where there is so much smoke there must be fire," holds good in the case of smoke about a novel. When a book moves many people of varying temperaments and in all circles of intelligence there is power in it. Behind such a book we have the right to imagine an author endowed with admirable gifts of imagination. The ancient saying, "The cup is glad of the wine it holds," was but another way of expressing the rule which judges a tree by its fruit and a man by his works; for out of character comes style, and out of a man's nature is his taste distilled. Every soul, like the cup, is glad of what it holds.

Mr. Major himself has said, in his straightforward way, "It is what a man does that counts." By this rule of measurement Mr. Major has a liberal girth. The writing of When Knighthood was in Flower was a deed of no ordinary dimensions, especially when we take into account the fact that the writer had not been trained to authorship or to the literary artist's craft; but was a country lawyer, with an office to sweep every morning, and a few clients with whom to worry over dilatory cases and doubtful fees.

The law, as a profession, is said to be a jealous mistress, ever ready and maliciously anxious to drop a good-sized stumbling block in the path of her devotee whenever he appears to be straying in the direction of another love. Indeed, many are the young men who, on turning from Blackstone and Kent in a comfortable law office to Scott and Byron, have lost a lawyer's living, only to grasp the empty air of failure in the fascinating garret of the scribbler. But "nothing succeeds like success," and genius has a way of changing rules and forcing the gates of fortune. And when we see the proof that a fresh genius has once more wrought the miracle of reversing all the fine logic of facts, so as to bring success and fame out of the very circumstances and conditions which are said to render the feat impossible, we all wish to know how he did it.

Balzac, when he felt the inspiration of a new novel in his brain, retired to an obscure room, and there, with a pot of villainous black coffee at his elbow, wrote night and day, almost without food and sleep, until the book was finished. General Lew Wallace put Ben Hur on paper in the open air of a beech grove, with a bit of yellowish canvas stretched above him to soften the light. Some authors use only the morning hours for their literary work; others prefer the silence of night. A few cannot write save when surrounded by books, pictures and luxurious furniture, while some must have a bare room with nothing in it to distract attention. Mr. Charles Major wrote When Knighthood was in Flower on Sunday afternoons, the only time he had free from the exactions of the law. He was full of his subject, however, and doubtless his clients paid the charges in the way of losses through demurrers neglected and motions and exceptions not properly presented!

One thing about Mr. Major's work deserves special mention; its shows conscientious mastery of details, a sure evidence of patient study. What it may lack as literature is compensated for in lawful coin of human interest and in general truthfulness to the facts and the atmosphere of the life he depicts. When asked how he arrived at his accurate knowledge of old London—London in the time of Henry VIII—he fetched an old book—Stow's Survey of London—from his library and said:

"You remember in my novel that Mary goes one night from Bridewell Castle to Billingsgate Ward through strange streets and alleys. Well, that journey I made with Mary, aided by Stow's Survey, with his map of old London before me."

It is no contradiction of terms to speak of fiction as authentic. Mere vraisemblance is all very well in works of pure imagination;

but a historical romance does not satisfy the reader's sense of justice unless its setting and background and atmosphere are true to time, place and historical facts. Mr. Major felt the demand of his undertaking and respected it. He collected old books treating of English life and manners in the reign of Henry VIII, preferring to saturate his mind with what writers nearest the time had to say, rather than depend upon recent historians. In this he chose well, for the romancer's art, different from the historian's, needs the literary shades and colors of the period it would portray.

Another clever choice on the part of our author was to put the telling of the story in the mouth of his heroine's contemporary. This, of course, had often been done by romancers before Mr. Major, but he chose well, nevertheless. Fine literary finish was not to be expected of a Master of the Dance early in the sixteenth century; so that Sir Edwin Caskoden, and not Mr. Major, is accepted by the reader as responsible for the book's narrative, descriptive and dramatic style. This ruse, so to call it, serves a double purpose; it hangs the glamour of distance over the pages, and it puts the reader in direct communication, as it were, with the characters in the book. The narrator is garrulous, and often far from artistic with his scenes and incidents; but it is Caskoden doing all this, not Mr. Charles Major, and we never think of bringing him to task! Undoubtedly it is good art to do just what Mr. Major has done—that is, it is good art to present a picture of life in the terms of the period in which it flourished. It might have been better art to clothe the story in the highest terms of literature; but that would have required a Shakespeare.

The greatest beauty of Mr. Major's story as a piece of craftsmanship is its frank show of self-knowledge on the author's part. He knew his equipment, and he did not attempt to go beyond what it enabled him to do and do well.

His romance will not go down the ages as a companion of Scott's, Thackeray's, Hugo's and Dumas'; but read at any time by any fresh-minded person, it will afford that shock of pleasure which always comes of a good story enthusiastically told, and of a pretty love-drama frankly and joyously presented. Mr. Major has the true dramatic vision and notable cleverness in the art of making effective conversation.

The little Indiana town in which Mr. Major lives and practices the law is about twenty miles from Indianapolis, and hitherto has been best known as the former residence of Thomas A. Hendricks, late Vice-President of the United States. Already the tide of kodak artists and autograph hunters has found our popular author out, and his clients are being pushed aside by vigorous interviewers and reporters in search of something about the next book. But the author of When Knighthood was in Flower is an extremely difficult person to handle. It is told of him that he offers a very emphatic objection to having his home life and private affairs flaunted before the public under liberal headlines and with "copious illustrations."

Mr. Major is forty-three and happily married; well-built and dark; looking younger than his years, genial, quiet and domestic to a degree; he lives what would seem to be an ideal life in a charming home, across the threshold of which the curiosity of the public need not try to pass. As might be taken for granted, Mr. Major has been all his life a loving student of history.

Perhaps to the fact that he has never studied romance as it is in art is largely due his singular power over the materials and atmosphere of history. At all events, there is something remarkable in his vivid pictures not in the least traceable to literary form nor dependent upon a brilliant command of diction. The characters in his book are warm, passionate human beings, and the air they breathe is real air. The critic may wince and make faces over lapses from taste, and protest against a literary style which cannot be defended from any point of view; yet there is Mary in flesh and blood, and there is Caskoden, a veritable prig of a good fellow— there, indeed, are all the *dramatis personae*, not merely true to life, but living beings.

And speaking of *dramatis personae*, Mr. Major tells how, soon after his book was published, his morning mail brought him an interesting letter from a prominent New York manager, pointing out the dramatic possibilities of When Knighthood was in Flower and asking for the right to produce it. While this letter was still under consideration, a telegram was received at the Shelbyville office which read: "I want the dramatic rights to When Knighthood was in Flower." It was signed "Julia Marlowe." Mr. Major felt that this was enough for one morning, so he escaped to Indianapolis, and after a talk with his publishers, left for St. Louis and answered

Miss Marlowe's telegram in person. At the first interview she was enthusiastic and he was confident. She gave him a box for the next night's performance, which Miss Marlowe arranged should be "As You Like It." After the play the author was enthusiastic and the actress confident.

At Cincinnati, the following week, the contract was signed and the search for the dramatist was begun. That the story would lend itself happily to stage production must have occurred even to the thoughtless reader. But it is one thing to see the scenes of a play fairly sticking out, as the saying is, from the pages of a book, and quite another to gather together and make of them a dramatic entity. Miss Marlowe was determined that the book should be given to a playwright whose dramatic experience and artistic sense could be relied on to lead him out of the rough places, up to the high plane of convincing and finished workmanship. Mr. Paul Kester, after some persuasion, undertook the work. The result is wholly satisfactory to author, actress and manager—a remarkable achievement indeed!

Mr. Major's biography shows a fine, strong American life. He was born in Indianapolis, July 25, 1856. Thirteen years later he went with his father's family to Shelbyville, where he was graduated from the public school in 1872, and in 1875 he concluded his course in the University of Michigan. Later he read law with his father, and in 1877 was admitted to the bar. Eight years later he stood for the Legislature and was elected on the democratic ticket. He served with credit one term, and has since declined all political honors.

The title, When Knighthood was in Flower, was not chosen by Mr. Major, whose historical taste was satisfied with Charles Brandon, Duke of Suffolk. And who knows but that the author's title would have proved just the weight to sink a fine book into obscurity? Mr. John J. Curtis, of the Bowen-Merrill Company, suggested When Knighthood was in Flower, a phrase taken from Leigh Hunt's poem, the Gentle Armour:

> "There lived a knight, when knighthood was in flower,
> Who charmed alike the tilt-yard and the bower."